A GATHERING STORM

JOANNA CHAMBERS

Joanna Chambers

A Gathering Storm

Copyright © 2017 Joanna Chambers

2nd edition, 2024

Published by Joanna Chambers

ISBN: 978-1-914305-12-2

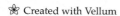 Created with Vellum

Author note: this book was released by the original publisher in 2017. The rights were returned to me in April 2024, however, since the book was part of a series of standalone novels set in a shared universe, I had to change various character and place names in this revised version.

Other than these minor revisions, the story is unchanged.

Joanna Chambers

∽

A Gathering Storm

"I want you to work with me, Mr. Hearn. And I'm not generally considered to be the sort of man who'll take no for an answer."

Grief-stricken after the death of his twin brother, unconventional scientist Sir Edward 'Ward' Carrick retreats to Trevathany, a remote village in Cornwall, to continue his work exploring the veil between the physical and spiritual worlds.

In Trevathany, he meets Nicholas Hearn, land steward to the Tremain family. When Ward learns that Nick's Romany mother was believed to be clairvoyant—and that Nick himself may have seen a ghost as a child—he becomes convinced that Nick is the perfect test subject for his work.

Unfortunately, Nick is unwilling to participate in Ward's experiments. However, as luck would have it, Ward finds himself in a position to force Nick to cooperate...

It's an inauspicious start. Nick is furious at having his hand forced by a high-handed aristocrat, while Ward grows increasingly frustrated at his lack of progress with his work. And yet, as the two men gradually learn more about one another—and discover their mutual physical attraction—they begin to form an undeniable bond.

But how strong is that bond? Is their fragile connection deep enough to withstand the gathering storm of Ward's growing obsession and Nick's doubts?

All our knowledge begins with the senses, proceeds then to the understanding, and ends with reason. There is nothing higher than reason.

—Immanuel Kant, *Critique of Pure Reason*

PROLOGUE

From *The Collected Writings of Sir Edward Carrick*, volume I

On the twenty-fourth day of June, in the year 1852, I was visited by my twin brother's spirit.

I was a passenger on a steamship, the *Archimedes*, sailing from Dublin to Anglesey, and it was close to midnight. The captain had told us they expected an electrical storm that night and that we should stay in our cabins, but I was most keen to witness the phenomenon of a great storm at sea, and so I ventured onto the deck despite his warnings.

It was like no other storm I had ever experienced. I could *sense* the electricity that saturated the atmosphere before a single bolt of lightning struck. Indeed, the very air seemed to hum with it, and the distinctive pungent odour of ozone gas —so named by Professor Schönbein, whose experiments into the electrolysis of water were of particular interest to me at that time—was all around me. When I glanced up at the sky, there was a faint, luminous glow over the brim of my hat, eerie and bluish white, and even though I knew it was produced by electromagnetism, it was no less beautiful or miraculous for that. I stared at that glow for long minutes, even discerning tiny sparks dancing there.

And then the lightning came. Mighty enough to tear the very heavens in two, it seemed, and I cried out in alarm, muttering some half-remembered prayer from my childhood as I clutched at the side of the *Archimedes*. Again the lightning struck, and again, each bolt seeming to disappear into the black depths of the churning sea. I admit, I was frightened then, and wished I had heeded the captain's words. But just as I was about to run below deck, a voice spoke to me, a voice as dear to me as my own. My brother, George. My twin.

"Ward," he said. "Ward. Can you hear me?"

I whirled on the spot, heart pounding, searching the empty deck for him. I called his name, over and over, and cried out, "I can't see you! Where are you?"

My rational mind supplied a rational answer: George was in Burma. His regiment had recently served at the Siege of Rangoon. He could not possibly be on a steamer to Anglesey with me, and yet I'd heard his voice!

"Everything will be all right, Ward," George said. "All will be well."

That was all he said. A moment later, a physical pain wrenched through my body, worse than anything I'd ever felt, even in the worst days of my long childhood sickness. I cannot do justice to that pain in mere words. It was as though one of those great lightning bolts had struck my very heart and sundered it in two. It sent me to my knees. I fell heavily to the wet wooden deck, crying out my brother's name.

I felt George's absence—the moment he was gone—much as I'd felt his presence. It was negative to positive, opposite and equal, an emptiness to match and cancel out his sudden, shocking appearance. He was dead. I knew it—felt it—with a terrible finality. And though I called his name, over and over, weeping, I knew he would not return.

I dragged myself to my feet and began to search the deck

of the *Archimedes*, hoping to find some lingering sign of George's fleeting visit, but it was not until I finally raised my eyes from the deck, beaten, that I saw it. Quivering at the very top of the ship's mast: a strange and luminous violet-blue light, like a huge flame atop some monstrous candle. Ethereal and otherworldly.

I knew what this was, had read reports of these *spirit candles*, as the Welsh sailors called them. Or *St. Elmo's fire*, as I knew it.

And as I stared, awestruck, I was filled with sudden certainty: that it was all connected somehow. The electric storm, the sea, the ozone, my bond with George. Some or all of these elements had combined to defy the laws of man as I knew them and bring my twin to me in the terrible moment of his death.

It was in that instant that my life's work was conceived.

CHAPTER ONE

2nd April 1853
Tremain House, Trevathany

The new mare was as fine a horse as Nick had ever seen. Proud and lovely with her dapple-grey coat, ivory mane, and delicate, high-stepping legs.

"What do you think of her?" old Godfrey asked, without looking at Nick. He leaned over the paddock fence, his eyes on the mare, but Nick could hear a betraying note of eagerness in his tone. "Do you think Isabella will like her?"

Nick, who'd been chewing on a stalk of grass, spat out a stray seed and said, "Those are two different questions."

Godfrey gave an impatient sigh and turned his head. At seventy-eight he was still hale, a big man with a shock of silver hair. There was a slight stoop to those broad shoulders these days, and the big hands gripping the top of the fence were spotted with pale brown marks, but he was as active as he'd always been. Still rode every day.

"Answer them separately then," Godfrey demanded.

Nick watched the mare canter round the field, in no hurry

to respond. He knew that Godfrey hated that Nick didn't rush to do his bidding like everyone else. In a way though, Godfrey liked that about him too. Or, at least, he respected it.

At last Nick looked at Godfrey and gave his verdict. "It's rare to find a *grasni* as fine as this one."

A brief flicker of distaste crossed Godfrey's face at Nick's use of the Romany word, but his satisfaction at Nick's approval soon chased it away.

"It is," he agreed. He respected Nick's opinion on horses more than anyone else's. Said that Nick had an instinct for them. Sometimes he said he should have left Nick in the stables, working with the horses, instead of educating him to take on the elevated position of Godfrey's steward. But that was usually only when he was irritated with Nick.

"I'm not certain, though," Nick continued, calmly, "that she's the right animal for Miss Isabella."

"Why ever not?" Godfrey demanded, his grin falling away.

Nick smiled, watching the mare as she tossed her head. "Just look at her. She's a handful."

"Isabella is a fine horsewoman," Godfrey snapped. "She has a wonderful seat—better than her brother."

Nick ignored that flicker of bad temper, his expression neutral. Godfrey was a domineering old martinet who controlled his household with an iron hand and sought to control everyone else who came into his vicinity too, but he couldn't control Nick. He might be Nick's employer, his landlord too, but Nick made sure Godfrey knew that if Nick had to walk away from his position and his cottage, he'd do it without a second thought. And he never let Godfrey see him getting riled. He reacted to all the old man's bluster with the same calm equanimity.

No matter what it cost him to do it.

"Miss Isabella has an excellent seat," he agreed now, his tone mild, "but you know she's careless with her hands at times. She damaged Acteon's mouth last month, pulling too hard at the reins. She didn't mean to hurt him, but she was showing off, being reckless."

He didn't waste his breath agreeing that she was indeed a superior rider to her brother, Harry. Godfrey was the only person permitted to criticise his heir.

Beside him, Godfrey gave a harrumph in poor-spirited acknowledgement of Nick's point, and they fell into silence, both turning back to the paddock.

The mare was cantering playfully round the perimeter now, and Nick found himself imagining what it would be like to ride her himself, to let her have her head on the long beach at Candlewick Bay with no saddle between them. He'd hug her flanks with his thighs and bend low over her neck as she galloped, and something of her would be in him and something of him in her as they raced.

Gaze fixed on the mare, Nick made a soft, clicking noise in his throat. Her pointed ears flickered, and she slowed her pace, turning her head in his direction. She paused, as though considering, then changed direction, swinging round to walk towards him. He reached into his pocket as she approached, drawing out a slightly shrivelled russet apple. He offered it to her from his flat hand, and she eyed it—then him—carefully. At last, though, she lowered her great head to accept the tribute, taking it almost delicately, her moist breath huffing against his palm. He patted her powerful neck as she munched the fruit.

Godfrey tutted. "Bloody typical. I couldn't get her to come near me when I tried earlier." His tone was light, but it carried an irritable edge. He and Nick shared a passion for horses, but Nick had an affinity with them—with all animals—that far outstripped Godfrey's mere knowledge, and at times, Godfrey seemed almost resentful of Nick for it.

The mare butted Nick's shoulder with her beautiful head

and whickered softly, demanding his attention, blatantly ignoring Godfrey.

"You're a flirt," Nick told her. "A bad 'un, through and through." Her neck was warm and powerful under his hand. She was quick with the magic of life, and again, he found himself wishing fiercely he could ride her.

The mare tossed her head, as though insulted by his words, but even as she did so, she stepped closer, bumping him affectionately with her nose.

Godfrey made a disgusted noise. "Christ, she *is* flirting with you. Bloody animal wouldn't even *look* at me!"

"*Ayes*, you like me fine, don't you?" Nick agreed, addressing the mare. "Maybe you've decided I'm husband material." He chuckled softly.

She gave him a look at that but stood her ground, docile as he patted her. When Godfrey stretched a hand out to her, though, she sidestepped, then turned and walked away. Slowly, as though to insult him.

Godfrey huffed a sigh. Nick took pity on him. "You did well to get her for the price you did," he said. "She should've gone for twice that."

That was all it took to cheer Godfrey up. Soon he was telling Nick the story of the auction for the second time that day, reliving the glory of his success.

Godfrey Tremain was a man who liked to speak far more than he liked to listen. He dominated every conversation he was part of, and though he was a fine storyteller, Nick had heard all his stories a dozen times or more. He was used to only half listening as the old man talked, and that was what he did now, grunting occasionally when Godfrey paused for breath. In truth, though, his attention was on the mare as she slowly circled the paddock.

After a while, another head butted him, below his knee this time. Nick looked down to meet the gaze of the white bulldog sitting at his feet, its unlovely face made uglier by a missing eye.

He smiled at the dog. "Did you think I'd forgotten you?" he asked Snow, bending down to ruffle the silky flaps of the dog's ears.

"That ugly mutt's still trailing after you, I see," Godfrey said disapprovingly. He kept a few hunting dogs, but was not a man to make a pet of an animal and couldn't understand why Nick would.

"He's a good dog," Nick said mildly. Godfrey just grunted, and they fell silent again.

Nick began tracking the mare's gait, fixing his gaze on her as she circled the paddock over and over. She had a slightly unusual high-stepping gait that made him wonder what she'd been used for before Godfrey had bought her.

He was about to ask just that, when Godfrey prodded his arm and said, "Well? Have you?"

Realising he'd missed something, Nick said, "Have I what?"

Godfrey's mouth tightened. "I knew you weren't listening."

Nick didn't bother to defend himself. As Ma used to say, *"No point saying sorry when you're not, is there?"*

"I said, have you seen Sir Edward?" Godfrey said.

"Who?"

Godfrey gave an impatient huff. "Sir Edward Carrick—the fellow who's built that new house up by the Zawn. He's calling it Helston House. Apparently he's some kind of *scientist*." Godfrey said 'scientist' as though it was the most ridiculous idea he'd ever heard, adding dismissively, "He must be a madman to build something up there—the bloody place's liable to fall into the sea!"

Nick used to play at the Zawn when he was a lad. The village children were all fascinated by it—an eighty-foot-high cavern that stretched from cliff top to seabed. When Nick was little, and Ma used to tell him stories about the *piskey* folk, she said the cliff had been gored by a giant bull. He'd believed her for years. That was just what it looked like after all, as though a huge horn had been driven into the cliff and torn back out again.

Back when Nick used to be friends with the village boys, they'd dare each other to stand at the edge, as close as they could get without falling in. They'd sway there, buffeted by the high coastal winds, waiting for the great rushes of seawater that would explode up through the rocky crevice at high tide, like spurts from a whale's blowhole, soaking them, sending them running away, shrieking with laughter.

He'd seen the new house—this Helston House—being built when he was out walking, and had wondered who it was for. It was a strange place to build somewhere to live. Not that the house was particularly near the Zawn itself. But still.

"I've seen the house," Nick said. "It's a handsome place."

Godfrey made a face. "You think so? I think it's quite ugly. But I suppose that's the modern style." He sniffed.

"It's not as beautiful as Tremain House," Nick agreed, shrugging, and that much was true. Tremain House was supremely elegant with its mullioned windows and long gallery, its weathered walls dressed in robes of ivy. The scientist's house was very different, square and strong, the edges of its brand-new sandstone bricks immaculate and sharp. Nick had been surprised to find that he liked the brutal, modern look of it, but he did.

"What's more," Godfrey continued, his tone displeased, "I don't know anyone who's even met this Sir Edward yet. Apparently he arrived in Trevathany a fortnight ago and hasn't so much as paid a call on anyone. Hasn't even been seen in the village yet."

That would bother Godfrey. As far as he was concerned, the Tremains were the most important family in the county, and he would certainly regard this Sir Edward's neglect of him as an insult.

Not to mention being wildly jealous of his title, Nick thought, suppressing a grin.

"Why d'you ask if I'd seen him if you know no one else has?" he asked, puzzled.

"I thought you might have caught a glimpse on one of your wanderings," Godfrey said carelessly. He cast Nick a sly glance. "Always up on those cliff tops, aren't you? Just like your mother. Must be her Gypsy blood coming through."

Nick smiled thinly. He knew Godfrey meant that as an insult, but Nick refused to take it as one. Even as a very young child, he had known he was different. His skin was darker than most people's round here, whether in summer or winter, and his hair wasn't merely black, it was so black it shone with a bluish lustre in the sun, like the plumage on a crow. The only sign of his *gadjo* side, his father, was his eyes. These were a distinctive and very light silver grey, bright against his tawny skin. They marked him as an outcast on both sides. Not Roma. Not Cornishman. Not... anything.

His mother hadn't ever belonged in Trevathany, but she'd had no choice but to stay. Her own father had refused to allow her to return to her people after she'd run off with the English *gadjo*. Not that it changed how she thought of herself —or Nick.

"We are Roma," she would tell him, fiercely. *"You should leave here and join the family when I am gone. When they see how you are with the* grai, *they will know you are Roma through and through, and let you travel with them."*

He'd hated when she talked like that, about dying. She'd been too young to talk like that. But she had died young after all, and now he wondered if somehow she had always known that was her fate. If the stories she spun about her fortune-telling had some kernel of truth in them, even though she'd told Nick they were just foolish nonsense she made up for the *gadjikane* villagers, to make a little money.

"Our secret."

Nick had never met his mother's people—he didn't know if he wanted to—but they came back to Cornwall every second year, and he knew they would be in Penzance this summer. Lately he'd found himself thinking about going to see them, to meet Ma's father and give him the news of his daughter's death. Nick wondered if he would care. Ma had always spoken of her father with loyal affection, yet he was the one who had cast her out and refused to allow her to return to her people when Nick's father abandoned her, forcing her to find another way to survive.

He wondered too if he would feel a connection to the old man. To any of them. If he would be tempted to travel with them if they asked him to. To leave Trevathany behind and take up a life on the road. That was what Ma had wanted. That was her dream for him.

Nick pushed himself back from the fence.

"I should be getting on," he said. "I've to see Jessop about that damaged wall."

Godfrey nodded, distant now. "Join me for supper in the library," he said. "Six o'clock. You can give me a proper report then."

Nick nodded, then turned on his heel and strode away, Snow lumbering and wheezing in his wake.

CHAPTER TWO

From *The Collected Writings of Sir Edward Carrick*, volume I

My brother George—my identical twin—preceded me into the world by six minutes. As boys we were as one, so much so that even our parents could not tell us apart. Our thoughts were as one too, and often we would speak the exact same words spontaneously. This changed forever, however, shortly after my eleventh birthday.

Father had taken George, being the eldest son and heir to the title, to town with him, and while they were away, my sister Honoria and I both fell ill with the disease now called diphtheria and in those days called the morbid sore throat.

My poor sister had the misfortune of falling ill first. As is well-known, victims of this cruel disease grow a putrid, grey, membranous substance in the throat that coats the tonsils and larynx. Within a week of taking to her bed, my sister could barely breathe and seemed like to suffocate. In desperation, and despite the warnings of our nurse, Mother called in a surgeon to try to cut some of the stuff away and ease the passage of air to her lungs. By all accounts, it was bloody work—certainly, I could hear Honoria's screams from the other end of the house. Unable to withstand the shock of the ordeal, she died a few days later.

I was spared this treatment but had to withstand endless days of struggling to breathe, dragging the tiniest threads of air through my clogged throat. I grew convinced my fate was to die from asphyxiation—something I cherish an utter dread of even now. At last, however, the membrane came loose and I could breathe again. The relief this brought was sadly short-lived as I was then afflicted by a weakening of the heart and paralysis, first of the face and then of the limbs. For weeks I could do nothing but lie and be tended to, like a newborn. Many times my parents were told they must expect my death. That this did not come to pass was, I feel quite sure, due to my mother's tireless care for me, and her determination that I would live.

Slowly, I recovered, but I was left with two permanent reminders of the disease. The first was a harsh, unbeautiful voice, my larynx having been permanently damaged. Even today, I cringe to hear my speaking voice and my laughter, which sounds like the barking of a dog. The second was the change in my similarity to my twin. While my body had been doing everything it could to resist death, George's had continued to grow. I never quite caught up to him. By the time we were one-and-twenty, he was five foot ten inches with broad shoulders and strong arms, while I was three inches shorter and far slighter.

~

4th April 1853
   Messrs Godritch & Jones, Solicitors, Trevathany

. . .

"Now, tell me," Mr. Godritch said, settling back in his chair, "how may I help you, Sir Edward?"

Ward regarded Mr. Godritch over the polished expanse of his desk. Godritch was the only solicitor in Trevathany, Mr. Jones having passed away some twenty years before. He was an unremarkable-looking man in late middle age, with a small paunch, thinning grey hair, and a rather rosy nose, the cause of which became plain when he insisted on breaking open a bottle of sherry, despite it still being afore noon. Ward's glass of amber wine sat on the desk before him, untouched, as Godritch sipped contentedly at his own.

"It is a rather unusual matter," Ward said. Godritch's gaze flickered briefly at Ward's harsh, toneless voice. That was a more restrained response than during their introduction a few minutes before. Soon Godritch would cease to react at all. It usually took a couple of meetings for people to become accustomed to it. Ward was used to such reactions, but still, they irritated him.

Godritch offered him a serene smile. "My practice is small but I am yet to be asked to deal with any matter beyond my abilities. Tell me—is it a question of property? Or perhaps you need to discuss your will? It is never too early to put arrangements in place—"

"I need subjects," Ward interrupted. "As many as you can get me."

"Subjects?" The solicitor frowned at him across his broad walnut desk. "*Subjects*? I'm not sure I follow."

"As you may have heard, I am a scientist, Mr. Godritch. I am also fortunate to come from a family of some considerable means. I visited this area last year and became convinced it was the ideal place in which to carry out my work. That is why I purchased the land on which I subsequently built Helston House."

"I was aware of that," Mr. Godritch said, inclining his

head in acknowledgement. "Having acted for Mr. Tremain in that transaction, as you will no doubt recall."

"Of course," Ward said, though in truth he hadn't known, nor did he care. He'd left all the legal business to Mr. Embleton, his solicitor in London.

"I first decided to purchase property in Cornwall," he went on, "due to the weather conditions here. The work I am doing now is concerned with the impact of atmospheric electricity and electromagnetism on... certain spiritual and psychic phenomena. Since this part of the English coastline is prone to storms, it's well situated for my experiments." Ward leaned forward, over the desk, warming to his subject now. "The particular reason I selected Trevathany, though, was because of the hole in the cliff, close to the edge of my property—"

"The Zawn, you mean?" Mr. Godritch interjected, his tone doubtful. "That was... an *attraction*?"

"Yes! Oh, I realise having a great hole in the ground, stretching all the way down to the sea, might be off-putting for most buyers, but for me, it was the very reason I wanted this land. The conditions inside that crevice would usually only be found during a storm at sea. The air is constantly saturated with droplets of sea water, and there are frequent surges from sea level. I fully expect that in the course of an electromagnetic storm, these unusual conditions will be enhanced, and indeed I hope to take steps to further enhance them myself. For one thing, I'm installing certain equipment at the base of the cavern to stimulate production of ozone gas. Are you familiar with ozone g—"

"Ah—Sir Edward?"

Ward blinked at that and for the first time noticed that Godritch looked... frankly bamboozled.

"Excuse me," the lawyer said, "but I'm not sure I am entirely following you. What does all this have to do with these *subjects* you want me to help you with?"

"I beg your pardon," Ward said, flushing. "I get a little ahead of myself sometimes, when I start talking about my work."

"That's quite all right," Godritch said. "And perfectly understandable. But if you could perhaps explain what it is you need my assistance with, that may... expedite matters."

"Very well." Ward paused and took a deep breath. This was the part he found more difficult. "It is my hypothesis— given the right person and the right conditions of electromagnetic and atmospheric activity—that it is possible for a living man to communicate with spirits."

Godritch's eyes widened. He opened his mouth. Closed it again. Then he picked up the sherry bottle, poured himself another large glass, and threw half of it back.

Ward waited. He was well aware, painfully so, of how most people, especially educated people, viewed his work. But he also hoped that Godritch, as a professional man with a living to make, would agree to help him regardless of his views regarding what Ward was trying to achieve.

Eventually Godritch said, "Are you a *spiritualist*, Sir Edward?"

Ward shook his head. "By no means. Make no mistake, Mr. Godritch, I am a scientist, first and always. I have witnessed some marvellous things in my life that others have ascribed to magic or religion, but there is nothing I have seen that I do not firmly believe may be perfectly explained by science, if not now, then someday."

Godritch considered that and finally said, "What is it you want me to do?"

"In order to conduct my experiments, I require various things"—Ward counted some of them off on his fingers— "electromagnetic activity, sea water, ozone gas. These are all things I am able to obtain in some form or other. There is one thing I need, however, that I have been unable to get: human subjects. It is this ingredient I require your assistance with."

Ward paused, then added, "I am willing to pay any volunteers you find me a generous sum for their assistance—and, of course, a fee to you for acting as my agent in this matter."

"What sort of person is it that you seek?" Godritch asked. "Do you require your subjects to be literate, for example? What will they be asked to do?"

Ward shook his head. "There is no need for them to be able to read or write. I will need them to tell me what they are experiencing, but that is all. My only real stipulation is that it would help if they have recently experienced a family bereavement." He saw the lawyer frowning at that bluntly stated requirement. "As for what they will be asked to do, well, nothing much at all: merely submit to being put into a trance—"

"A trance?" Godritch sounded taken aback. "Do you mean mesmerism? If you mean to put them to sleep and press pins into them or some such thing, I'm afraid I could not countenance assisting you with any such endeavour." He gave a dry chuckle to lighten his words, but Ward could see he meant it seriously.

"No, no, of course not," Ward reassured. "Nothing like that, Mr. Godritch. I am not a circus performer. The reason I put my subjects into an hypnotic trance—which is in a fact a very subtly altered state from the usual—is not to deprive them of the ability to sense things, as the mesmerists purport to do, but rather to enhance their mental concentration. By focusing my subjects' minds in this way, I hope to unlock what I believe is a latent ability we all have to reach beyond the boundary of the visible world we perceive around us."

As usual when he spoke of his work, Ward began to feel happier, excited at the prospect of the efforts that lay ahead, and of the tantalising possibility of success. He realised he was smiling, and that Godritch was considering him with what looked like curious interest, no longer the wary man of business, but one man taking his measure of another.

At length, Godritch nodded. "Very well, Sir Edward. Let us give this a try. I will do what I can to help you find some subjects, and we will see how we go." He rang the bell at the side of his desk and seconds later, the young man who had greeted Ward when he first arrived popped his head round the door.

"You rang, Mr. Godritch?"

"Ah, Mr. Pascoe. Please come in," Godritch said. "We have a contract of agency to draw up."

Godritch was as good as his word, but over the next several weeks, the few subjects he was able to send Ward's way proved to be worse than useless.

Agnes Penrose, a frowsy woman of about forty, blushed every time Ward asked her a question, could barely stammer out an answer, and was impossible to hypnotise due to her inability to maintain her gaze where Ward needed it to be to achieve the requisite state.

Thomas Cadzow, a strapping young farm labourer, appeared a better prospect, at least at first. He succumbed to the trance state with ease, but it transpired he'd never suffered a bereavement in his life—not only were his mother, father, and six siblings alive and well, but all four grandparents and two great-grandparents were in fine fettle too. The man hadn't lost so much as a pet cat.

The worst, though, was Jago Jones, a sullen man who'd recently lost his place on one of the local fishing crews after being drunk and incapable one too many times. Silent at the outset, in his trance he grew tearful and spoke like a frightened child till Ward, alarmed, woke him. On waking, Jago was mortified to find himself cowering and wet faced. He claimed to remember nothing of what had occurred and grew angry with Ward, though all Ward had done was ask him to call to mind his dead father. He stormed out of Helston House insisting Ward had been trying to possess him with witchcraft.

A few days later, Godritch called on Ward.

Pipp showed him into Ward's study, and he dropped into the chair opposite Ward's desk with a heavy sigh.

"Is something wrong?" Ward asked.

"Mr. Jones's family are swearing blind he's been abed since he returned from undergoing your experiments," Godritch told Ward flatly. "They say he's unable to see, hear, or speak since you put him in a trance."

Ward frowned. "Well, I can assure you, he was able to do all those things when he walked out my house shouting at the top of his voice."

Godritch nodded wearily. "I pointed out to them he must've got home somehow. Nevertheless, that's what they claim. And if they start spreading that rumour, your chances of getting any more subjects for your experiments will dwindle to nothing, I'm afraid."

Ward gave a harsh bark of laughter. "Well, that couldn't be much worse than what I've had so far."

Godritch sighed again. "Yes, I know and I'm sorry for it, but the truth is, the villagers have been more wary of your experiments than I expected them to be. It's not so much the hypnotism that bothers them as the rumours that your work involves electricity. Most people round here have lost men to storms at sea at some time or another, and they don't consider that such things are to be trifled with."

"Believe me, no one has more respect for the power of an electrical storm than I," Ward replied. "I wouldn't consider putting anyone in any kind of danger. For God's sake, I'm erecting lightning rods round the Zawn so that when I'm working in storm conditions, any strikes will be harmlessly discharged!"

"That's not how the villagers see it," Godritch said, shrugging. "So far as they're concerned, your lightning rods attract lightning, and they can't understand why on earth you'd want to do that."

"Oh, for God's sake!" Ward exclaimed, throwing up his hands. "That's ridiculous!"

"But that's how they think," Godritch pointed out patiently. "And that's why I've not been able to find anyone else willing to be a subject. Mind, I'll keep looking, but in the meantime, if you want the Jones family to be quiet, I suspect you're going to have to pay them some money."

As much as that rankled, Ward hadn't spent months building Helston House and planning the work he would carry out there, only to throw his efforts away now by allowing the Jones family to defame him the length and breadth of the county. Besides, as much as he doubted the truth of their claims over Jago's incapacity, he still felt faintly guilty every time he remembered the sight of the man weeping like a babe. And so, in the end, he instructed Godritch to offer the Jones clan twenty pounds in exchange for their silence, and they happily took it.

Jago Jones was, of course, walking and talking as well as anyone else within a day of the money being handed over. He blew the lot at a boxing match at Trebudannon, got spectacularly drunk, overturned his buggy on the way home, and caved in his skull. He died three days later.

Within a week, the whole county was whispering that his death was down to Sir Edward Carrick's mysterious electromagnetic experiments.

After that, there were no more subjects from Mr. Godritch.

CHAPTER THREE

28th April 1853
   The Admiral's Arms, Trevathany

"Well now, me 'ansome, what will you be having this fine day?"

Martha Trevylyn winked at Nick over the scarred wood of the bar and thrust her ample bosom out a little further. She was known to be a lusty one, Martha, and she'd made it plain to Nick on more than one occasion that she fancied him.

"A pint of ale, if you please, Martha."

"No smile for me today?" she teased, lifting up on tiptoe to unhook a metal tankard from the beam above her. Nick just grunted in reply, and she sighed dramatically. "It's a sin, is what it is, a man like you never cracking a smile. I daresay you'd be twice as lovely to look at if you did."

"I'm hardly lovely to look at," Nick scoffed, but Martha laughed.

"What've you to be so glum about anyway?" she demanded as she pumped out the frothy ale. "It's a lovely day. The blossom's on the trees, it's warm as high summer, and the maypole's going up today for May Day on Sunday. If it stays like this, we'll be dancing late into the night."

"That so?"

"It is—not that you're one for dancing." She set the tankard down in front of him and lifted the coins he'd laid there.

He took a swig of the ale. "That's true enough—I've two left feet."

She eyed him, unimpressed. "No use lying to me, Nick Hearn. I seen you dance with Jenny Lamb three years ago, and you were fine. Better than fine."

Nick forced a smile. "Jenny was a determined lass."

Martha laughed. "Oh, she's determined all right! I'll wager you're relieved she married the schoolteacher and laid off you. We was all sure she'd set her cap at you."

Nick's smile felt fixed and stiff, and he didn't know what to say. He'd felt a lot of things over Jenny's marriage to Gabe Meadows, but relief wasn't one of them.

"Promise you'll give me at least one dance, Nick," Martha wheedled. She sent him a wicked look from under her lashes, the sort of look that should have given him a cockstand, but never would.

"We'll see," he said at last. "Mayhap I'll fancy a jig come May Day, if I can get five minutes' peace and quiet to drink this good ale."

Martha put her hands on her hips and glared at him, mock-offended. "I swear you prefer the company of that ugly dog to me."

Nick glanced down at Snow, who lifted his head and gave a little grunt, as though he knew he was being talked about.

"Well," Nick said. "He talks less."

Laughing, Martha sauntered off to see to her next customer, and Snow set his heavy head back down on his paws.

The inn was busy, despite it being the middle of the day.

On a warm day like this, a working man liked a cool pint of ale to quench his thirst, and the place was full of labourers, fishermen, and other men who worked in the village and on the surrounding farms. There were a number of men his own age who Nick had attended the village school with and played with as a lad. Till the interest Godfrey Tremain had taken in him had marked him out as different from them.

Nick turned round to face the room, leaning one elbow on the bar behind him. He raised his tankard and drank deeply, enjoying the light, hoppy ale. He'd been out riding round the estate all morning and had been nursing his thirst in anticipation of this drink.

When he finally lowered the tankard, he glanced around the inn, nodding a few civil greetings at the other patrons without bothering to initiate conversation. He was a man of few words. He knew some people reckoned he thought he was better than everyone else because he'd risen from being Darklis Hearn's bastard to being steward to the Tremain family, but that was their lookout. He couldn't help what people thought or didn't think.

When Nick finished his ale and turned to set his empty tankard down on the bar, Jim, the innkeeper, caught his eye. He raised a questioning brow at Nick.

Another? was the unspoken question.

Nick swithered briefly, then nodded, and Jim brought a fresh tankard to him a minute later. He was halfway through his second ale when the door of the inn opened and a newcomer arrived—or rather, two newcomers. The first man was plainly a toff. He was elegantly dressed, all in shades of brown, and had the typical air of a rich man—the air of someone used to getting what he wanted, whenever he wanted it. He strode inside and looked boldly around, not bothering to shield his curiosity about the gathered clientele. The second, older man seemed to be the first man's servant. He appeared far less comfortable, his gaze flicking nervously about the room from behind his half-moon spectacles.

Gradually, the taproom fell silent. The toff removed his hat and regarded the inn's patrons with bright-eyed interest. He had a willowy sort of youthful grace—Nick guessed him to be somewhere in his twenties. His neatly side-parted hair was dark blond and his golden-brown eyes shone with intelligence and unconcealed curiosity. There was a delicacy to his clean-shaven face, with its fine, symmetrical features, yet there was firmness there too. Determination in the sharp jut of his jaw, boldness in the unshirking gaze.

Unexpectedly, desire rolled in Nick's belly, cresting like a wave that broke and flooded through him. The strength of his reaction took him by surprise, and he had to glance away briefly to consciously school his expression before he allowed himself to look back.

The toff offered the assembled company a smile. "Good afternoon, gentlemen," he said. Or rather barked.

Christ, that voice. The man might be fair, but his voice was scraping and hoarse. Nick waited for him to clear his throat, but he didn't, merely continued in the same harsh tone.

"Allow me to introduce myself. I am your new neighbour, Sir Edward Carrick. I live close to the Zawn—I'm sure you all know it. You may be aware that I've built a house there, where I carry out my work." He offered another of those engaging smiles. "I am a scientist."

"We know what you are," a voice assured him from the back of the inn. "You're the one messing around with 'lectricity and putting up lightning rods."

Sir Edward craned his neck, trying to find the owner of that voice. "Well, that's rather an oversimplification, but in essence, yes. I am investigating certain effects of electromagnetism, amongst other things. It is, as I'm sure you all know, an area that is being studied in some depth at this time. No doubt you're all familiar with the work of Mr. Faraday."

"Oh, to be sure!" someone else said, with a snort. "We're regular professors here at the Admiral's Arms."

That voice was closer, and familiar to Nick. Jed Hammett, one of Nick's boyhood friends. These days he was a fisherman—at least, he was when his brothers could extract him from the village hostelries. He liked his rum, did Jed, and he was a belligerent drunk as Nick knew too well, having had more than one run-in with the man when he was in his cups, when Jed would decide that Nick had gotten above himself and needed taking down a peg or two.

There were a few muted chuckles at Jed's comment. Sir Edward frowned, as though not quite sure if he was being laughed at, which he was, of course—at least as blatantly as a group of working men would ever laugh at a titled gentleman in broad daylight. Nick glanced about the taproom, taking in the shared glances and grins of the other patrons. On the other side of the room, Sir Edward's servant looked like he wished the ground would swallow him up. Nick lifted his tankard and took another swallow of ale, waiting to see what would happen next.

"Well," Sir Edward said, turning his head to address his comments to Jed. "Perhaps you might be interested in assisting with my experiments then? For that is my purpose today—I am seeking volunteers, and I am, of course, prepared to pay. Generously."

He gazed at the assembled company with a bright, expectant look that made Nick's gut twist. There was a spark of something in that hopeful look, something vital and rare. Something that he knew the other men in the taproom would see as nothing more than foolishness. That thought bothered Nick more than it ought to have, and he turned determinedly away to face the bar again, setting his tankard down on the wet wood and hunching over it, wanting nothing to do with that handsome, intriguing young man. Beside him, Snow pressed in close, his short, powerful body warm against Nick's calf.

"So, milord, what would these volunteers 'ave to do?"

That was Jed again, the rich, round burr of his Cornish accent a stark contrast to Sir Edward's upper-class rasp.

"Very little. Merely allow me to put them into an hypnotic trance, then open their minds to whatever messages might come to them from—" He faltered.

"From?" Jed prompted.

When Sir Edward spoke again, his voice sounded even harsher than before. More brusque. "From the spiritual plane —beyond the veil, if you will."

"*Beyond the veil?*" Jed repeated, his words infused with real amusement now. There were some subdued chuckles from the other patrons too, and a few more backs turned on Sir Edward as some of them grew bored with the scene, preferring to buy themselves more beer. Jim took a flurry of orders while Martha began gathering in the empty tankards that were pushed forward.

"You want us to speak to spirits? What do you think we are?" the first voice from the back of the room called out. "Gypsies with crystal balls?"

More laughter greeted that, a little less subdued this time. Some ineffective shushing followed. Tense and angry, and still facing away from the excruciating scene between the toff and Jed Hammett, Nick gripped his tankard so hard his knuckles turned white. As though sensing his emotions, Snow rubbed his head against Nick's leg, and Nick leaned down to give him a reassuring pat.

"Well now," Jed chuckled behind Nick, "if it's a *Gypsy* you're looking for, milord, we've got someone right up your street."

Nick stayed where he was, his back firmly to the room, but he knew from experience that more jibes would likely be coming, which probably meant that one of his regular half-joking, half-aggressive confrontations with Jed was inevitable. He really wasn't in the mood for it today. Not in front of this comely young man with his devil's bark of a voice who seemed to be oddly oblivious to being mocked.

But perhaps Sir Edward wasn't as oblivious as Nick thought, for when he answered Jed, his voice was all icy anger. "Kindly do not *presume* to tell me what I'm looking for," he snapped.

The impact of that was instantaneous. The muted chuckles died away, replaced by a newly respectful silence, and as pleased as he was to hear Jed being set down, Nick couldn't stop his lip curling at that. This was typical, wasn't it? The rich, titled gentleman presenting himself, uninvited, in the taproom of the local inn and expecting respect to be handed to him on a silver platter. Then reminding them all of his power when he didn't get it.

Nick half expected Jed, a notorious hothead in his cups, to snap back. But perhaps the fisherman hadn't yet had enough rum for that since, after a tense moment, he chuckled again and said, "I beg your pardon, milord, I didn't mean to offend you. Why don't you tell us what you're looking for, and we'll see if we can 'elp you."

"As I said, I'm looking for volunteers," Sir Edward replied stiffly. "I need subjects to work with me on my experiments—as many as I can get. I'll take anyone who's willing, but—and I apologise for the indelicacy of this—the recently bereaved would be especially welcome."

Nick blinked at those succinct and coolly spoken words.

"The recently bereaved would be especially welcome."

The toff said that as though it was an incidental thing. As though being recently bereaved was like having a particular colour of eyes.

"The bereaved?" Jed parroted, unconsciously reflecting Nick's thoughts. "Why would they be *especially* welcome?"

"It's been theorised that the recently bereaved are more receptive to communications from... the other side," Sir Edward explained stiffly.

"Oh, I see, it's been *theorised*, has it? Well I never!" Jed's clumsy sarcasm mimicked the man's upper-class intonation— so perhaps he'd had enough rum to be foolish after all. But this time no laughter greeted Jed's mockery, only silence. An uncomfortable, difficult silence that stretched and waited for Sir Edward's reaction.

"It seems," Sir Edward said at last, his rasping voice pricking at Nick's jagged nerves, "that I was mistaken in coming here. Furthermore, it seems—" and here he paused, before continuing in a louder voice that addressed everyone in the taproom, not only Jed "—that the men of Trevathany don't have nearly as much backbone as I'd thought they would. To be frank, I'm astonished to find that there is not one among you that isn't too craven to take part in a few simple scientific experiments."

The nature of the silence in the room shifted at that and the men slouching against the bar beside Nick began, slowly, to turn around to face Sir Edward again. With a muttered curse, Nick turned too, resenting his own foolish inability to mind his own business, while Snow circled Nick's legs anxiously, butting his head against Nick's calves.

The scientist stood in the middle of the taproom, his angry gaze travelling over the men gathered around him. His golden-brown eyes glittered with injured pride and his deter-mined jaw was rigid—perhaps from biting back yet more ill-considered words. Again, Nick's senses tingled in response to the man. He had a spark in him that called to Nick. Like the quickness of Godfrey's new dappled-grey mare, or the glimmer of life he'd seen in Snow when he'd first laid eyes on the dog's torn-up body in that alleyway in Truro. Why that should be, Nick had no idea. It made his brows draw together with displeasure till he was fairly glaring.

Jed said quietly but ominously, "Did I 'ear you right, milord? Did you just call the men in this taproom cowards? After what you did to Jago Jones?"

Jed was a big man. He topped Nick by at least three inches and Sir Edward by more like six. In bulk, he probably outweighed the scientist near enough two to one. Yet Sir Edward was uncowed. He glared at the big Cornishman with scorn in his eyes.

"Any man in this room who won't accept my offer because of Mr. Jones isn't just a coward, he's a fool," Sir Edward spat.

There were a few intakes of breath at that, and some uneasy murmuring.

"Now, now," Jim said from behind the bar. "Let's ease up 'ere, shall we?" He looked at Jed. "No more accusations from you, Jed." Then he glanced warily at Sir Edward, adding, "He don't mean nothing by it, sir. I'm sure none of us really know what happened to Jag—I mean, Mr. Jones."

Sir Edward eyed the innkeeper. "Well, *I* know what happened," he snapped. "Mr. Jones overturned his cart and broke his head open because he was drunk. The only part of it that I had anything to do with was that I gave him the money that he drank himself into a stupor with."

Jed greeted that blunt statement with silence, but his expression was ugly. He eyed Sir Edward with blatant, naked dislike and a couple of the onlookers standing nearest to the scientist took a step away from him, as though to disassociate themselves from whatever Jed might do, or perhaps just to avoid Jed's fists. Sir Edward's servant was eyeing the crowd carefully, as though weighing up the situation, and all the while, Sir Edward kept glaring at his aggressor, not giving an inch.

This was going to come to blows if someone didn't step in. Nick mightn't altogether mind the thought of Jed Hammett being dragged up before the magistrate again, and Sir Edward might be behaving with the usual high-handedness of the rich, but still, Nick found he didn't like the thought of that comely face being marked with bruises from Jed's fists.

With an inward sigh, he slammed his tankard down on the bar. The clatter of metal on wood caused half the heads in the taproom to turn his way.

"Well, Jed," Nick said. "Even you must admit that driving your buggy arse over tit is apt to do you in."

There was a little uneasy laughter at that. Slowly, menacingly, Jed turned his attention from Sir Edward to Nick. Nick offered him an insouciant grin, feigning relaxed amusement, though in truth he was holding himself loose and easy, ready for violence should Jed rush him.

There was little love lost between him and Jed these days, but there was, at least, a modicum of respect if it came to a fight. When they were boys, they'd run wild together, playing and arguing and yes, brawling a few times, until Jed had finally realised that, despite being much bigger, he couldn't guarantee he'd beat the Gypsy's bastard every time—and he certainly couldn't cow him, as he could so easily the other boys.

"Well now, if it isn't Nick 'Earn!" Jed said, all aggressive friendliness. "I was just speaking of you to milord here." He turned back to the scientist. "Mr. 'Earn is the Gypsy bast—sorry, *gentleman* I mentioned to you, milord. He is just the man for you, is Nick. For these 'speriments of your'n."

Sir Edward's jaw tightened, eyes flashing with irritation as he anticipated more mockery, but Jed held his hands up in a *wait a moment* gesture.

"Now, hear me out, milord. You'll like this, what with you looking for someone who might be closer to the *veil* an' all." He pointed at Nick. "This 'ere Gypsy, not only did his old mother pass away just last year—which is one of the partic'lars you're looking for, you said—but better'n that, he *sees ghosts*. Ain't that the truth now, Nick?"

Nick's gut clenched. He itched to ram his fist into Jed's smirking face, and only the knowledge that that was precisely what the fisherman wanted stopped him. By sheer force of will he maintained a neutral expression, opening his mouth to disavow Jed's words, only for Sir Edward to beat him to it.

"You've seen ghosts?" Sir Edward said, fixing that golden-brown gaze on Nick for the first time. His expression was curious. Avid. And somehow, without intending to, Nick found himself answering.

"I was practically a babe when it happened." He shrugged. "Probably imagined the whole thing."

Jed gave a chuckle and wagged a finger at Nick. "Oh no. I remember that night like it were yesterday. You saw something right enough. The look on your face was a sight to see." He turned back to Sir Edward. "None of *us* saw anything, you understand. But, well, Nick's a Gypsy, see? And them Gypsies? Some say they're related to the devil hisself, don't they? Stands to reason Nick 'ere would be able to see spirits."

Sir Edward didn't even acknowledge Jed's words. He canted his head a little to one side, studying Nick intently. Nick felt that unfaltering gaze like a physical touch, his cock stirring in his drawers as another wave of desire broke in his belly. *Christ.* Why did the man affect him like this?

"What did you see, Mr. Hearn?" he asked.

Nick pressed his lips together and shook his head, annoyed with himself for not laughing off Jed's charge immediately as he'd usually have done. "Nothing," he said flatly. "It was a child's fancy, nothing more."

"Don't listen to him," Jed told Sir Edward. "He saw the Physic, a ghost as has been walking this village for nigh on two hundred years. He saw it as clear as I see you now, milord. We was"—he glanced at Nick—"what do you think, Nick? Seven? Eight? And you told me everything about that ghost, didn't you? From the square buckles on his shoes to the beaky mask he wore on his head to keep out bad humours. When I told old Granny Hammett what you said, she said to me, 'That Gypsy's bastard's seen the good doctor, all right! He's got him right in every partic'lar.'"

Nick gave a tight laugh. "I'd probably heard your granny talking about what the Physic looked like and repeated it all back to you. She always did blather on."

Jed ignored that, his attention on Sir Edward again. "And what's more, Nick's mother—God rest her soul—she told fortunes," he continued, jerking his thumb at Nick. "Read them fancy picture cards to tell people's futures. Tea leaves too. Nick 'ere probably gets the sight from her."

Nick's hands tightened into fists at his sides. If there was one thing he couldn't stand, it was the likes of Jed Hammett talking about his mother. But before he could spit a word out, Sir Edward distracted him, his own words tumbling out in a hoarse, rasping rush.

"Mr. Hearn, I must say, this all sounds very promising— would you consider coming to Helston House to discuss these matters with me in more detail? I promise I will pay you generously for your time."

Nick turned back to Sir Edward. The man's eyes shone with hopeful eagerness as he spoke and for an instant, Nick contemplated their unusual hue. They reminded him of acorns, he thought. That smooth, nutty colour. It wasn't just the colour that arrested him though. It was how *unguarded* that gaze was. Where was the caution in this man's soul? Did he always show his thoughts like this? So plain on his face for all to see? He seemed already to have forgotten his brief alter-cation with Jed Hammett—now he was entirely taken up with Nick, and this nonsense Jed had started about Nick having *the sight*.

Nonsense Nick had no intention of indulging.

Somehow, finally, Nick found his voice. "Thank you for

the offer, Sir Edward," he said politely. "But I already have a position that pays me well enough. I really have no need of any other employment."

And with one last nod, he walked out of the taproom, with Snow lumbering at his heels.

CHAPTER FOUR

1st May 1853

Three full days after his disastrous visit to the inn in the village, Ward decided to go to speak to Nicholas Hearn in person. He told Pipp he was taking an evening stroll and set off for the cottage on the outskirts of the village that he'd learned Hearn occupied.

It had been a lovely spring day and even now, at seven in the evening, it was pleasantly warm. The sun, which was still some way off setting, was low in the sky and tiny insects danced in the hazy sunbeams that shafted through the tree canopy.

As Ward strolled, he thought about Nicholas Hearn. A few days before, the man had poured cold water on Mr. Hammett's claim that Hearn had seen a ghost when he was a child. But even at the time, Ward had felt sure in his bones that there was something to the story. He'd seen Hearn's face when Hammett had spoken of those long ago events, and somehow he had known Hearn had been genuinely shaken to be reminded of them.

It wasn't even that Hearn's face had given him away—in fact, to the casual observer, he would have seemed remarkably unaffected by the whole incident—but something had flashed in his eyes before he blinked it away and resettled his calm expression. It was the briefest of betrayals, but Ward had seen it. Difficult to miss, he supposed, given how intently he had been staring at the man by then.

"Even you must admit that driving your buggy arse over tit is apt to do you in."

What had prompted Hearn to chime in with that irreverent observation? As the conversation had continued, he hadn't struck Ward as a joker. Quite the opposite, with his serious, intense expression. Christ, those eyes! With Hearn's dark colouring, Ward would have expected the man to have eyes like sloes. But no, Hearn's eyes were a light, silvery grey. That unusual gaze of his, coupled with his quiet stillness, made Ward think of a wolf. Watchful, intelligent, wary.

Wild.

Given the stories of ghost sightings and clairvoyance in his family, Ward couldn't help but speculate that Hearn might well be sensitive to spirits—that he could, in fact, be the perfect subject for Ward's experiments. Annoying then, that he seemed determined not to participate. Well, Ward had no intention of accepting his refusal so easily. He was at least going to give persuading him another try.

It wasn't going to be easy to bring Hearn around. Most of the villagers had probably already decided Ward was a lunatic, or at the very least an eccentric, with his talk of breaching the veil between the physical world and the spirit world. That in itself didn't come as a surprise. After all, hadn't his own peers reached exactly that conclusion? Hell, each and every one of them had abandoned him following the debacle over Mrs. Haydn.

Unthinkingly, Ward's hand went to his inside pocket. With his fingertips, he grazed the edge of the wallet that contained last year's newspaper clipping. He didn't need to take the clipping out to remember what it said. Every word of Professor Arnold's letter to *The Times* was burned into his memory.

Sir—I was most surprised to read Sir Edward Carrick's letter of 16th inst. regarding the recent séances he has attended conducted by a Well Known American Medium. Sir Edward is a learned young gentleman who has justifiably earned, at the tender age of five-and-twenty, a considerable reputation amongst his peers, principally for his work in the physical and natural sciences. I have the utmost respect for Sir Edward's work in this field, and it was therefore with the greatest dismay that I read his letter. Not only did he defend this lady, he even went so far as to suggest that her claims to have powers of clairvoyance were true, despite Dr. Jeffrey's reports of clear evidence to the contrary during the séance he attended. Sir Edward's letter reveals not only a lack of personal judgment in this instance, but a careless disregard for the responsibility men of learning bear towards their less educated brethren. It is for this reason that I feel I must denounce it, and him, in the most unambiguous terms...

Ward's stomach churned just thinking of that letter—never mind the other five that had been published that week along the same vein—but he forced himself to remember every word. He refused to flinch from what had happened. He had to remember what he had vowed to himself: that he must be prepared not only to think the unthinkable, but to apply his knowledge to finding explanations for the unthinkable. Because there *were* explanations, of that he was quite sure.

Ward had hoped that money would be enough to persuade the people of Trevathany to help him, but fear and superstition seemed to be keeping those who might need the money away, and it turned out Nicholas Hearn didn't fall into that category anyway. Despite being referred to as a *Gypsy's bastard* by Hammett, Hearn held a respectable position as land steward to the Tremains, the first family of the county. Ward could see that a man in that position might not wish to be seen to be helping a seemingly eccentric scientist with his work. But what if Ward met with Hearn alone? Made a personal plea for his assistance and explained properly what his work entailed? Surely Ward would have at least a chance of persuading him, particularly given what he was willing to pay?

He had to believe so.

It was only two miles from Helston House to his destination and so, less than half an hour after setting off, Ward found himself approaching Hearn's home, a white-painted cottage with a black slate roof. He made his way through the overgrown garden to the front door, scents of camomile and thyme drifting on the warm evening air.

Lifting his hand, he gave a peremptory knock on the heavy, old wood, and waited.

There was no answer.

He knocked again, then again, waiting several minutes. He tried, rudely, to peer through one of the tiny windows, but it was gloomy inside and he couldn't see much of anything.

Damn it all, was the man out?

Where might he be? Back at the village inn? No doubt a lot of the village folk would repair there in the evenings for refreshment and conversation, and of course, Hearn lived alone. Perhaps he grew lonely, as Ward sometimes did? It could be isolating, living alone. Even for a man like Ward who was so very busy with his work.

He wasn't sure he fancied venturing back to the inn. That scene with the fisherman who'd seemed determined to taunt him—and to rile Hearn while he was at it—hadn't been at all comfortable, but he did want to see Hearn. Ward considered what to do, chewing his lip a moment, but at length he decided to go into the village, just for a look.

He set off down the road. Here at the edge of the village, it was terribly quiet. Just a handful of cottages and no children out playing, no neighbours chatting or pottering around. It seemed, in fact, unusually quiet for such a warm evening. Once he'd gone a little further though, Ward realised that it was quiet because something was happening in the village. The strains of some ramshackle music carried on the breeze. Distant voices too, and laughter, and the shrieks of children playing. Frowning, he wondered what the occasion was, then suddenly remembered: it was May Day.

May Day was an important occasion round these parts— Pipp had mentioned something about a festival, he seemed to recall. No doubt the celebrations would have been going on all day, with a May Queen being crowned, perhaps dancing round a maypole, and much eating and drinking.

Hearn must be there. Possibly cheerful with ale and sunshine. It mightn't be a bad time to try to get him alone so that Ward could make his plea.

As he drew closer to the centre of the village, the noise grew, the clamour of voices becoming more distinct. He followed the sound of fiddles, pipes, drums, and singing through the narrow streets and lanes of the oldest part of the village till eventually he emerged onto a wide open stretch of village green.

It looked as though everyone in Trevathany was there. Families were scattered around the grass, eating and drinking and laughing, while a group of men danced some ancient country dance, hopping and crashing wooden staffs together. Beside them, a few girls played a complicated skipping game, while a pack of smaller children ran wildly around, darting between blankets and dancers and skipping girls and screeching whenever they caught sight of what looked to be a tall man with a horse's skull for a head, shaking a staff decorated with ribbons and jangling bells at them.

The village women were all dressed in simple light-coloured gowns while the men were all hatless and lounging on the grass in their shirtsleeves. Suddenly Ward felt very out of place in his high-crowned hat, elegantly tailored coat, and four-in-hand necktie, especially when he saw the curious looks being sent his way. Despite his growing discomfort though, he stayed where he was. He hated to give up, having come this far in the hopes of seeing Nicholas Hearn.

Just then, he caught sight of a familiar face. A young man walking towards him with a pretty young lady on his arm. It took him a moment to place the fellow, then he remembered —it was the clerk from Mr. Godritch's office, the one who had written up the agency agreement.

He stepped forward, catching the surprised young man's eye. "Good evening, Mr.—" he hesitated an instant, then it came to him, tumbling from his mind to his lips with only the barest pause "—Pascoe. How nice to see you again."

"Sir Edward—" Pascoe looked stunned at Ward's unexpected recognition of him before hurriedly saying, "Ah—good evening!" He glanced briefly at the young lady at his side, adding, "This is Gracie—I mean, may I introduce Miss Grace Evans?"

Ward bowed politely to the young lady, who nodded back wide-eyed, then bobbed an inelegant curtsey.

Ward turned his attention back to Pascoe. "I wonder if you can help me, Mr. Pascoe? Do you know Mr. Hearn? Mr. Nicholas Hearn?"

"Yes, of course."

"Oh good. Have you seen him this evening?"

Pascoe turned his head to scan the villagers dotted about the green, before returning his gaze to Ward. "He was certainly here earlier, but I don't see him now. He might've gone home, I suppose, or he might have gone down to the mill stream. There was talk among some of the men about jumping over it for a wager. Gid Paget was in on it, and he's a friend of Nick's—Mr. Hearn, I mean."

Ward smiled. "Thank you, Mr. Pascoe. That's most help-ful. I'll try the mill stream. Could you direct me there?"

~

Pascoe's directions took Ward just outside the village and onto a bridle path that, when followed to its end, brought one to the next village. Ward had only been strolling a few minutes when he encountered three men coming the other way. One was soaked to the skin and was being held up by the other two. All three were singing a song about someone called "Lovely Molly."

"I beg your pardon," Ward said, stopping them in their tracks. With his ugly voice, he never sounded polite, always harsh and probably angry—not the best when accosting three really rather drunk men. Ward smiled to make up for his unfriendly tone. "Will I find Mr. Nicholas Hearn down this way?"

The three men stared at him for a moment, then one of them said, "'Bout another quarter mile down this path. Unless him and Gabe Meadows have gone off walking the other way, that is. He's a reg'lar wandering Gypsy, our Nick."

"Well, he certainly wandered over that stream easily enough," another added. "Not like you, Bert!"

"'Wandered'? 'E bleddy flew!" the soaked one slurred indignantly, his Cornish burr thick. "Like a bleddy airy-mouse, 'e was!"

"Airymouse"?

The other two laughed at that and they set off on their way again. They'd scarce walked the length of themselves before the one in the middle hissed to the others, with the too-loud care of the very drunk, "That's 'im as sent Jago Jones to his death."

One of the other men shushed him quickly, darting a quick glance back at Ward before starting up the "Lovely

Molly" song again. And then they were weaving away, stumbling round a bend in the path, their voices already fading. Ward sighed and set off in the direction they'd come from.

The trees grew thicker the further down the bridle path Ward walked, creating a leafy canopy over his head through which the evening sun gently streamed. After a few minutes, he couldn't hear the men he'd met at all. Only the twittering of a few birds coming home to roost disturbed the peace. Ward removed his hat and strolled on, enjoying the warmth and the silence.

And then, just as he drew close to the bridge, he heard the low murmur of new voices. Male voices.

Later, he would wonder what it was that made him slow his step at that point. Consciously hush his own movements. Perhaps it was the edge of anguish in those voices. But at the time, he was only acting instinctively.

He moved carefully forward, listening attentively.

At first he couldn't make out words, only that there were two voices, and something... contentious was being discussed. But this was no ordinary argument between two ordinary men. This was something much more intimate. One voice was implacable, a little angry, the other pleading. As Ward drew closer, the first words he discerned were "No"— this from the angry voice—and from the pleading one, "Nick, *please*."

Nick. Nicholas Hearn.

Ward moved closer still. Just a few feet ahead, there was a turnoff from the main bridle path, a smaller footpath that led to the mill stream, and to the little bridge over the water. Carefully, quietly, Ward stepped onto the footpath and walked a little further, his steps tentative. The voices were becoming more distinct now, and when he saw the sun-dappled outline of a figure ahead, through the trees, he stopped, heart in his mouth. Glancing around, he saw a shadowy copse on the same side of the path where the two men stood. He would be out of sight there, but able to see, and to hear.

This was very wrong—he knew it was—and yet Ward found himself stealing into the copse, holding his arms close to his body and turning his hips so he could slip between two trees without so much as brushing a leaf.

"I saw you looking at me, Nick. I know you still want me."

Ward's heart thundered so loudly it was amazing he could hear what was being said. But oh God, he did. He heard every word.

"So what if I do?" This voice was bitter. "It's hardly the point. You are *married*."

Ward was so close, he didn't dare move his feet, but he swayed there, tilting his head till he found the best view from between the thick, leafy branches.

Now he could see them. Standing there, illuminated by the evening sun, while he stood, like a thief, in the shadows. Nicholas Hearn was dressed like the other villagers. His shirt sleeves were rolled up to his elbows, revealing well-made forearms, his tawny skin contrasting with the white cotton. His dark waistcoat was open, and his simple shirt had no collar. The top button was undone, and Ward's gaze went straight to the twin points of his collar bones at the base of his throat, and the deep dimple between them, before moving up to take in the furious expression Hearn wore as he glared at his companion.

From this vantage point, Ward could see Hearn's face quite well, but of the other man he saw little more than a head of reddish-brown hair and a sliver of his profile. Nothing of his expression. This man was a bit taller than Hearn, and a bit leaner too. He was dressed more formally than Hearn, though not so much as Ward. He wore a coat at any rate, and looked to have a tie about his neck.

"Nick, please, I'm going back to Truro tomorrow," the

man said, his voice gentle now. "Can't we have one more time together? There's only you in the cottage now." He lifted his hand and set it on Hearn's shoulder, and Hearn closed his eyes, his expression almost pained.

"Gabe," he whispered. "Don't."

"But I can't stay away," Gabe murmured back. He lifted his other hand and curled it round the nape of Hearn's neck, leaning in and pressing his mouth against Hearn's lips.

Hearn's hands were fisted at his sides, the knuckles white, as though he was fighting with himself not to put his arms round the man kissing him, even as he let his mouth be taken.

Ward stared at them, appalled and aroused and now drenched with guilt. He rubbed at the placket of his trousers, trying to discourage his stiff cock from hardening further. This was not for his eyes. This was not for anyone's eyes but the two men standing in front of him. And Christ, how foolish were they to do this here, where they might be seen by anyone happening along? They were lucky—damned lucky—it was him and no other.

It was past time he left. Past time he retreated a good way back. He readied himself to do just that while they were still caught up in the tight, desperate kiss, but before he could move, Hearn lifted those arms—not to pull Gabe into a closer embrace, but to thrust him back. So hard that the taller man stumbled.

"Nick," Gabe gasped. "Bloody hell, what's wrong with you?"

Hearn's expression was all disgusted misery. He wiped at his mouth with the back of his hand. "Just go," he spat. "Go on, fuck off back to your wife."

"Why can't you forget about her?" Gabe demanded, his voice edged with frustration. "If I can, you should be able to. Jesus, Nick, it's not as though she'd care! She doesn't want me anywhere near her since the baby came."

Hearn gave a bark of laughter. "Ah, now I see why you

followed me up here. Jenny's not letting you tup her, so you're looking for another bed to warm?" His lip curled up in a sneer. "Not even that probably—it's not as though we ever needed a bed before, is it?"

"Christ, Nick—"

"Tell you what, if you want it so much, I'll let you suck my cock. You can do it here, on your knees, the way I used to for you. You spilling down my throat while I spilled in the dirt."

Hearn's vitriolic words shocked Ward, so much so he felt physically winded by them, as though he'd been thrown by a horse and had all the air knocked out of him. He had to lay his hand on the tree beside him to steady himself, taking in a shaky breath as quietly as he could manage. He heard the pain in those words, registered Hearn's hurt, accusatory tone, but even as he did so, his mind was supplying vivid images of this Gabe—or was it himself?—dropping to his knees while Nicholas Hearn unbuttoned his trousers... and God, but it was a picture that made his cock stiffen and throb. The thought of that fierce face staring down at Ward as Ward leaned forward, opening his mouth...

Ward swallowed thickly, blinking the fantasy away, focusing his attention back on the two men facing each other.

Hearn glared at Gabe, those silvery eyes burning a cold fire as he waited for some kind of response, but Gabe said nothing and eventually, after long moments of silence, Hearn gave a mocking laugh. "I thought not."

He turned away so he faced the stream, giving Gabe—and Ward—his back.

When next he spoke, his voice was low and weary. "Go back to Truro, Gabe."

"*Nick*—" Gabe's voice cracked with some emotion, and behind Hearn's implacable back, he lifted his hand, as though to touch him. He never made contact though. His hand hovered there, trembling in the air while Hearn stood, unmoving, looking out over the water.

Eventually, Gabe sighed and let his arm drop.

"I'm sorry," he said, with what sounded like real sorrow. "I shouldn't have followed you here."

"No," Nick said, without turning. "You shouldn't."

Unseen by Hearn, Gabe nodded, shoulders slumping. Then without another word—not even a farewell—he turned and began to walk towards Ward. Towards the path that led back to the village.

Alarmed, Ward drew further into the shadows of the dense copse. He was standing off the footpath itself and well hidden by the trees; nevertheless, he couldn't help but worry he'd be seen. When Gabe passed him though, just a few feet from where Ward himself stood, he didn't so much as glance Ward's way, merely trudged away down the footpath.

Heart thudding, Ward watched him leave. He watched till Gabe had turned off onto the bridle path and vanished entirely out sight, and he kept watching for several minutes afterwards, all the while staying as still and silent as he could amongst the shadowy trees.

When finally he looked back at Nicholas Hearn, he saw that the man hadn't moved so much as an inch. He stood in the exact same spot he'd been in when Gabe had left, still staring out over the little stream.

Heart thudding, Ward considered the best way to extricate himself from his predicament—he'd given up on the idea of talking to Hearn as soon as he'd realised what he was witnessing. Best to slip away and never speak to anyone of what he'd seen and heard this evening. The prudent thing to do would be to wait for Hearn to leave, then give it a few minutes before making his own escape. The only trouble with that plan was that Hearn was showing no sign of going anywhere. In fact, now he was sitting himself down on the grass and there was something about the set of those broad shoulders, and the stillness of his lonely figure, that made Ward suspect he was settling in for a while.

At last, deciding he had no choice but to try to sneak away as quietly as possible, Ward took a deep breath and stepped carefully back towards the footpath—immediately cracking a stick loudly beneath his boot.

Hearn whirled round at the sudden sound, scrambling to his feet. "Who's there?" he cried. He glared into the shadowy area where Ward stood, and suddenly Ward felt like the worst sort of creeping voyeur—he'd known from the beginning he should've walked away as soon as he'd realised what was going on, but instead he'd let his curiosity about Nicholas Hearn take over.

Now he would have to own his shameful behaviour.

Ward forced himself to step out of the shadows—to walk past the line of trees that disguised him and meet Nicholas Hearn face-to-face. His cheeks flamed with heat as he saw the expression on Hearn's face: wary fear and incipient fury.

"What were you doing? Were you *hiding* in there?" Hearn demanded. He stepped forward, and Ward immediately took a step back, stumbling a little. Already he was regretting his brief moment of courage—Hearn wasn't much taller than Ward, but he was broader, and right now, looked very fierce. What's more, he wasn't as alone as Ward had initially believed. The ugly white dog that had been with him in the inn was here too. It trotted over from wherever it had been nosing around to stand beside Hearn and stare at Ward with its single baleful eye.

In the face of Ward's stumbling retreat, Hearn halted, pulled back a little, and the dog glanced up at his master as though for instruction.

"Well?" Hearn demanded. He seemed to find an answer to his question on Ward's face—perhaps in the intensifying heat that Ward felt flare on his cheeks—and added more softly, more dangerously, "How long were you there?"

Ward coughed—a nervous habit of his. Trying to clear a throat that could never be cleared.

"A while," he admitted at last in his usual rasping tone.

Hearn studied him, his face oddly expressionless. At last he said flatly. "I don't know what you heard, but—"

Ward interrupted. "It's none of my business." His throat ached, the way it sometimes did when he'd overused his voice, which was ridiculous when he'd barely spoken to anyone all day.

Hearn remained impassive, though Ward saw his throat bob just before he asked, "Why are you here then?"

"I was looking for you in the village," Ward replied carefully. "Someone told me you'd come up to the mill stream, so I followed you. When I realised you weren't alone—" he broke off, sudden shame flooding him "—I should have left. I'm sorry, I didn't intend to… witness anything."

Hearn was pale now. "So you overheard?"

Ward's cheeks blazed even hotter. "I didn't intend to," he repeated miserably, then, compelled to honesty, "But yes, I did overhear your… disagreement."

Hearn swallowed again and ran his hand over the back of his neck, agitated. Beside him, the white dog snuffled, bumping its head against his lower leg.

"Mr. Hearn," Ward said, holding up his hands, palms outwards. "The reason I wanted to speak with you was because I *very* much want you to help me with my studies. Ideally I would like to work with at least half a dozen subjects, but if I can only get one, you seem to me to be a particularly suitable candidate." He paused, then added, more firmly, "In short, I *need* your assistance, Mr. Hearn."

Hearn turned his silvery gaze back on Ward. A watchful, wild wolf.

"Is that so?"

"It is," Ward replied, nodding vigorously. "I want you to work with me, Mr. Hearn." He offered what he hoped was a winning smile. "And I'm not generally considered to be the sort of man who'll take no for an answer."

There was a brief pause, then Hearn laughed. It wasn't a real laugh though. It was an angry, unamused sound that made Ward's own smile wither.

When Hearn spoke, his voice was bitter. "Christ, you must be thanking your lucky stars you stumbled on me and Gabe."

For a moment, Ward was bewildered by Hearn's furious words. Then the light dawned.

Hearn thought Ward was blackmailing him.

Ward nearly laughed aloud—only the disgusted expression on Hearn's face stopped him. Ward opened his mouth to reassure him that he had no such intention... but no words came out. He remembered their last encounter. Hearn's words.

"Thank you for the offer, Sir Edward. But I already have a position that pays me well enough. I really have no need of any other employment."

He realised then that there was no chance of Hearn agreeing to help him with his studies willingly. Saw too that this was... an opportunity, and as ignominious as it might be to take advantage of it, it was likely his only chance to obtain Hearn's assistance.

His work mattered.

George mattered.

Heart thudding, Ward spoke slowly.

"I would like us to help each other, Mr. Hearn."

CHAPTER FIVE

From *The Collected Writings of Sir Edward Carrick*, volume I

George and I were sent away to school when we were nine years old, but after my illness, I had to stay at home. A tutor was secured for me as a temporary measure, but it was intended I would return to school when I was well enough. As it happened though, under my excellent tutor's watch, I became, for the first time, a devoted student and began to excel in my studies. As a keen geologist, Mr. Lucas instilled within me a passion for the sciences that would prove to be lifelong.

When I confessed to my mother how much I had hated being away from home when I first went to school, she decided she would prefer me to remain at home. No doubt, she was influenced by her conviction that I was now of a delicate constitution and required gentle handling, a misconception I am ashamed to say I took ruthless advantage of. She spoke to my father, pointing out that under Mr. Lucas's tutelage, I had progressed far quicker than George and the other boys in our age group at school, and suggested it would be better to allow me to complete my studies at my own swift pace. At length, my father, despite being a Winchester fellow through and through, agreed I might be educated at home. And so it came to pass that I was ready for university two years before George, but never learned how to row, box, or bowl anyone out at cricket nearly as well as him.

∾

8ᵗʰ May 1853

As soon as Nick awoke the following Sunday morning, before he even came to full alertness, he knew there was something he had to do that day. It took a few moments before he remembered what it was, but when he did, he groaned aloud, throwing an arm over his face. He had to go up to Helston House.

For a while he lay in bed, mulling over the stories he'd heard in the village about what Sir Edward did to his "subjects." It was all rather vague. Tom Cadzow claimed he couldn't even remember what happened, but he was a dozy lad, that one. As for Jago Jones, his family claimed that Sir Edward had put him into a trance and shocked him with electricity. They said that was what made him so addled he'd overturned his own buggy. Nick didn't believe that for a minute—he'd known Jago for years, and he was fairly sure that Sir Edward's version of events was nearer the truth. It was brandy and ale that had addled Jago's brains that day.

But what if it was true? What if Sir Edward wanted to shock Nick? The very thought made Nick shudder. Men didn't benefit from being struck with lightning, did they? And then there was the prospect of being put in a trance. Being in someone else's control. He hated that idea. It was almost enough to resolve him to defy Sir Edward, until he considered the other, more pressing danger he faced. If he was brought up on charges, at worst he'd be looking at the noose, at best prison. Maybe even a spell in the stocks. The local mob wouldn't stay its viciousness against a sodomite.

Just thinking about that made Nick keenly aware of his aloneness in the world. Growing up, he'd been the Romany boy—the Gypsy woman's bastard. As if that hadn't been enough to set him apart, Godfrey Tremain had stepped in when he was twelve years old, plucking him out from the pack of village boys to educate him and elevate his station in life. Now, his position was far above the men he used to play with when he was a boy, and he knew that at times he was resented for it. He wasn't one of them anymore, but nor did he belong with the Tremains and their sort. Sir Edward Carrick's sort. People like them would never see Nick as an equal. In their eyes, he was no more than a well-paid, well-educated servant, one with a distinct disadvantage in his far-from-respectable birth.

As for his Romany family. Well, he didn't even know them.

He belonged nowhere, and to no one. If he was sent to gaol, no one would be waiting for his release. If he was broken and beaten in the stocks, no one would be there to mend his hurts. Those stark truths were painful to contemplate.

When he'd first met Gabe, things had been different for a while. Gabe had come to Trevathany to take up the position of village schoolmaster. Like Nick, he hadn't really fit in with anyone else, and they'd drifted into spending time together—sharing a table at the Admiral's Arms in the evenings, walking or going fishing down at the mill stream on Sundays. They'd become friends. Then, one night when Gabe was drunk and Nick stupid, Nick had learned that he wasn't alone in his desire for his own sex, and they'd become more than friends. For a short while, things had been good. And then Gabe had gone and married Jenny Lamb, without so much as a word of warning to Nick before he did it.

It was that thought that finally got Nick out of bed. No matter what lay ahead of him today, anything would be better than lying in bed brooding about Gabe. He threw back his bedcovers and jumped up, shivering in the cold morning air. Snow lifted his head from his bed in the corner of the room, regarding Nick for a moment before yawning, stretching, and wandering over for some attention, grunt-snuffling his dear, ugly face into Nick's hand.

Nick patted him affectionately, running his hand idly over the dog's velvet-soft ears.

"You'll have to wait here today," he told Snow apologetically. "I can't take you with me."

Snow looked disgusted. He turned away and lumbered back to his rumpled blanket bed, circling three times before settling himself down with his head in his paws, his single, heavy, rheumy eye fixed reproachfully on his master.

Nick sighed. "Sulk if you must then." He crossed the room and lifted the water ewer, pouring a basinful of freezing water. Gritting his teeth against the cold, he grabbed the soap and washed himself thoroughly. Then he wet his thick black hair so he could comb it down neatly. He hadn't liked the avid gleam in Sir Edward's eyes when Jed had been going on about Nick being a Gypsy, and he was determined not to look like anyone's idea of a Gypsy today. Today he would be Godfrey Tremain's respectable, educated steward, and Sir Edward could like it or lump it.

He dressed in his usual tweeds, tied his necktie neatly, pocketed his silver watch, and fastened the silver watch chain in place between his waistcoat button and pocket. Godfrey Tremain had given him this watch three years before. Nick had been summoned to the old man's study, and when he'd entered, it had been to find Godfrey leaning back in his wingback chair with a long black leather box sitting on the gleaming desk in front of him.

"Open it," Godfrey had said. "It's for you."

When Nick had lifted the lid and seen what lay inside, he'd been astonished. "What's this for?"

"You've worked hard," the old man had said gruffly. "I had it made for you. Jacob had one just like it."

Jacob. Godfrey's son, dead and away. Nick's—

"Of course, his was gold."

Nick had looked up at those sharp words, and the old man's expression had been flat and hard. Unhappy in a way Nick wasn't sure he understood. His heart had ached with something like pity, even as his gut burned with resentment at the point the old man seemed to be making.

Sometimes he wished he'd thrown the watch back in Godfrey's face there and then, but it would have been more of a reaction than he'd ever have been willing to let the old man see.

And besides, it was a good reminder, the watch. Of what he was.

So he'd kept his anger tamped down, his expression blank, and thanked Godfrey in a neutral tone that betrayed neither pleasure nor hurt. Giving the old man nothing in return.

Nick checked his reflection in the mirror. The silver watch chain gleamed at his waist. He looked respectable in his smart tweeds, but not wealthy. A difficult man to place, perhaps, if you passed him in the street.

Well, perhaps that was no bad thing, he decided. For the day he had ahead of him.

Sir Edward's new house was built on land he'd bought from Godfrey Tremain. It was part of a much larger plot of unused land that Nick had spent the last two years trying to persuade Godfrey to start farming himself. He'd been close to achieving his objective when Sir Edward had turned up out of nowhere and made an unsolicited, and very generous, offer for a number of acres surrounding the Zawn. For now, the rest of the plot remained fallow, and Nick was biding his time before starting in on Godfrey again.

Sir Edward had sited his new house about a quarter mile from the Zawn, where Nick and the other village children used to play when he was a boy. It struck Nick as an odd place to choose to build a house—beside an eighty-foot chasm going down to the sea—but Nick supposed the house must be far enough away that there was no concern about subsidence. Certainly, when Sir Edward had first purchased the land, some men had come up to survey the ground. Nick had seen them when he was out walking, pacing around with charts and mathematical instruments. He supposed they must have satisfied themselves on that score.

Helston House itself was a blunt, unapologetic edifice. To Nick's eyes, it looked defiantly modern, the edges of the masonry sharply perfect, the sandstone bright and unweathered, the great bank of windows at the front of the house glittering with brand-new glass. As he walked up to the front door, his belly churning with a mix of nerves and resentment, it swung open.

"Good morning, Mr. Hearn," said the man who stood there. He had neatly combed greying hair, a neatly trimmed moustache and beard, and a neat pair of gold-framed half-moon spectacles perched on his long nose. Nick recognised him as the servant who had been with Sir Edward in the Admiral's Arms.

Nick cleared his throat. "Good morning." He gave the servant a brusque nod, and added, "I've an appointment with your master."

The servant inclined his head. "I am aware, sir. Please do

come in." He stood aside in invitation, and Nick stepped past him, walking though the small porch and emerging into an imposing hallway.

His immediate impression was this had to be the brightest house he'd ever been in. The ceiling of the hallway was the height of the whole house, and on its rear wall, a wide bank of arched windows let through copious sunlight. A grand central staircase led up to a first floor balcony that ran round the perimeter of the hall like a sort of minstrel's gallery. After a moment, Nick realised a man was standing up there, leaning over the balustrade, looking down at him.

Sir Edward.

This was the man-at-home then, informally attired in fawn trousers and waistcoat with his shirtsleeves rolled up to his elbows and a floppy necktie tied carelessly about his neck. He was even more comely like this, a little mussed, with a stray lock of hair falling over his forehead.

"Mr. Hearn," he called down in that devil's bark. "You came." He smiled happily, for all the world as though this was a pleasant surprise, and there hadn't been a bit of coercion on his part.

Nick regarded him coolly, not offering an answering smile. "Good morning, Sir Edward."

If the man noticed Nick's flat tone, he didn't show it. "Come on up," he said, beckoning with his arm. "We can have some tea in my study while I explain a bit more about my work."

God, that voice of his. So hoarse and ugly. It didn't fit how he looked at all. Again Nick felt that deep, disconcerting thrum of attraction. He'd never felt such a profound pull to another person, but Sir Edward Carrick wasn't just comely, he had that fierce, elusive spark of *life* that seemed to burn brighter in a very few people. Nick wanted to curse—why this man of all men?

"Mr. Pipp," Sir Edward said, addressing his servant now. "We'll take tea and scones in my study."

"Very good, sir," the servant said, as Nick made for the staircase.

Nick was absurdly aware of Sir Edward's gaze on him as he climbed, and he hated how that made him feel, how it made him wonder if the man felt any attraction to Nick in return. As though that was likely.

Sir Edward waited at the top of the stairs, bathed in the sunlight that streamed through the arched windows. He stepped forward as Nick reached the top, offering his hand, gilded by the sun. He was quite a sight, standing there, all golden, and somehow Nick knew this moment was going to become a life-long memory. Like the way Nick remembered his mother, long, black hair flying as they ran along a windy beach when Nick was small, or Gabe by moonlight in the dunes, his eyes gleaming with lust as he leaned over Nick's prone body to kiss him.

This memory wouldn't be of wind or moonlight though. It would be of sunbeams and dust motes dancing. A rich, golden youth, slender and elegant, offering his hand with a confident smile, all easy privilege.

Nick took the offered hand and gave it a quick workman-like shake before he dropped it.

"Follow me," Sir Edward said, smiling. "My study's in the east wing."

He led Nick to a door off the gallery. "I have my private apartments and laboratory in this wing," he explained as he preceded Nick down a spacious corridor. Nick stared for a moment at the tight perfection of the man's arse as he walked, before dragging his gaze up and following.

"Everything was built to my precise specification," Sir Edward continued. "The other wing has the drawing room, dining room, kitchens, et cetera." The tiny hand wave he gave as he mentioned the contents of the west wing left Nick in no doubt that Sir Edward had little interest in such tedious details. "Here we are—this is my study."

He opened a door, then stood aside to allow Nick to pass him.

The study wasn't at all what Nick had expected. He'd been imagining something like Godfrey's library: a gloomy room with dark wood furniture and heavy, velvet drapes. But this room, like the hallway, was surprisingly bright and spacious. The walls were the colour of freshly churned butter, the drapes covering the window the yellow-green of the gooseberries that grew in Nick's garden.

Other than a large walnut desk, a couple of armchairs, and two full walls of bookshelves, the room was curiously sparse. The only decorative object anywhere in the room was a large, beautifully framed photograph of a man in military uniform. He looked very like Sir Edward, though noticeably bigger and more muscular. Nick hadn't seen many photographs before, and he stared at the picture, fascinated both by its eerie realism and by the similarity of the subject to his host.

"Is this your brother?" Nick asked.

"My twin," Sir Edward confirmed. "George."

They didn't look like twins. Not that there wasn't an obvious family resemblance between Sir Edward and the man in the photograph, but *twins*? The man in the photograph appeared more physically imposing than Sir Edward. Older too, especially with those whiskers he'd been sporting at the time the photograph was taken.

"Won't you sit down, Mr. Hearn," Sir Edward said, his harsh voice making Nick jump. He turned round to find that the man had already taken a seat behind the walnut desk and was gesturing at the comfortable-looking leather armchair on the other side.

Nick sat down, making a conscious effort to mask his immediate irritation at that order disguised as an invitation. No doubt Sir Edward thought he was being the soul of magnanimity, inviting Nick to take tea with him in his private study, but Nick had had a lifetime of sitting on this side of a rich man's desk, and it bothered him that his first interview with Sir Edward was taking place in these circumstances. His fingers strayed to his silver watch chain, fiddling with the fine links.

"First of all, thank you for coming today," Sir Edward began. He offered a wide smile, eyes glinting with excitement, plainly eager to begin. Nick tried to ignore his body's undeniable reaction to the man. Yes, he found him appealing. Who would not? But it was an unwelcome distraction and one he must ignore.

"No need to thank me," Nick said in the neutral tone he used with old Godfrey. "It's not as though I had a choice."

Sir Edward flushed at that, and Nick was reminded of their last encounter down by the mill stream when the man's cheeks had been stained scarlet with embarrassment almost the whole time, even as he made his outrageous demands. Well, good. Nick was glad he was discomfited, even knowing the cause of his feelings was likely disgust at what he had witnessed between Nick and Gabe, rather than shame over his own actions.

Sir Edward looked away under the guise of reaching across the desk for a notebook. Pulling it towards him, he opened it and leafed through a few closely written pages till he reached a fresh one. Smoothing his hand over the clean, white paper, he cleared his throat—or rather tried to, since, when he ultimately spoke, it was with the same barking intonation as always—and said, "Perhaps we could start with you telling me about your background, Mr. Hearn?"

"What do you want to know?"

"Well," Sir Edward began, slowly, tentatively, "that fellow at the inn said your mother was a Gypsy?"

"Roma," Nick said flatly. "My mother was Roma. Romany."

Sir Edward looked up at that, his gaze curious. Today his eyes had a greenish tinge to them, like new wood. Nick frowned at that wayward thought, pressing his lips together into a firm line as though to stop it spilling out.

"I'm sorry, do you not like me referring to your mother as a Gypsy?"

"It's a *gadjikane* word."

"*Gadjikane?*"

"Non-Roma," Nick said shortly, annoyed with himself. Why was he telling Sir Edward this? He usually didn't bother to object to whatever people called him. Had long ago decided that would be a waste of time.

Sir Edward canted his head to the side, regarding Nick curiously. "You feel... insulted by the term?"

Nick scowled. At length, when it became plain Sir Edward was going to wait for his answer however long it took, he muttered, "My mother didn't like it."

"You didn't object when that fellow was using the term the other day, in the inn," Sir Edward observed mildly.

"You mean the one who kept calling me a 'Gypsy's bastard'?" Nick asked, his tone deceptively pleasant. "Do you think a man like Jed Hammett's going to stop talking to me like that if I say 'Oh, I say old chap. I'd really rather you didn't call me that. Would you mind awfully?'" He used the accent of an upper-class buffoon to make his point, edging the words with a little personal contempt.

Sir Edward blinked at Nick, plainly startled. "Oh, I didn't —" He broke off, considering for a moment before starting again. "Well, it's clear you don't like that term, so I'll be sure not to use it again. I apologise for doing so before."

In the circumstances, Nick supposed it was a generous apology. He shrugged, saying somewhat grudgingly, "You weren't to know. I don't bother objecting when Jed says it, because he uses it deliberately to goad me. He's the sort that, once he knows a man hates a particular name, he'll make a point of using it every time he sees you. When we were lads, I went after him every time he called my mother a Gypsy or a whore—needless to say, we were always brawling. But no matter how many times I punched Jed in the mouth, he wouldn't give up saying it."

Sir Edward looked shocked. "Why on earth not?"

Nick gave a harsh laugh. "Because he *likes* fighting. Every time I went after him, I was just giving him what he wanted."

"So instead you let him win?"

Nick bristled at that, but he said evenly, "He hasn't won if he isn't getting what he wants."

Sir Edward considered that. "But you haven't got what you want either. And meantime, he's still using a term you dislike."

"So, neither of us win," Nick replied, shrugging. "That's how some games are. Sometimes the best outcome you can hope for is to lose less badly. Or maybe not to play at all, if the rules are so stacked against you, you can't ever win. So that's what I do with Jed, mostly—I refuse to play his game." He paused, met Sir Edward's gaze, and added, "But there are some games you're forced to play, even when you don't want to."

Sir Edward said, "What do you do when that happens?"

Nick gave him a steady look. "We're about to find out, aren't we?"

CHAPTER SIX

Ward stared at Hearn's grim face.

At some point over the last week, he had almost convinced himself that Nicholas Hearn was a semi-willing participant in his plans. It had been easy to get him to agree to come to the house today. That evening, down by the mill stream, Ward had merely said that if Hearn could see his way to assisting Ward with his work, he saw "no reason for any embarrassment." To his relief, after a short though uncomfortable silence, Hearn had replied he would come to Helston House on his day off—today—sparing Ward the mortification of having to spell out what he wanted in more detail.

Ward had rather been hoping they might go on like that. If they didn't speak of the reason for Hearn's agreement, Ward could even pretend that Hearn had been willingly recruited rather than press-ganged.

Vain hope. Hearn was plainly not pleased to be here. This was a game he was being forced to play.

Just then, a knock at the study door announced the arrival of the tea and a welcome diversion from the tension that had arisen.

"Come in," Ward called out, and Pipp entered, bearing a

large silver tray bristling with crockery.

Pipp deftly arranged cups, saucers, plates, and cutlery on the desk. He set down a tiered china stand, crammed with delicious fancies, followed by crystal dishes of black currant preserves and thick cream. Typically, Mrs. Waddell hadn't just sent up a couple of her delicious scones, she'd put out half a dozen of them, added a similar number of delicate quince tartlets, and topped the lot off with a pile of Ward's favourite sugar biscuits. Pipp lifted the teapot and poured them each a cup of tea before finally tucking the empty tray under his arm.

"May I be of further service, sir?" he asked, eyebrows raised in enquiry. When he and Pipp were alone, Pipp was a benevolently nannying tyrant, but in front of others, he acted the perfectly obedient servant.

Ward shook his head. "Thank you, Mr. Pipp," he replied gravely. "That will be all."

"Very good, sir."

Pipp slipped silently out of the room, closing the door behind him with the barest click while Ward gave his attention to the scones on the china stand, examining them as though selecting the best one was a matter of life and death. He grasped one with the silver tongs Pipp had provided and held it up, asking hopefully, "Would you like a scone, Mr. Hearn?"

Hearn looked distinctly unimpressed. "No, thank you."

Ward wasn't even hungry but nor was he ready to resume their conversation—and he had to do something with the bloody scone—so he put it on a plate and busied himself with cutting it open and heaping it with dark purple jam and unctuous, pale-yellow cream.

It was probably as delicious as Mrs. Waddell's scones always were, but it might as well have been ashes in his mouth for all he tasted it. He set it down after two bites, swallowing drily, unsure how to go forward.

Hearn took the matter out of his hands. "Before we go any further, I want us to agree precisely what it is I am going to have to do here," he said in the flat, emotionless tone he'd used before. "I do not wish to be at your beck and call permanently, Sir Edward. Tell me what you want of me and let us agree a number of visits, or hours, or whatever is most appropriate, and the limits of what you will ask of me. In return, provided you're reasonable, I will comply with what you ask."

Ward stared at him, appalled. It was one thing to imply threats in the hope of getting what you wanted; it was quite another when your victim—and yes, he admitted to himself, Hearn was the victim here—faced up to you and made you talk about what you were doing. Ward's cheeks warmed and he knew he must look as awkward as he felt. "I—I'm not sure how long it may take," he managed to stammer as his mind raced. "It's difficult to estimate—"

Hearn sighed. "Let's start with what will be involved. Perhaps then we can agree the terms of our arrangement."

"That's a good idea," Ward replied, relieved. "Once you grasp the purpose of my work, you may understand why I am a little—" he paused, searching for the right words "—a little *single-minded*, at times." He offered a tentative smile, but Hearn merely waited for him to go on.

Ward took a deep breath, trying to settle himself before he began. "These are exciting times for men of science, Mr. Hearn. New discoveries are being made every day, some of them in fields that didn't even exist a few years ago. My own field is the physical sciences. For the last number of years, I have been studying electricity and related phenomena—" He broke off when Hearn held up a hand. "Yes?"

"This is all very interesting," Hearn said, though his weary tone suggested the exact opposite. "But perhaps we could stick to the question I asked, namely what it is that you want to *do* to me."

The image that sprang, unbidden, to Ward's mind in response to that question—Ward on his knees, unbuttoning Hearn's trousers, reaching inside to take hold of his shaft—had his cheeks flushing again. Somehow though, he managed to thrust the mental image aside and say, "I want to hypnotise you. Hypnotise you and ask you some questions—that's all at first. Then, gradually, I'll introduce some other variables."

"What does that mean? What 'other variables'?"

"Other factors that might influence your ability to contact or attract... well, *spirits*, for want of a better word. In this case, the variables I am principally looking at are electricity and ozone gas."

Hearn blinked at that. For several moments he was quiet, then eventually he said faintly, "I'm beginning to wonder if the Jones family have a point about you."

Ward bristled. "I'm not sure what you mean by that, but I can assure you that whatever you may have heard, nothing untoward occurred with Mr. Jones. I hypnotised him precisely once, for approximately half an hour, and he was fully conscious and quite unharmed when he left this house. I didn't get anywhere near the stage of introducing other variables, and I *certainly* didn't give him electric shocks as the Jones family have been telling everyone."

Hearn's eyebrows rose at that, and a hint of a smile momentarily played about one corner of his mouth. "All right," he said mildly. "I don't disbelieve you about Jago Jones. But that doesn't change the fact that I don't like the idea of you mesmerising me. I don't want to lose control of my mind to a man I barely know."

"It's hypnosis, not mesmerism," Ward corrected him. "And it won't be like that. What you must understand is that I have no wish to control you—that's the last thing I want, in fact."

"What do you want, then? Why put me in a trance?"

"I want to try to unveil something that is already in you.

It's something I believe may be in all of us, but there are a few indications that you may be more receptive than others to the subtle influences of the spiritual plane."

"And what indications would those be?" Hearn asked. "The fact that my mother was a *Gypsy*?" He used the word himself this time, lacing it with a touch of bitterness.

"No," Ward replied carefully. "But I do take into account that she was considered by the villagers to be clairvoyant, and also that you reported seeing a ghost when you were a boy. Those strike me as highly relevant factors."

Hearn gave a humourless laugh. "You shouldn't believe everything that people tell you," he said flatly, and Ward wondered which one of those factors Hearn was alluding to.

He forced himself to stay quiet though—he could see from Hearn's face that the man was pondering what they'd discussed. Surely that, at least, had to be a good sign?

After a while, Hearn said, "What do you mean when you say you'll 'introduce' the other variables? I don't want you shocking me with electricity when I'm in a trance."

Ward huffed a laugh. "You needn't worry. I have no such intention, I assure you. At some point, I would wish to expose you to the *presence* of electricity and ozone gas, but I have no intention of applying them to your person. My hope would be that I could put you into a trance during a real electrical storm. If that is not possible, I can only do my utmost to re-create such conditions as best I can. We will have to see what the weather brings. In any event, I promise you, on my honour, I will not be 'shocking' you with electricity."

Hearn nodded and fell into another contemplative silence.

After a while, Ward said, "Does that answer all your questions?"

Hearn looked up. A small, puzzled frown pleated his brow. "To be frank, I don't understand how any of this relates to what you are trying to achieve. How is this supposed to help you contact spirits? And why do you even want to?"

Ward stared at him. The sudden lump in his throat surprised him. He had to swallow against it and felt sure Hearn must see him doing so. Somehow, that was humiliating. He wanted to seem impervious to Nicholas Hearn. Strong and confident and sure. But all he'd done today was blush and stammer like a green boy. And now he had to speak of something that might even make him weep.

A part of him wanted to refuse. A part of him whispered that he should tell Nicholas Hearn in no uncertain terms that Ward was the one who held the power here and Hearn had better start falling into line and stop asking questions. But he couldn't have done that, even if he wanted to. The fact was, he wouldn't have a chance of hypnotising an unwilling subject. Somehow, he was going to have to persuade Hearn to assist him.

"I believe it will help because it happened to me," he said at last. "I spoke to a spirit. My brother, George."

Hearn's gaze flicked to the photograph on the wall and back.

"He was with the 80th Foot in Rangoon," Ward went on. "On the night he died, he—he visited me. I heard his voice, Mr. Hearn, and it was unmistakably him. A visitation from my brother—from beyond the veil."

Hearn's expression was difficult to read, but Ward detected a glimmer of pity in those bright-silver eyes, one he'd seen before in others' eyes. He didn't like that sort of pity.

He continued, determined now to get it all out. "On the night it happened, I was on the deck of a ship, the *Archimedes*, in the midst of a huge electrical storm."

"And so," Hearn said, a hint of a question in his tone, "you have concluded this visitation occurred because of the storm?"

"That's a possibility, yes, but there were a number of other variables in play that night too, so it may have been a combination of factors that created the necessary conditions. For one thing, the storm was an unusually fierce one, with more electrical activity than one would ordinarily see, probably because it took place at sea. As well as lightning, I witnessed St. Elmo's fire that night—are you familiar with that phenomenon?"

Hearn shook his head.

"Have you heard of spirit candles?"

This time Hearn nodded. "The sailors speak of them. Unholy flames that hover on top of masts."

"Quite so. That is St. Elmo's fire, a phenomenon of electrical activity. There was also ozone gas that night too. The air reeked of it—once you know the smell of ozone, it's unmistakable, and often present during electrical storms. And then there was the fact that it was the moment of George's death, and that there was an unusually strong connection between us. We were twins after all, though we looked quite different after my illness."

"Your illness?"

"When I was a child I contracted diphtheria."

A brief silence as Hearn absorbed that. Then, curiously, "How old were you?"

"Eleven. George was away with our father when it struck, so he escaped the outbreak. My sister died, but I survived, though with some damage to my vocal chords and throat, as you will have heard." He offered a twisted smile. "It took me a long time to recover. Half a year just to be out of bed, longer still till I felt well again. During my recuperation, I fell behind George in my growing and never really caught up to him again."

Hearn's gaze returned to the photograph on the wall. "The likeness is unmistakable, though I certainly wouldn't have taken you to be twins."

"He was taller than me and broader in the shoulders," Ward admitted. "But we were practically identical facially.

You can't really see it in the photograph because of George's whiskers." He smiled sadly. "He was extraordinarily proud of those whiskers."

Hearn sipped his tea. The bright sunshine that flooded through the study window made his hair gleam black-blue.

After another pause, he said, "I still don't understand why you need to hypnotise me."

Ward took another deep breath. "The hypnotic state is the other factor I believe may be significant here. On the night my brother visited me, I am sure I was in a trance."

Hearn looked puzzled at that. "Someone hypnotised you on board the ship?"

Ward shook his head. "No, I was alone that night—I believe I inadvertently hypnotised myself."

Hearn's brows rose in frank disbelief, and Ward smiled. "I realise how that sounds, but I can assure you, autohypnosis is perfectly possible. In fact, it was through hypnotising himself that Mr. Braid, the author of the seminal work on the subject, worked out how to induce a trance in others. I believe that is what happened to me on the *Archimedes*. I also believe that it was due in part to my trance state that George was able to reach me."

"You hypnotised yourself," Hearn said flatly.

"Yes, I believe so," Ward insisted. "Mr. Braid talks of bringing about an 'upwards and inwards squint' in his subjects, a particular fixing of the gaze that produces a degree of eye strain and a consequent entry into the hypnotic state. That night, in the midst of the storm, I saw a glow above the brim of my hat—"

"A glow?"

This time, the blunt scepticism in Hearn's tone irritated Ward. "Yes, a glow. I saw it. It was there, physically *there*. That glow was caused by the same phenomenon that produces spirit candles, a regular sight in electrical storms at sea. In any event, it was very beautiful and of course, quite unexpected.

It transfixed me and, by maintaining a studied concentration on the sight, I believe I entered the self-induced hypnotic trance state that Mr. Braid describes."

Hearn looked no more credulous than he had before. "So, you were in a trance but still able to walk and talk as normal?"

"Quite so. The hypnotic state is much misunderstood. It is not, as the mesmerists would have you believe, a case of a weaker person falling under the influence of a stronger one, then doing their bidding like a slavish automaton. It is rather the entering into of a state of acute concentration so that all other distractions are muted. I felt thoroughly awake and quite myself when I heard my brother on board that ship, but I was also entirely focused upon what was happening to me. One hypothesis is that it was because of this heightened concentration that my brother was able to reach me. Another is that the electricity in the atmosphere or the ozone gas coming off the sea, or both of them, created some sort of ideal medium through which his message could be conducted to me. A third is that all these elements combined somehow to produce this effect." He smiled and shrugged. "There are others—but these are some of the theories I hope to test with the assistance of yourself and any other subjects I am able to recruit."

Hearn's bright gaze searched Ward's face, and Ward wondered what he sought there.

At length, Hearn said, "This sounds like a great undertaking, Sir Edward, and despite what you have heard of my history, I must tell you that I am not a spiritual man. I like the good ground under my feet, and I only believe in things I can see and touch. I have no wish to wake the dead."

Ward felt a sinking sense of disappointment at that. He looked down at the polished desk, readying himself for the rejection that must surely follow.

But all Hearn said was, "So, you must consider yourself

warned. I may not prove to be at all what you are hoping for in a subject."

Ward's gaze snapped back up. Hearn's expression was as forbidding as ever, and he was plainly not eager to start, but it seemed he had no intention to test Ward's resolve.

"Let us agree at the outset, though," Hearn went on, his voice firm, "what my whole commitment is to be. As I said, I do not want to be at your beck and call forever."

"Of course not," Ward said hurriedly. "I perfectly understand."

Hearn's expression was difficult to read. "I have Sundays off," he said. "So here is my proposal. I will come here each Sunday that you want me, but only for the course of the summer—till the last Sunday in August. How is that?"

It was far better than Ward would have hoped for at the start of this conversation. "I—ah, yes, that will—that will be fine," he stammered.

"All right, then that's agreed. Now—" Hearn held up a warning hand "—I will do what you ask, within reason and in accordance with what you've just explained to me, on the days that I come, but it must be clearly understood that whatever results you get make no difference to our arrangement. You can't demand more days from me if things don't turn out how you hope. Agreed?"

"Yes, of course. That's perfectly reasonable." Ward wanted to whoop at the unexpected triumph, but tried instead to look serious and as though none of this was a surprise.

Hearn nodded. "Fine. We may as well get on with it then. Do you plan to hypnotise me in here?"

Ward eyed Hearn's tense frame and tightly clenched jaw. The man wasn't remotely ready to be hypnotised. He was plainly still in a somewhat combative frame of mind. Somehow Ward had to relax him before they could think of making a start. Ward rose from his chair.

"Why don't I show you my laboratory first?"

CHAPTER SEVEN

From *The Collected Writings of Sir Edward Carrick*, volume I

In 1840, when I was fourteen years of age, Mr. Lucas and I took our first trip to the capital, something that would become an annual event for the next several years. On that first occasion, we must have visited every museum and library in the city, and Mr. Lucas took me to several public lectures besides, culminating in one given by Professor Daniell at the Royal Institution. The professor was speaking about the principles of electricity and I was immediately entranced. My tutor's particular interest was geology, and I had thought myself similarly inclined, but when I heard Professor Daniell speak of electrical currents and magnets and induction, a fire was lit within me. This was around the time of the first commercial telegraphs—only a few years before, the idea of sending a message over a long distance near instantaneously would have been unthinkable, but now it was a reality. And these machines were powered by Professor Daniell's own invention, the Daniell cell.

∽

"So, this is where I do most of my scientific work."

Nick followed Sir Edward into the enormous room. It was the size of several chambers and fitted out with high benches built into the walls, shelves crowded with bottles and jars, and tall bookcases tightly packed with volumes. A large, rectangular table in the middle of the room was covered with all sorts of equipment: a pile of rough-looking wooden frames, loosely coiled strands of copper wire in different thicknesses, blocks of blackish iron, and an abundance of glass jars and ceramic pots. There were various devices too, made up of these and other materials, though what purpose they served, Nick couldn't tell. Another, smaller, round table at the back of the room was surrounded by high-backed chairs and covered with papers and books and sheaves of notes.

"Watch your feet!" Sir Edward cried as Nick approached one of the shelves, intent on reading the labels on the bottles crammed there. He halted and looked down, blinking at the contraption on the floor. Half a dozen copper cylinders set inside a wooden case, each cylinder filled with another, smaller pottery cylinder that had a whitish metal rod poking out.

Sir Edward got down onto his knees beside it. "This shouldn't be on the floor. There's still some acid in the elements. Will you help me lift it up to the bench?"

Nick dropped down to his haunches. "What is it?"

"A battery of Daniell cells," Sir Edward replied. "If you lift here." He pointed where Nick's hands should go. "Be careful."

It wasn't particularly heavy, but it seemed Sir Edward's request for assistance was more about keeping the contraption steady. They lifted it cautiously together, slowly rising to their feet and transferring it onto the nearest bench at Sir Edward's nod.

"What's it for?" Nick asked once the contraption was safely moved.

"It's an electrochemical cell—or rather a battery of cells." He pointed at one of the copper cylinders. "Each of these cylinders is an individual cell with a chemical reaction happening within it. Those reactions create energy that can be used to power machines. Like the electric telegraph."

"The telegraph?" Nick repeated. He looked at the puzzling arrangement of metal, pottery, and wood with new eyes. "This is how they are able to send the messages?" He shook his head. "I wondered what powered the telegraphs. It seems like magic."

He'd only read about telegraphs in the newspaper— instant messages sent over great distances. Already there was talk of telegraph offices opening all over England.

Sir Edward grinned quite suddenly, as though something on Nick's face, or in his tone, had pleased him. "Not magic," he said, shaking his head. "Science. Before I came to Cornwall, one of the things I was working on was developing an improvement on this device. The Daniell cell is very good, but its life is quite short. I had been experimenting with some other electrolytes…" He trailed off, then sighed. "I don't have time for that now though."

"Why do you still have one in your laboratory then?" Nick asked.

"I use it to power equipment I've installed at the base of the Zawn. A wheel of sorts. It's an attempt to produce ozone gas." Sir Edward smiled. "I'll take you down there and explain more about it another day."

Nick raised his brows. "So it's true what they're saying in the village about you doing experiments down there?"

"At the moment, I'm only working on producing ozone at sea level, at the base of the Zawn," Sir Edward said. "But yes,

I plan to do more there, inside the crevice. The sea water surges are particularly interesting. In a storm, I believe the conditions may be similar inside the crevice to those on the open sea."

Nick strolled over to the large, central table, pausing at a round tin full of squarish lumps of dark metal. "What are these?"

"Magnets," Sir Edward said, coming up behind him. "Look."

He reached past Nick, his sleeve brushing Nick's and causing Nick to give a tiny involuntary shiver. He plucked a couple of small metal blocks out of the tin and proceeded to demonstrate how they reacted to one another. How they adhered and repelled. Nick knew about magnets, but he'd never handled any before, and when Sir Edward passed them over, he played with them for several minutes, fascinated first by the strength of that pull of attraction, how one block would leap across thin air to click against the other. That sheer physical force, invisible as it was, was astonishing and palpable. Even more fascinating was the repulsion. He moved the magnets around, exploring the shape of the invisible boundary between them. How it *curved*. Invisible, intangible, but *there*.

When at last he looked up, it was to find Sir Edward watching him with a small smile.

Such a comely boy this one, he thought, then realised he was staring and that his thoughts were going in entirely the wrong direction. He glanced quickly away, fastening his gaze on the magnets again, reminding himself that Sir Edward Carrick was a manipulative and ruthless man, not an innocent lad.

Sir Edward didn't seem to notice how distracted Nick was. He was already reaching for another box. "Iron filings," he said, showing the contents to Nick. He held one of the magnets over the box and the filings jumped out, as though they were alive, fastening themselves to the dark metal like a layer of fur.

Nick couldn't help but laugh at that and for a while, they messed around like a pair of schoolboys, using the magnets to make the tiny shavings of metal dance and move, building tiny bridges and towers.

From time to time, Nick cast a sidelong look at Sir Edward, marvelling at his carefree grin and easy manner. Nevertheless, Nick had no intention of allowing himself to forget what had brought him here today. He felt better now—more in control—knowing that there would be an end to this after August. On that point, he was prepared to take Sir Edward Carrick at his word. But that was as far as his trust went, and he wasn't going to let go of the lingering resentment that simmered inside him over how the man had got him here.

After a while, he decided it was time to stop letting Sir Edward charm him. Setting the magnet in his hand down on the bench, he said, "Well now, this has been very interesting, I must say, but don't you think we should get started?"

Sir Edward looked up at his words, seeming surprised, and perhaps even a little nervous. "All right. Let's go back upstairs then."

He led Nick out of the laboratory and back upstairs. He ushered him into the study, then closed the door behind them and crossed the floor to draw the curtains, making everything restful and shady. He turned the armchair Nick had sat in earlier so it faced away from the large desk and into the middle of the room instead, drawing up a smaller upright chair for himself.

"Make yourself comfortable," he said, and Nick tried to do so, though his gut churned with nerves.

"How does this work?" he asked as he settled himself down.

"Have you ever seen a mesmerist perform?" Sir Edward asked.

"No," Nick admitted, though he knew all about them—the newspapers were always full of their exploits. Nick took what he read with a pinch of salt though. He had reasons of his own to be sceptical of such sensational stories. He knew how easy it was to deceive with a few simple tricks. "Isn't the whole thing just a fraud?"

"Yes and no," Sir Edward said. "The mesmerists believe that there is an invisible force—animal magnetism as they term it—that influences all living things. They claim to be able to manipulate this force and thereby put their subjects into a trance state during which various phenomena may be witnessed—extreme pain endured by the subject without complaint, for example."

"I've read stories," Nick confirmed.

"The interesting thing," Sir Edward continued, "is that some of the mesmerists' claims are irrefutably genuine. This is what confounded so many of the detractors of mesmerism. At least until Mr. Braid came along."

"Oh yes? And what did Mr. Braid do?"

Sir Edward's eyes were bright with enthusiasm now, an expression entirely at odds with his harsh voice. "He realised that something was genuinely happening to these subjects, but that it must be something other than what the mesmerists claimed. And in quite short order, he discovered that there were indeed simple processes that could be followed whereby almost anyone could be induced into a trance state—provided they were willing participants. It was nothing to do with the mesmerist and everything to do with the techniques employed."

"Techniques? What techniques?"

"There are a few that can be used, but for my part, I stick to the simplest one, which is to have the subject look at an object for a period of time and ask them to fix all their attention upon it."

"What sort of object?" Nick asked, his nerves sharpening now that the moment was approaching.

"Anything will do really," Sir Edward said, reaching into his pocket. "Though I find something shiny is good, since it naturally draws the eye." He drew out a silver box, about the size of his palm. It was, Nick saw, a match-safe box. He held it up, a little above Nick's head, and watched as Nick followed it with his eyes.

"Look at this box," Sir Edward said. "Keep your gaze fixed upon it, please." He shifted the box a couple of times and Nick faithfully followed it, as instructed.

"Yes," Sir Edward said at last. "Just like that. That's perfect."

∼

"Wake up."

Nick stirred.

He had been asleep, he realised, surprised. Now he felt amazingly alert, though his eyelids remained closed.

"I'm awake," he said.

"Good. How do you feel?"

Sir Edward's voice, when he spoke, sounded further away than he expected.

"I feel fine."

"And are you comfortable?"

"Yes." He was conscious—very conscious, in fact—of considering his responses to Sir Edward's questions. No loss of free will there. On the other hand, his hands felt heavy, weighed down on the arms of his high-backed chair, and the very idea of opening his eyes was unthinkable. He wondered if that should alarm him. It didn't. In fact, he'd rarely experienced such a feeling of well-being as the one buoying him up now.

"Shall we begin?" Sir Edward asked.

"Yes."

"All right. Why don't you begin by telling me about your mother?"

Nick thought about that. "She loved the seaside," he said at last. "She loved the wind." He could see her, vividly, in his mind's eye, yanking her skirts up to her knees and calling to him to race her along the sands, black hair flying about her face, teeth flashing in a mischievous smile. "We used to go to Candlewick Bay when I was a boy. Then we'd walk past Tremain House on the way home."

Sadness flooded him at that memory, an unexpectedly visceral feeling.

"Didn't you like going there?" Sir Edward asked.

"I liked the bay," Nick said. "Not Tremain House."

"Why not?"

"We went because Ma wanted to rub my sire's nose in his mistake. And he hated when he saw us. He hated me." Nick rolled his head from side to side against the leather headrest in mute denial. There were no words, at least he had no words, for the remembered turmoil of pain and anger that had flooded him each time his father had laid eyes upon him.

Sir Edward's voice was hesitant, almost reluctant, as he asked, "Are you speaking of Mr. Tremain? Your employer?"

Nick shook his head. "No, Jacob. Godfrey's son." He said flatly, "Jacob's dead. Like Ma."

There was a long pause. Nick didn't open his eyes. He didn't feel any need to do so. Was happy to simply sit, with his eyes closed. Relaxed.

"Do you miss your mother?" Sir Edward asked at last.

"Yes," Nick whispered, and right then, the way he missed her was a space in his solar plexus that ached and grew. It was white and terrible. Nick rolled his head again, side to side, and something wet rolled from the outer corner of his eye down his face. Clods of sorrow in his throat choked him.

Sir Edward said, "Mr. Hearn, are you all right? Can you hear me?"

When Nick said nothing, only choked with misery, Sir Edward used his given name.

"Nicholas? Nicholas, *please*. You must breathe for me. In... and out. In... and out." He demonstrated what he wanted as he spoke the words—*In... and out*—and at last, Nick managed to do as he said, taking several choppy breaths, then a few longer, slower ones, till it felt as though the white space inside him had contracted and he could send air to his lungs and let it back out again, unimpeded.

"Good," Sir Edward said, his harsh voice strained. "That's good, Nicholas. Now keep breathing."

Nick liked the way the man said his name. Taking the time to say it all, every syllable—Ni-cho-las. He thought about that as breathed.

In... and out.

Ni-cho-las.

Gradually, he calmed. So much so, that he could barely remember having been upset at all. For a while, he drifted.

At last, Sir Edward spoke again, just a gentle murmuring. "Nicholas—"

That utterance of his name was like a signpost in the road, a reminder that time had indeed passed. How much, Nick didn't know. It could have been hours, or minutes. He wasn't sure and didn't much care.

"I'm here," he said, eyes still closed. His voice was surprisingly ordinary.

"Do you want to try to reach out to your mother?" Sir Edward asked.

No.

No, no, no!

Nick's gut tensed with absolute physical refutation.

"Nicholas? Did you hear me?"

"No," he bit out. "No, I don't want to. Not at all."

The silence that greeted those words was profound. After a minute, Sir Edward said, slowly, "That's all right. You don't have to do anything you don't want to."

Nick laughed at that.

"I mean it," Sir Edward said. His harsh voice could never soothe, but it was at least reassuringly devoid of tone. No hint of disappointment or disapproval, or indeed anything else, at Nick's refusal.

"Perhaps you could tell me about her instead," he said. "She could speak to the spirits, you said."

"*I* didn't say that." Nick sounded surprisingly petulant to his own ears.

A pause. "I'm sorry. Was it the other man who said so? Hammett?"

"Yes. Jed."

"And *could* she speak to spirits?"

Nick was silent for a long pause, then he bit out, "I don't know. She never did so in front of me."

Surprised silence.

"Do you want to talk about something else?"

"Yes."

"All right. Can you tell me about the ghost you saw when you were a boy? The Surgeon, was it?"

"The Physic," Nick said, and his voice was strangled. "He was a doctor here, during the plague. So they say."

"Sorry, yes. The Physic. Did you really see him?"

Nick opened his mouth to scoff. To say, no, of course not, it had just been his imagination. Instead a whisper came out of him. "Yes."

The Physic was vivid in Nick's memory in that moment, as clear as he had once appeared before his childish eyes. The ghost's old-fashioned clothes—long waistcoat, cassock coat, wide-brimmed hat, and square-toed buckled shoes—had been enough in themselves to mark out the shadowy figure as something strange. But it was the leather birdlike mask the ghost wore over its face—the round glass-covered eyeholes and long "beak" Nick had later learned would have been packed with aromatic herbs to keep out the putrid air—that had caused the creep of rising gooseflesh on the back of his neck and made him realise he was looking at someone, something, that... did not *live*.

The worst moment though, had been when the ghost had seemed to become aware of Nick, turning to look directly at him, with that blank, inhuman face. Those empty, soulless glass-lens eyes.

That was when Nick had begun to scream. When he'd run away, bawling at the top of his lungs with Gid Paget and Jed Hammett on his heels, calling his name.

"Tell me about him," Sir Edward murmured.

"He knew I was there," Nick said. "He looked at me." Impossible to convey how terrifying that had been.

"Were you frightened?"

"Yes. I was very young—I think I would be frightened even now, though. Seeing him felt... wrong."

"What do you mean, 'wrong'?"

"Wrong like... that two-headed calf born on Yellow Cove Farm that lived but an hour."

"Unnatural, you mean?"

"I... suppose." He wasn't sure that was what he meant. He meant a wrongness that reached right into his gut and twisted him up inside. Perhaps a better word was *horror*. But he didn't say so.

"Have you ever seen another ghost?" Sir Edward asked.

Nick shook his head slowly. "Just that one time. I ran home to Ma, and by the time I got there, I was feverish. She put me to bed and I stayed there three days. I remember in my fever state..."

"What? What do you remember?"

Nick said, almost wonderingly, "Ma told me she'd speak to the ghost and tell him he must leave me alone. She said I'd never see him again."

"And did you?"

"No. I never did." After another moment, he added, "It turned out I was ill that day. It was probably just the fever that made me imagine it." But even as he said the words, he wasn't sure they were true.

That thought unsettled him, and he decided to let the memory of the ghost go, turning away from it. Immediately, he felt calmer. He concentrated on the feel of the chair beneath him, the leather-upholstered seat under his thighs, the wooden arms under his hands, the chairback cradling his shoulders. He felt it all, but he felt too as though he floated. Like a dandelion clock drifting on the air. Or maybe a kite, tethered to the world only by Sir Edward Carrick's unmistakable voice.

Was it strange he didn't want this to end?

"I think that's enough for now, Nicholas," Sir Edward said, as though he'd followed Nick's train of thought. "Rest for a few minutes. Then, when you're ready, open your eyes, and wake up."

Nick almost laughed. Rest indeed! He wasn't the least bit tired. He'd never felt so awake.

But yes, perhaps he would drift on the breeze a little longer before he opened his eyes.

CHAPTER EIGHT

Ward watched Nicholas Hearn sleep. He'd slid into a light slumber just a minute or so after they'd stopped talking. Whereas before, he'd been sitting upright, with the curious alertness of the hypnotised subject, all inward-focused, now his whole body was relaxed, his head lolling to one side as he breathed, deep and slow.

Ward let his gaze travel over the man. He was not conventionally handsome, but he was very attractive. There was something about his stark, fierce features that drew one's attention. He had something of the hunter about him. Something intense and single-minded. Perhaps it was that disconcerting silver gaze, veiled now by thick black lashes as he dozed.

Nicholas—it was already impossible to think of him as Hearn after what had just passed between them—had surprised Ward with his easy slip into the trance state. The man's plain reluctance to be here had made Ward wonder if he would go under at all, but it seemed he'd reconciled himself to the idea in his own mind, because after a little while, he'd surrendered willingly enough. He'd answered Ward's questions with reasonable frankness too. There had been some resistance, of course. Notably his refusal to even attempt to try to reach his mother, but there had been surprising revelations too. Not least that Godfrey Tremain was his natural grandfather.

That had shocked Ward.

Ward wondered whether Nicholas would remember what he'd shared when he awoke. Ward had hypnotised over a dozen subjects himself now, and he'd witnessed many more demonstrations by others, including the great Braid himself. In his experience, subjects tended to remember what they said, on the whole, though Jago Jones, he recalled, had not. Or, at least, that had been his story.

If Nicholas remembered, would he be mortified? Angry to have revealed so much? Or would he take it in his stride? Ward hoped he would not be distressed. He had already caused Nicholas Hearn enough grief.

At last, Nicholas stirred, shifting slightly in the chair before slowly opening his eyes. He gazed at Ward unseeingly for several long moments, then blinked and seemed to come back to himself.

"I was asleep," he said, sounding surprised.

"Yes, for almost forty minutes."

Nicholas's eyes widened. "I wasn't even tired."

"It's not uncommon," Ward assured him. "How do you feel?"

"Fine." Nicholas frowned and smiled at the same time, an oddly charming expression that made him look puzzled and pleased all at once. "Actually, better than fine. I feel good. As though I slept a whole night through." He glanced at Ward, curious. "Is that usual?"

"For some people, yes. Tell me—do you remember any of it?"

Nicholas frowned, thinking. "Yes, I believe I spoke of my mother—" He broke off, closing his eyes. "I refused to try to contact her, didn't I?"

"Yes."

Nicholas shook his head. "Sorry, I didn't—"

"Please don't apologise," Ward said hurriedly. "It must come freely, I think. I would certainly not wish to force the issue, even if that were possible. We can try again next time."

"Oh. Yes. Of course." Nicholas sat up properly and set about straightening his clothes.

After a moment, Ward said, "If you don't mind me asking, Nicholas—" He halted, realising he'd used the man's given name again. "Sorry. Mr. Hearn, I mean."

Nicholas looked at him. He was frowning slightly, remembering perhaps. Then his frown cleared and he said, "You called me Nicholas when I was in the trance."

Ward nodded. "You became distressed at one point and were not responding to me, so I took the liberty of using your given name in order to get your attention. It seemed to work, but you had not invited me to use it, and for that I apologise."

Nicholas just shrugged. "I don't mind. You can call me Nicholas if you want."

Ward felt an unexpected rush of awkward pleasure at that invitation. Perhaps Nicholas was thawing at last? "Well, then you must call me by my given name too."

Nicholas didn't respond to that. Instead he said, "What was it you were you going to ask me anyway?"

"I was wondering what else you remembered of our discussion while you were in the trance." Ward considered asking particularly about the ghost, but decided not to. Better to see what Nicholas offered.

"I think I remember most of it," Nicholas said. He frowned, then something seemed to occur to him, and a flush rose in his cheeks. "Ah. I think I told you rather more than you needed to know about my family background."

"You mean about Jacob Tremain being your father?"

Nicholas let his head fall back against the headrest. "Yes."

"I won't gossip to anyone about it," Ward reassured him. "You don't need to worry about that."

Nicholas laughed. "Oh, I'm not worried about that. Everyone round here knows already."

Ward smiled sympathetically. "It did help explain a few things."

"Such as what? Why Godfrey Tremain offered me his patronage?"

"That would be one."

Nicholas gave another mirthless chuckle. "Yes, he's not the sort that would ordinarily give a Gypsy bastard a leg up in life."

Ward winced inwardly at that dry comment. "No, but he's your grandfather."

Nicholas's mouth twisted up at one side. "He's Harry Tremain's grandfather. I think of him more as my sire's sire."

Ward's stomach clenched in pity.

"How did your parents meet?" he asked.

Nicholas shrugged. "Jacob Tremain met my mother when he was visiting a friend in Derbyshire. My mother's people were travelling through the county at that time. Jacob was already married, but he decided he'd fallen in love with my mother and they ran away together to London. When he ran out of funds and found himself with a squalling brat on his hands, he decided he wasn't quite as in love with her as he'd thought, and came back to Cornwall to his wife and his money—or rather, Godfrey's money."

"Leaving you and your mother behind?"

Nick offered a mocking smile. "Not only that, he abandoned us in London with the rent unpaid. Left us to the mercy of an angry landlord and a hoard of other unpaid creditors."

"Good God," Ward breathed, hardly able to believe such villainy.

Nick's lip curled. "He underestimated my mother, though.

She sold the ring he'd bought her and made her way from London to Trevathany, confronting him with me in her arms. She only wanted money from him, but then she discovered that Godfrey was the one holding the purse strings, not Jacob."

"And he supported her? Your grandfather?"

Nick gave a bark of laughter. "In a manner of speaking. Being Godfrey, he refused to agree to her proposal that he settle a decent sum on her in exchange for our disappearance. Instead, he gave her a life interest in a cottage at the edge of the Tremain estate and a tiny annual stipend—just about enough to live on, but not enough to escape on. So we ended up being trapped here."

"Why did he do that instead of just paying her off?"

Nicholas shrugged. "Punishing her for her gall, would be my guess, and Jacob too, for his behaviour. Maybe even my father's wife, for being barren. He likes to control people."

"Does he recognise you now? As his grandson?"

"Are you joking?" Nicholas asked. He grinned, but it was like the grin of a fox, feral and snarling. "No. But he gives me employment, and I have Rosehip Cottage rent-free."

It didn't sound like much to Ward, but he said nothing more, only asked, "What about your mother's family? The Hearns?"

"What of them?"

"Have you met them?"

Nicholas shook his head. "They shunned Ma when she ran off with Jacob Tremain." Then, sounding almost wistful, he added, "I've been thinking about tracking them down. My mother wanted me to go to them once she was gone. She worried about me being alone."

"It can't have been easy for her," Ward said. "A lone woman with an illegitimate child."

Nicholas shrugged. "We were protected to some extent by the connection with the Tremains. At least, no one in the village was blatantly hostile to us. Oh, there were always snide remarks, and I was forever getting into fights with the village boys, especially Jed, when he called my mother a whore."

Ward winced. Children could be cruel.

"And of course, people were wary of her because she was Romany and they thought she might put a curse on them. But that was also what brought them to her door—because they thought she could speak to dead people, and make love potions, and tell them their futures. And they would pay her a few pennies for that. It helped us get by."

"They thought she could speak to dead people..."

Did Nicholas believe his mother could do those things? Ward wanted to ask him, but that really would be an impertinent question and he'd asked enough of those today, so with some difficulty, he quelled the urge.

"Is that the time?" Nicholas said suddenly, sitting forward, eyes fixed on the clock on the wall.

Ward looked over his shoulder, noting with surprise that it was after five already.

"Goodness, I hadn't realised how late it was. You must be starving! We had no luncheon. Would you care for something to eat now?"

Nicholas got to his feet. "Thank you, but—"

"Really, you must let me call for something. I'll be wretched if you don't let me feed you after such a long day."

"Sir Edward, I—"

"Come now, you're not allowed to call me that anymore," Ward interrupted, holding up his hand. "We agreed. If I'm calling you Nicholas, you have to do likewise and call me Ward."

"'Ward'?"

"Short for Edward," Ward explained. "Edward was my father's name, so I got Ward."

"I see," Nicholas said slowly, as though he wasn't quite

sure what that had to do with anything. "Well, I'll try to remember. In the meantime, I'd best get back. I left my dog at home to fend for himself today. He'll be getting anxious."

Ward remembered the one-eyed creature that had been with Nicholas in their previous encounters. "This is your white bulldog, I take it?" he said, as he too rose from his chair. "What's his name?"

"Snowflake. Snow for short."

"Do you generally have him with you?"

"Always," Nicholas said. "He doesn't do well alone. He was badly mistreated before I got him."

"Well," Ward said impulsively, "when you come back next Sunday, bring him along. There's no need to leave him at home when he could be here with you. I certainly have no objection."

Nicholas looked surprised, and for an instant, a faint smile tugged at one corner of his mouth, till he suppressed it. He cleared his throat. "Thank you," he said stiffly. "That would be... helpful. Snow's wretched when he's without me."

"All right then," Ward said, meeting his gaze. "That's settled. And perhaps next week you will stay for dinner, since you are bringing Master Snowflake?"

To Ward's amazement, Nicholas actually chuckled at that. "*Master Snowflake*? He's a dog you know, not a child."

Ward flushed, but he didn't mind the teasing at all. He was just relieved that Nicholas, who had seemed so distant and cool when he first arrived today, had unbent so much as to make a joke at his expense.

It was only once Nicholas was gone that he realised that Nicholas hadn't answered his question about staying for dinner next week. Or yet uttered Ward's name.

"You haven't touched your dinner, Master Edward."

Ward looked up from the journal he'd been writing in. "I wish you wouldn't call me that, Pipp," he said, but he spoke without heat. He well knew he would always be *Master Edward* to Pipp, at least in private. It was the name by which the family servants had called him when he was a sickly boy and Pipp, then a footman, had been assigned as Ward's personal servant. Now Pipp was—Well, Ward wasn't sure there was a name for what Pipp was. Part butler, part secretary, occasionally part nanny to Ward's irritation. Pipp's rôle in Ward's household was beyond the usual master and servant one, though they went through the motions of Ward pretending to give instructions and Pipp pretending to follow them.

"My apologies, sir," Pipp said insincerely. "Nevertheless, you will observe your dinner remains uneaten."

Which was Pipp's roundabout way of demanding an explanation.

Ward eyed the congealed plate of food at the edge of his desk without enthusiasm. "I didn't notice you bringing it in."

"That's because Martha brought it in and she's too frightened of you to speak."

Ward shrugged unrepentant. "I'll just have some tea and toast."

"Certainly not," Pipp said, glaring. "You've had nothing since that half-eaten scone when Mr. Hearn first came this morning. If you're going to be as distracted as this every time he comes, you'll fade away to nothing."

"Oh, for goodness sake, Pipp!" Ward snapped. "I'm six-and-twenty, not six."

Pipp stared at him for several long moments over the tops of his half-moon spectacles, plainly offended by Ward's sharp tone. Then he sniffed.

"A man of twenty-six wouldn't ask for toast for dinner."

Ward just shook his head, infuriated and amused in equal measure.

"How about a nice bit of roast fowl with some Duchess potatoes?" Pipp wheedled.

"All right," Ward sighed. "Have a tray brought up."

Pipp didn't bother to hide his triumph. "Very good, Mast—sir," he said, and swept out of the study.

Ward looked down at the journal. He'd written pages and pages of notes, recording every detail of the day that he could remember, then, at even greater length, his thoughts and follow-up questions. Nicholas Hearn was a fascinating man and Ward had only just begun to explore the complicated layers of his nature and history. Whether or not the man had any natural abilities so far as spirits were concerned remained to be seen, but he was intelligent and sensitive, and those two characteristics together gave Ward hope that Nicholas would be able to help him, even if he was only one subject and Ward had been hoping for at least half a dozen.

When his dinner arrived—delivered by Pipp himself this time—Ward polished off both the roast fowl and a dish of ginger pudding, discovering with some surprise that he was hungry after all.

Pleasantly full, he bathed and retired to bed, expecting to drift off directly.

He did not.

Instead, he lay awake in the darkness, and his mind returned to Nicholas Hearn.

He was painfully aware of the irony of having black-mailed Nicholas into assisting him under the implied threat of revealing his true nature, when Ward himself was a shameless, unrepentant sodomite.

Oh, the things he would do to Nicholas Hearn, if he could...

Ward's cock thrummed at just the hint of such thoughts, stiffening under his nightshirt at the memory of Nicholas Hearn walking up the stairs this morning to greet him, taking Ward's hand in his own and meeting his gaze.

Nicholas was a few scant inches taller than Ward's five foot seven, his build lean overall but with broad shoulders. When he'd been standing in front of Ward, his hair had shone with the lustre of a magpie's plumage. And then there were those disconcerting, silver-bright eyes.

Everything about Nicholas Hearn tugged at Ward, attracting him closer, in the same way his magnets drew the iron filings. Something about the man demanded Ward's attention, some kind of energy perhaps. That lean, lithe form seemed to Ward to hold a fierce and palpable power that called to him.

There had been a few occasions that day when he'd wondered if he'd felt Nicholas's gaze on him while Ward wasn't looking. It was possible he'd imagined it. One did imagine things, sometimes, especially when one lusted after someone the way Ward lusted after Nicholas.

With a muffled cry of frustration, Ward pushed his sheets aside and yanked up his nightshirt, baring his slim body to the cool night air. His nipples hardened in the chill, goose-flesh rising as he took hold of his shaft in his right hand and began to stroke himself.

His mind's eye went straight to a visual memory of Nicholas: standing before Ward down by the mill stream, a somewhat shadowy presence in the waning light. Only his white shirt stood out, almost luminous in the dusk, a bright contrast to the strong brown throat and lean forearms exposed by his open collar and turned-up cuffs.

Today, Nicholas's arms had been covered, but when Ward had taken his hand in greeting, he'd discovered something new he hadn't known before: that Nicholas's hand was calloused, far rougher than his own.

Ward's hands—certainly the one that was sliding over his shaft anyway—were very far from calloused. His hands were soft from lack of manual work. Hardly surprising, he supposed, given how little he did with them, other than leaf through books and write up notes.

Just these thoughts—of Nicholas fully clothed, of the callouses on his hands—had Ward's shaft impossibly hard before he even started pleasuring himself in earnest. A bead of fluid blossomed at the eye of his cock, and he collected the bounty with his thumb, groaning as more oozed up. He smeared the wetness around his cockhead, distantly fascinated by the way the fluid dried so quickly and stickily.

Nicholas.

His strong, lean body.

His barely reined-in anger that evening at the mill stream.

His smile at the end of today, half-hitched and oddly warm.

In his imagination, Ward kissed Nicholas, even though he'd never shared a kiss with another man. Not that he was innocent—he'd done plenty of much more wicked things than kiss, but only with Alfie. Alfie was handsome and skilled and very expensive, but when he'd asked Ward, at their first meeting, if Ward would want to kiss him, Ward had found himself declining. Even now, he wasn't entirely sure why. If Alfie had simply done it—kissed him without asking —he certainly wouldn't have objected. It was the fact that he *had* asked, and perhaps too that there had been a tone to the question, a silent expectation that the answer would be no. Perhaps even that it ought to be no.

So no, Ward had never known a lover's kiss, but that did not stop him dreaming of sharing one with Nicholas Hearn now. As he stroked himself rhythmically, he let his mind dance over the possibilities. Having undressed the clothed Nicholas of his memory, Ward knelt at his feet to suck his cock, bent himself double to take him deep in his body, fucked him hard in return.

With that fevered swirl of images in his head, he was very soon ready to come and, recognising that, began to regret his own too-quick efficiency. At the last, he tried to pull back, banishing his more lustful thoughts and endeavouring to think only of the man as he'd first seen him, down by the mill stream. But it was no good. Even the thought of Nicholas's mocking smile and angry gaze pushed Ward closer to his climax. Those perfect, lean forearms crossed over the man's chest.

The moody slope of his broad shoulders.

Ward came with a hiss and a stifled groan, his blood-warm spend spattering his pale torso. For a moment he was all tension—arched back, stiff arms, clenched fingers—and then he was all softness, his tight grip loosening on his shrinking cock, his heavy arm slumping to the mattress.

His body throbbed with the woolly good feeling of having climaxed, and he let himself enjoy it fully. That was one thing his days of childhood sickness had taught him: that moments of pleasure and comfort ought not to be squandered. So he relished his pleasure, not hurrying to wipe the mess away, just lying there as the final pulses ebbed to nothing.

CHAPTER NINE

From *The Collected Writings of Sir Edward Carrick*, volume I

When I returned from that first London trip, my father allowed me to set up a very basic "laboratory" of my own at home where I was able to carry out some simple, practical experiments. These enabled me to witness in operation the scientific principles expounded by Mr. Faraday and other eminent gentlemen of the time. Although George and I were apart during the school term, we were as close as ever when he came home for the holidays. He would spend hours with me in the "laboratory," listening patiently as I explained the principles and theories that fascinated me, exclaiming with gratifying wonder at the experiments I performed. Occasionally, I would allow him to drag me outside. Through his determined efforts, I eventually became both a tolerable horseman and swimmer, although there was nothing he could do for my cricket.

~

The whole of the next week, Nick was preoccupied with thoughts of the day he'd spent at Helston House. Or perhaps, more accurately, he was preoccupied with thoughts of the master of the house—his master too now, he supposed—Sir Edward Carrick.

"If I'm calling you Nicholas, you have to do likewise and call me Ward."

Ward. It suited him, Nick thought, though he still found it difficult to imagine using it to the man's face. Names could be strangely intimate things. It was one thing for Sir Edward to address him as Nicholas—he didn't care about that at all. No one else called him by that name anyway—but somehow the invitation to call Sir Edward *Ward* was troubling, smudging the clear boundary that Nick had set up in his mind between them.

Ever since the invitation had been issued, though, Nick found he couldn't think of the man as anything *but* Ward. That bothered him more than it should have.

Nick also found himself revisiting, over and over, the strange, timeless period he had spent in a trance, tethered to the world only by Ward's devil-harsh voice. To his surprise, he hadn't hated it. Hadn't felt, as he'd feared, as though he was in Ward's power. He'd been clearheaded and coherent throughout when he'd expected to feel out of control and confused, as though he were drunk or half asleep.

Nevertheless, it had been a distinctly odd experience. His words had come out, unbidden, without him deciding what to say beforehand. It was as though a door had closed on the part of Nick's mind that made him stop and think and reason, so that the words that tumbled from his lips were painfully true. Except, that wasn't wholly accurate, because there had been times too when he'd refused to answer questions, rudely even, like a recalcitrant child. He smiled at the memory, and at how surprisingly patient Ward had been. Perhaps it was more that a different side to Nick had been unlocked by the trance, a more spontaneous fellow, who answered as he wished without weighing the consequences first?

All in all, it had been a strange day. Certainly not as unpleasant as he'd feared, other than that excruciating talk they'd had in Ward's study when he'd first arrived. Up until then, Nick had been thinking of Ward as a shameless black-mailer, but whilst blackmailer he might be, he was far from a shameless one. The man had plainly been mortified when Nick had raised the subject, unable even to look him in the eye as Nick forced him to address it, all red-faced and stumbling over his words. Nick had almost felt sorry for him, which really was ridiculous. But Christ, that was the only explanation he could come up with for his absurd offer to go there every Sunday for the whole summer. He was certain now that Ward would have accepted less. What had he been thinking?

Worse than that thought, though, was the little voice in his head that whispered that it wouldn't be so bad to spend a day every week at Helston House, would it? Last Sunday had been diverting in the end. Ward was knowledgeable and enthusiastic about his passions, and when it had come, at last, to the hypnosis, he'd been gentle in his manner.

You want to go back, the voice in his head whispered. *You're looking forward to it.*

And to his mortification, it was true. Despite his lingering resentment at being blackmailed into this, he did want to go back, and God help him, he wanted to see Ward again. When he thought of Ward—standing at the top of the stairs at Helston House all bathed in sunshine, or later in the laboratory, animated as he explained how magnets worked—he felt almost giddy, and then he would be miserable, because he knew very well how foolish it was to have such thoughts about another man. Especially this man. This wealthy, powerful, and untrustworthy man.

Even Nick's sleep was affected by his preoccupation with

Ward. One night he dreamt that he was running along the sands at Candlewick Bay with Ma. They came upon a wide band of washed-up stones and Ma said, "Look, Nick, wishing stones!"

Wishing stones. That was what she called any stone with an unbroken ring of white running right round it. When Nick was small, he'd make wishes on them, then throw them back in the sea. Ma said if he was lucky, he'd get one with the wish still in it, but a lot of them were no good because their wishes had already been used up by mermaids.

In the dream, they bent down to look at the stones and Nick started filling his pockets with them. After a while, a devil said, "The white parts aren't wishes, they're lightning."

Nick glanced up. Ma was gone. Instead, it was Ward standing there, perfectly elegant in his well-cut clothes, that errant lock of hair falling over his forehead.

Nick looked down at himself—he was dressed like a tinker in his oldest breeches, no stockings even, just his bare feet, all spattered with wet sand. He felt ashamed.

"Lightning?" he said. He lifted the stone he held in his hand to peer at it more closely. It was a very ordinary grey colour, but the uneven band of white did seem to glint with tiny sparks. "How do you know?"

"I cut them open to let it out," Ward replied in his characteristic rasp. "Once I get enough sparks, I'll bring your mother back from the dead." He looked so very serious.

Nick wanted to kiss that serious mouth.

Instead, he asked, "Will she be like she was before?"

Ward said, still serious, "I don't know—what are ghosts usually like?"

"I don't know."

"Yes, you do. Look."

Ward pointed and Nick followed the direction of his arm, towards the wet sand where the waves lapped the shore. And there he was: the Physic, unmistakable in his cassock coat, beaky mask, and low-crowned, wide-brimmed hat, moving with that eerie glide that Nick still remembered from when he was small and terrified.

Why that gliding movement should fill Nick with such sickening, appalled horror, he couldn't have said, but it did. And when the ghost turned to look at him, staring at him with unfathomable, glassy eyes, he was overwhelmed by terror. Could have sworn he felt his very heart slowing, his blood growing sluggish, like the mill pond in winter when it bloomed with ice crystals.

Fear gnawed at his belly as he gazed upon the Physic—there was something so profoundly and obviously *wrong* with him. So wrong it made the hair stand on end on Nick's body and a bone-deep shudder run through him. Just the *deadness* of him, in the living world.

It was then Nick realised that Ward was walking towards the ghost, his elegant, well-tailored figure full of purpose. Nick tried to scream, to call him back, but he couldn't make his mouth move. He tried to stumble after the man, but he was weighed down with stones. They were in his pockets, tumbling out of his hands. He fell to his knees, among the stones, and tried to call after Ward, but couldn't manage anything but a gibbering sort of sound—*gah-gah-gah*—and the man didn't even turn, just kept walking inexorably towards the ghost.

Ward was going to die. The deadness of the ghost was going to infect him—Nick was so suddenly sure of that, he finally he found his voice and screamed, a wild, unhinged scream that ripped from his throat—and woke him up, sweat-soaked and tangled in his blankets, in his own bed, in Rosehip Cottage. Trembling and panting, in the early light of dawn.

~

After Nick woke from his nightmare, there wasn't much point in going back to sleep. He got up, dressed in his oldest clothes and, with Snow at his heels, walked the coastal path right round the headland, then back to the cottage, across fields that were wet with dew.

He changed his damp breeches and oldest boots for something more respectable before walking over to Tremain House. The kitchens were already busy. Mrs. Hughes, the cook, was kneading dough at the big table while her maids ran around, attending to her orders as they chattered.

"Mornin', Mr. 'Earn," the cook greeted him. "Take yoursel' a seat at table." She nodded at his usual place, then lifted her chin and called, "Polly, fetch Mr. 'Earn's breakfast."

Ten minutes later, a plate of eggs and ham with a thick slice of bread, still warm from the oven, was set down before him. Hungry from his long walk, he ate quickly, then tarried over his tea, listening to the maids gossip and watching as Mrs. Hughes worked another batch of dough with her massive arms.

After breakfast, he headed over to the stables. Leaving Snow with Tom, the youngest stable lad, Nick asked one of the grooms to saddle up Valentine, a big, powerful chestnut gelding. While he waited for the horse to be readied for him, he decided to look in on Isabella's new mare, now named Callista.

When he leaned over the half door of her stall, the mare turned her head, all haughty disdain. Seeing it was Nick, though, she approached him. He reached into his pocket, drew out one of the sugar lumps he'd purloined from the kitchens, and offered it to her on his open palm.

She considered the treat for a moment before lowering her great head and taking it delicately, huffing hot, moist breath against his hand.

"I saw that, you knave," said an amused but faintly cross voice behind him. "You're bribing my horse."

Nick glanced over his shoulder at the pretty girl who stood there, pert in her pale-blue riding habit, an outrageously impractical confection of a hat perched on her bright curls.

"And good morning to you, Miss Bella," he replied evenly. He turned back to the mare, patting her powerful, dappled neck.

Isabella joined him at the stable door, reaching up a gloved hand to pat the animal too. The mare gave her a scornful look and sidestepped.

"Oh!" Isabella exclaimed, dropping her hand. "Callie, you're so infuriating! You let Nick fawn over you but turn your nose up at me? *I* am your mistress!"

Callie ignored her, instead butting Nick's shoulder with her head and whickering softly.

Nick chuckled. "Nobody can be master or mistress of an animal like this. You should be pleased that she graciously allows you to admire her."

"Well, that is not how it is supposed to be," Isabella grumbled. "Grandy says one must always be master of one's horse. I should thrash her soundly."

"I'll thrash *you* if you try it," Nick replied, though he didn't think for a minute she meant the threat. Bella was spoiled and thoughtless at times, but not unkind. "Besides, there's a difference between being able to guide and persuade a horse to do what you want and mastering it the way old Godfrey means. You are able to guide Callie, aren't you? You rode her beautifully the other day."

"I suppose," Isabella muttered.

"Well then, that should be enough for you. You don't need to master her as well."

Isabella rolled her eyes. "Guiding, persuading, mastering —however you put it, it all comes down to the same thing."

She was wrong, but Nick just shook his head, uninterested in arguing the point further. He was fond of his spoiled cousin in his own way, but he wasn't much in the mood for her company today. She needed too much entertaining. Was always prattling on when he wanted to be quiet.

Theirs was an odd bond, delicately balanced. When Nick had first come to work in the stables at Tremain House, Harry had already been sent away to school, leaving his younger sister with no playmates. Little Isabella had taken a shine to Nick and followed him around like a puppy. Even now she had an annoying tendency to dog his heels from time to time, claiming to want to know more about the workings of the estate. In that sense, she was the supplicant between them. But she knew, too—had always known—that she was above him, and that knowledge coloured all their dealings. He couldn't help but resent her at times.

"You'll have to excuse me. I need to be off," he said now, spying the groom approaching with Valentine. "I've a busy morning ahead."

"I'll ride with you, if you'll wait till—" Isabella began, but he didn't even wait to hear her out. Just strode away.

"Can't today," he called over his shoulder. "I'm already late."

That wasn't true and the scowl on Isabella's face told him she suspected as much, but he didn't care. He was a steward here, not a nursemaid. Isabella would have to find her own entertainment.

Besides, she was the last person he wanted with him today. He planned to drop by each of Godfrey's tenants, in an informal way. It was a few weeks till the next quarter's rent was due, and since Godfrey was a stickler about prompt payment, Nick liked to ferret out any possible difficulties in advance. It was an approach that had proven invaluable last year when Abel Pendleton had been short for Michaelmas rent and Nick had had a chance before rent day fell to soften Godfrey up to letting the man have another month to pay the full amount. The tenants were reluctant to admit to any difficulties as it was—the last thing Nick needed was Godfrey's granddaughter hovering at his shoulder and making them clam up altogether.

Thankfully though, it seemed that none of the tenants had any such difficulties this quarter. Nick had a good long talk with each of them to satisfy himself on that score and carried out a myriad of other tasks besides—examining a suspect ewe for foot rot, inspecting the crumbling end of a boundary wall, making a list of repairs needed to the barn on Pendleton's holding and giving the man a much needed talking-to about proper upkeep.

By early afternoon he was done, though not quite ready to return to Tremain House and Godfrey's irascible company over the ledgers. Instead, he took Valentine down to Candlewick Bay and rode him up and down the wide stretch of beach, right on the edge of the waves so that his fetlocks splashed through the salty water.

The wind ripped through Nick's thick hair as he rode, and though it was an overcast day for the most part, from time to time the sun would split through the clouds, bathing the beach with sudden, unexpected sunshine. It was glorious. Glorious to ride the big, powerful gelding and feel all the world about him. Everything brimming with life and energy.

Eventually, Valentine tired and Nick dismounted. He led the gelding into town by his bridle, as much to stretch his own legs as to spare the horse's. Thirsty now, he tied the horse up at the hitching post outside the Admiral's Arms and went inside.

The first person he saw was Jed Hammett, leaning back against the bar, a tankard held loosely in one meaty fist. When he caught sight of Nick, his eyes gleamed with his usual expression—mingled pleasure and malice. No doubt the man was already anticipating taunting him.

"Jed." Nick nodded at him briefly, then turned his attention to Jim who was stepping up to the bar to serve him.

"How do, Jim?"

"Aw'right, Nick." The hulking innkeeper was already reaching up for one of the tankards that hung from the hooks on the beam above the bar. "Ale, is it?"

"*Ayes.*"

As he usually did when he was speaking to one of the villagers, or Godfrey's tenants, Nick fell back into the rhythms of his childhood speech. They were a laconic people round here for the most part. No words wasted. Ma, who had travelled all over England, said people in Trevathany rolled their words up together to get them out with as little effort as possible.

"Not like the folks up north. They talk slow, like they're chewin' on the words like tough mutton. Takes 'em all day jest to ask 'ow you are!"

Nick was a magpie when it came to speech. As a lad, he'd had one voice for the villagers, another for Ma, and a third for Godfrey—a careful, proper English one, that one, quite close to Godfrey's own, though with enough of the Cornishman in it to avoid being accused of mimicking, or getting above himself.

That proper voice was the one he'd used with Ward last Sunday. He'd fallen into using it without thinking, probably because, even though Ward's own voice was harsh and rasping, it was still precise and upper class, reminding Nick inevitably of the Tremains, with those clipped consonants and distinct vowels. Nick's proper voice was all at the front of his mouth, at the tip of his tongue, the words falling from his lips like silver pins. His Cornish burr felt entirely different. It bubbled up from under his tongue, like water from a spring.

His Roma voice, the one he'd used only with Ma, felt like a secret part of him. One he didn't even hear himself anymore.

"'Ere you go, Nick," Jim said, setting a pewter tankard

down on the bar in front of Nick before moving away to serve another customer.

Beside him, Jed turned to face him, leaning one elbow on the bar.

"What you been up to lately then, Nick 'Earn?"

"Nothing much," Nick answered shortly. He lifted his ale and drank deeply.

Jed chuckled. "*Giss on!*" he said, and when Nick glanced at him in query, winked at him. "I did hear tell you was up at that lunatic scientist's house last week. Did he 'lectrify you?"

Nick sighed. He might've known word would have got out about that.

"Sorry to disappoint you, Jed, but no. No 'lectrifying at all," he answered, and lifted his tankard to his lips again.

"I was right surprised to hear you'd been there," Jed persisted. "You told 'im right 'ere to his face you wouldn't go." He raised one thick eyebrow. "Why d'you change your mind?"

"None of your business," Nick replied flatly.

Jed chuckled again. "You're not bein' very friendly today, Nick. What's got you so teasy?"

"Nothin'," Nick bit out. "What d'you want, Jed? I'm in no mood for your nonsense today."

It was foolish to let his temper show. Jed had an instinct for sore spots and was the type to keep pressing them out of sheer badness. But the thought of the man finding out the real reason Nick had agreed to help Ward with his experiments made Nick feel ill.

Jed's pale-blue gaze narrowed at Nick's tone and his lips curled in a knowing smile. "Oh you *are* teasy," he murmured. "What's got your Gypsy breeches all twisted up, Nick?"

Nick forced himself to stay calm, grinding his jawteeth together till he felt able to paste a semblance of a smile on his face.

"Truth to tell, Jed, I'm having a right day of it today—old

Godfrey's in a bleddy awful mood. But Carrick?" He made himself wink. "Fact is, he's paying me good money for my time, and all I've had to do so far is listen to him gab on."

Jed chuckled. "Is that a fact?"

Well, no, it wasn't. Nick hadn't had and didn't *want* a penny from Ward—the last thing he needed was to feel even more like the man's servant—but his answer seemed to satisfy Jed, who leaned in closer, his expression all avid curiosity.

"What's the 'ouse like inside?" he asked. "Is it as fancy as Tom Cadzow says?"

Nick shrugged. "Didn't see much of it," he said, then added, untruthfully, hoping to kill Jed's interest, "It's nothing like as fancy as Tremain House."

Jed looked disappointed. He turned away to catch Jim's eye, lifting his empty tankard. The innkeeper, presently serving another customer, gave a nod of acknowledgement.

"You want to watch out, you know," Jed told Nick as he turned back. "Carrick might only be talkin' at yer for now, but at some point 'e's likely goin' to want to put 'lectricity through you, and everyone knows that was what made Jago Jones's brain go scrambled." He jostled Nick with his elbow. "Course, Gypsy brains is likely already scrambled, I reckon."

Nick gritted his teeth. If he stayed here much longer, he was going to end up punching the big oaf, and given Jed was twice his size these days, Nick would likely end up spitting up teeth.

He finished his ale in one long swallow, setting the tankard down on the bar just as Jim arrived to pick up Jed's empty one. The innkeeper caught Nick's eye.

"Another for you, Nick?"

Nick shook his head. "No, it's back to work for me. If I drink anymore I'll be falling asleep in front of old Tremain, and we can't have that or I'll be getting my marching orders."

Jed laughed. "Gawd, I'm surprised you've not 'ad 'em

before now. Must be right tricky for you, goin' in that 'ouse and not comin' out with 'alf the silver in your pockets. You Gypsies are that light-fingered, the temptation must be somethin' awful for you." He offered Nick one of his leering grins, practically inviting him to plant a facer on him.

"Ignore 'im, Nick," Jim said mildly as he pumped beer into Jed's tankard. "'E's jest tryin' to get a rise out of you. Bugger's only after a fight."

"I know," Nick said, affecting unconcern. "Else he'd have his teeth down his throat already."

"Ah, I'm only funnin', Nick," Jed protested as Nick turned away and made for the door. "You Gypsy folks take offence too easy, ain't that so, Jim?"

"Shaddup, Jed," Jim replied.

As Nick walked through the door, Jed's jeering voice followed him out. "You watch yerself with that Carrick. You don't want to end up like Jago now, do you?"

CHAPTER TEN

The week that followed Nicholas Hearn's first visit to Helston House dragged by for Ward. Usually he was happy to immerse himself in reading—there was so much still to learn about this new field—but he found the days very slow. Pipp was practically the only person he saw all week, other than the local vicar who'd taken to popping round every Tuesday afternoon, ever hopeful of persuading his newest parishioner to attend church. Ward had spent an hour with the good vicar yesterday, doing little to disguise his boredom. Afterwards, as Pipp had cleared the tea things away, he'd taken Ward to task over his rudeness.

"Would it hurt to observe the social niceties, Master Edward?" he'd asked drily. "Just a little?"

"If I observed the social niceties, I wouldn't be allowing you to talk to me like this," Ward had pointed out, before returning his attention to his journal, ignoring Pipp's offended sniff.

Even by Ward's standards, it was a pathetic amount of human contact for a whole week: a little under an hour of the vicar's unwanted company and daily bickering with his over-familiar servant.

Perhaps that was why he could barely contain his excitement at the thought of seeing Nicholas again on Sunday? Or perhaps it was merely that he was eager to finally make some progress with his experiments, even if he did only have one subject to work with. After buying this land, building this house, erecting lightning rods, and doing the other works at the Zawn, he was anxious to see some return for his efforts.

As he got dressed on Sunday morning, Ward felt full of renewed vigour. He would make a real start now. He might only have one subject to work with, but Nicholas was at least a promising one, and in the meantime, Ward was working towards finding others. He'd written to a spiritualist society to enquire whether they knew of any mediums in Cornwall, or indeed anyone who might be more sensitive to the spiritual plane. If he had to bring subjects to Helston House from Truro or Penzance, he would do so. Hell, he would bring them from John O'Groats if he had to. Whatever it took, the work would be done. It was too important, too vital to be allowed to slide.

Nicholas arrived while Ward was having breakfast.

Pipp opened the door of the breakfast room and announced him. "Mr. Hearn, sir." He paused, no doubt for dramatic effect, before adding, "And his *dog*."

He stepped aside, holding the door open for the new arrivals. And yes, there was Nicholas, with his absurdly ugly dog standing beside him.

Ward's chest felt suddenly tight, his breath a little constricted. It was the oddest feeling. Distantly, he was aware that he was standing up, his chair scraping against the parquet flooring, and then he was moving towards Nicholas, and Nicholas was coming forward to meet him, his face curiously expressionless, so that Ward wasn't at all sure if the man was pleased to be here or not. He'd thought Nicholas was content to return when they'd parted last week. Had he been wrong?

Suddenly, Ward wasn't sure what to do. He dithered about offering his hand, then stuck it out too quickly. Couldn't find the easy greeting that he was quite sure any other man would have uttered. Instead, he rasped, "It's good to see you again, Nicholas," wincing almost instantly at the ugly croak of his voice.

Nicholas shook his hand briefly. "You said I could bring Snow—is that still all right? I can take him home if you prefer."

"Of course, no trouble at all." Ward turned to Pipp. "Mr. Pipp, will you bring some tea for Mr. Hearn? Oh, and a bowl of water for Master Snowflake." When Pipp looked confused, he added, "The dog."

Pipp's eyebrows rose but he murmured, "Very good, sir," before melting away.

Ward turned back to Nicholas.

"Would you like some breakfast?" He gestured at the dishes on the sideboard.

"No, thank you. I've already eaten."

"I hope you don't mind joining me while I finish breakfast?"

"Not at all, I'm happy to wait," Nicholas replied evenly. And still, frustratingly, Ward could glean no sense of how happy or otherwise he was to be here.

"Please, take a seat," Ward said, returning to his own place. "Mr. Pipp will be back directly with fresh tea."

Nicholas selected the chair to the right of Ward's own. Snowflake trotted as close to his heel as could be, before settling himself down at his master's feet with a few whuffling breaths.

"He stays very close to you, doesn't he?" Ward observed. "It's as if he's afraid to let you out of his sight."

When Nicholas looked down at the dog, his stiffness eased, a small, fond smile curling the tight line of his mouth. That smile had a remarkable effect on his face. The man's fierce features softened. He was handsome when he smiled, his expression very appealing. There was much, in fact, about Nicholas that was appealing: the lean, tough body; the obvious, unshowy intelligence. And something too, about that quiet, self-contained reserve that Ward greatly liked. It was soothing, that stillness.

"He prefers to be with me," Nicholas said, bending down to caress the dog's ears. "Poor fellow was near death when I found him, and I doubt he'd known a moment's kindness in his life before that. He doesn't trust easy."

"He was injured when you found him?"

"*Ayes*," Nicholas said, his soft Cornish burr gentle as the dog gazed devotedly up at him, big, round head cocked at an odd angle so he could keep that single eye on Nicholas. "He was a fighting dog. Came off worst in a bout and was left to die in an alley. When I found him, he was in such a terrible state, I thought it would be kinder to kill him, but I was too much a coward—I couldn't do it."

Ward stared at the dog's empty eye socket, the hollowed space softened by a layer of white fur. He saw that the dog bore other scars on his unlovely face.

"It's not cowardly to shirk at killing a living being," Ward said.

"Yes, well, I'm glad I wasn't able to do it now. Snow's the gentlest companion you could wish for. Has the sweetest soul."

Ward was immediately intrigued. "Do you really think a dog can have a soul?" he asked. He was genuinely curious, but as usual, his awful, wrecked voice made his words sound harsh, so that the question came out sounding like an accusation. He opened his mouth to apologise or explain—something—but when Nicholas looked up to meet his gaze, he didn't seem offended.

"I'm certain of it," he said simply. "Whatever a soul is—

I'm not sure I know." He shrugged. "Perhaps you will find out from your experiments."

Ward smiled, relieved that not only had Nicholas not found his question offensive, he seemed to find it interesting. "Perhaps I will. I don't see why a soul or a spirit—whatever you want to call it—shouldn't be capable of being observed and measured. It's only a matter of finding the right way to do it."

Nicholas canted his head to one side, considering Ward curiously. "Is that right, though? A soul isn't like a—a rock or a butterfly. It's not something you can stick in a glass case and put a label next to."

"You're the one who said you saw a soul in Master Snowflake," Ward pointed out. "If you can identify a soul just by looking at a dog, is it so unreasonable to suggest I might be able to identify one using sound scientific methods?"

Nicholas's brows drew together at that, not in a frown as such, but in a thoughtful expression. "I'm not sure those are the same kinds of seeing. What I'm talking about is… more fleeting. A momentary flash of recognition that you feel here." He touched his solar plexus. "That's not the sort of seeing you're talking about."

"Oh? And what sort of seeing am I talking about?"

"I think you're talking about capturing something, then peering at it. Studying it. Taking it apart and putting it back together again till you know exactly how it works."

Ward felt oddly thrown by that assessment, which struck him as not entirely approving. "Well, that *is* how scientists understand things."

Nicholas nodded. "I know, but I'm not sure everything can be understood in that way. Some things are too fleeting, or—oh, I don't know—too *shadowy*."

"Nonsense," Ward replied. "Everything is capable of being studied and understood. I have to believe that. What do we have otherwise? People going around declaring this or that to be a truth based on some nebulous *feeling* they get? How could you ever disprove such a supposed fact, if you didn't agree with it? And how would we ever progress without the ability to disprove and offer new, better explanations? The discipline of science—the drawing of logical conclusions from objective evidence—is the only reliable way we have of understanding anything."

"So what is it that you wish to understand?" Nicholas asked. "From these experiments of yours?"

Ward blinked, taken aback by the question. "Well," he said after a pause, "I want to understand how my brother's spirit spoke to me on that ship. Where he was and how that plane of existence he was on interacts with our own world. The known, visible world."

"And you think you can find evidence that will explain those things using scientific methods?"

"Yes," Ward replied. "Why not?"

Nicholas was silent for a long time. At last, he said, "I can believe that Snow has a soul without having to understand what a soul really is. But what you're talking about..." He paused, frowning. "It sounds to me as though you're searching for a way to *allow* yourself to believe."

Ward stared at Nicholas. He couldn't think how to respond to that, and his gut began to churn uneasily as he turned over the words in his mind. He was relieved when Pipp knocked at the door, interrupting them.

"Come in," he croaked, and Pipp glided in. While he poured tea for Nicholas and asked if he would like anything to eat, Ward looked down at his own half-eaten breakfast. He'd forgotten about it while he and Nicholas had been talking, and now it was cold and unappetising.

"You can clear this away, Mr. Pipp," he said when Pipp was finished with Nicholas, ignoring the man's purse-lipped disapproval as he lifted the plate and left the room.

Once Pipp had left, Nicholas said, "May I ask you something?"

"Of course," Ward replied, though in truth he was wary now of what Nicholas might ask, given what had gone before.

"Do you believe in God?"

The question surprised Ward, and he didn't answer immediately, studying Nicholas for several long moments.

"No, I don't," he said at last. "But that is not to say I couldn't be persuaded if there was evidence. Do you?"

"I don't know," Nicholas said. "But sometimes, when I'm walking along the cliff tops, I look out over the sea. The wind will be wild and the birds circling above, gulls and kittiwakes and guillemots, and the sky will have a thousand clouds in it. It's all so... immense and so grand and it all fits together just so. And I get the strongest feeling—a sort of yearning, I suppose— as though part of me is trying to burst out of my body and join with it all." He smiled uncertainly at Ward. "When that happens, it's difficult to believe there isn't something."

Ward wasn't sure what Nicholas meant by that. Was he saying he believed in God or not? He considered asking, pressing the point, but in the end, he left the thought unspoken. Instead he just watched while Nicholas bent down to pet the dog again, his gaze lingering on the sharp sweep of the man's firm jawline. The bluish lights that the sunshine streaming through the window picked out in his black hair. The way his strong, capable hand gently fondled the ugly dog's ears.

After breakfast, Ward suggested they walk over to the Zawn. It wasn't far from the house, and there were things he wanted to show Nick.

"I'm having a series of platforms constructed inside the

crevice," he explained as they strode over the scrubby, wind-tugged grass. Nick realised he was growing used to the man's odd rasping voice. Already he barely noticed it.

"What purpose will they serve?" he asked.

"They're for my ozone gas efforts," Ward said, as though that explained everything.

Nick could see, up ahead, that the Zawn was now encircled by a makeshift wooden fence, about three feet high. What on earth?

"You'll have to watch out," he warned. "If the village children find out there's platforms in there, you'll have them crawling inside, and you'll get the blame if one of them falls to their deaths."

Ward frowned. "Surely they won't come all the way up here? This is private property, and it's a fair walk from the village just to play in a hole."

Nick laughed. "If you think the village boys won't walk a couple of miles to climb inside a crack in the ground that stretches all the way from the cliff top to the sea *and* spurts up great bursts of water without warning, you need your head looking at. Of course they'll come! God knows I used to, when I was a boy."

"Did you?"

Nick glanced at Ward, perplexed by his disbelief. Lord, hadn't the man ever played as a child? He was looking at Nick with the same expression he'd worn that first day in the Admiral's Arms, his acorn-brown gaze all earnest and his hair glinting in the sunshine.

Nick cleared his throat and forced himself to go on. "Of course I did. I used to come up here with Jake Odell, Gid Paget, and Jed Hammett. We'd dare each other to stand at the edge and wait for the sea spurts, see if we could run away without getting drenched."

They had reached the Zawn now. Nick laid a hand on the flimsy fence. "You might be better taking this down.

There's nothing draws an adventurous lad like a fence round some works. You'd be better off putting a proper fence up along your entire boundary. Dissuade any would-be trespassers from getting near enough to even see these platforms exist."

Ward frowned thoughtfully.

Nick vaulted over the fence with ease, then leaned back over, gesturing to Snow and making a clicking noise with his mouth. "C'm'ere, boy." The dog trotted up to the fence and jumped into his waiting arms. Nick set Snow down again on the other side and patted his thigh to let the dog know he wanted him close.

Nick stepped up to the mouth of the crevice, Snow padding cautiously beside him. He looked down the long, craggy tunnel to the patch of glittering grey-blue below where the sea undulated and foamed. There was something bobbing down there in the water. Nick squinted—it looked like several wooden crates, bound together. Further up the crevice, perhaps twenty feet from the bottom, there was a wooden platform. It looked to be three feet wide and perhaps six or seven feet long. Very solid. Another platform had been started further up, thick beams already secured in place on which the thinner platform boards would be set.

Nick glanced at Ward who was now standing beside him, peering down too.

"How many of those are you going to build?"

"Three near the bottom and three near the top. To begin with, anyway."

"What have they got to do with ozone gas then?"

Ward pointed down the hole. "Do you see the wooden cases right down at the bottom? In the sea?"

"Yes."

"Those contain cells, not unlike the ones I showed you last week. Batteries of them—some other equipment too. In essence, I'm trying to produce ozone gas by passing electricity into water, a process that happens naturally during storms. I'm attempting an artificial synthesis."

"And have you been successful?"

Ward made a face. "Slightly. It's not very difficult to produce a small quantity—it's a question of volume."

"I see. And the platforms?"

"Those are mainly for carrying out observations. As and when I get to the stage of producing a reasonable quantity of ozone, I'll be taking measurements to see how it travels, what effect the sea surges have, and so on." He looked at Nick, catching his eye. "And of course, the platforms will be useful for working with subjects too. This crevice is a natural funnel. I'm hoping I can take advantage of that to re-create the atmospheric conditions present during a storm at sea, even when the weather is fair." He glanced at Nick. "In fact, if you like, we could hold our session out here today?"

Nick raised his brows. "You want me to climb down there so you can *hypnotise* me?" he exclaimed.

Ward grinned. "Does the prospect alarm you?"

That grin, so brilliant and bright with humour, momentarily floored Nick. He could do nothing but gaze at the man, rocked by a sudden surge of helpless longing.

When he realised he was staring, heat flooded his face and he looked quickly away, but not before he saw Ward's own brows draw together in faint puzzlement.

Frantically, Nick searched his mind for Ward's last words. "Alarm me?" he repeated. He cleared his throat. "Yes, it does rather. I'd far prefer to be hypnotised in your study, in that nice comfortable armchair." He made himself smile, though he feared it was a stiff and awkward thing. "Speaking of which, isn't it about time we got back and made a start?"

Without waiting for a reply, he strode back to the fence, praying that Ward would follow him, and that he wouldn't ask Nick why he was suddenly so anxious to be put into a trance.

CHAPTER ELEVEN

From *The Collected Writings of Sir Edward Carrick,* volume I

Some of the first experiments I conducted involved the production of chemical reactions by the application of an electrical current to an electrolyte. My father allowed me to purchase a simple electrostatic machine and I used this firstly to electrolyse water, splitting it into its two constituent gases, and then a variety of other electrolytes. It was the reverse process, though—producing electricity from the energy released by spontaneous chemical reactions—that truly fascinated me. As Professor Daniell had explained in that first lecture I attended, exciting new inventions were already being powered with the portable power source he had invented, the Daniell cell. It was clear to me, even then, that far greater things would be possible in the future, as more power was harnessed into smaller and ever more durable batteries of these cells. That, I felt sure, was the key to the future.

∾

12th June 1853
   Four weeks later

"Is she there?" Ward asked. "Can you sense her?"

Nicholas sat on the high-backed armchair opposite Ward in the study. His eyes were closed, his posture curiously alert yet somehow still relaxed, forearms and hands resting on the arms of the chair. A few moments earlier, he had called out to his mother. *"Ma? Can you hear me?"*

At Ward's question, a tiny frown appeared between Nicholas's brows. It was an expression Ward had become very familiar with over the past five weeks. That and a hundred others. When he wasn't in a trance, Nicholas's resting expression was, well, no expression at all, which made it all the more fascinating that his features gave so much away when he was in a trance, as though a mask had been stripped away.

For a long time, Nicholas was silent, sitting very upright. He looked as though he was listening just as hard as he could. At last though, he sighed and answered Ward's question.

"No," he said. "I can't sense her."

At least he had tried—really tried, Ward was sure—this time. That was an improvement.

Ward noted it in his book. *NH cooperative in trance. Attempted to contact deceased mother. Attempt unsuccessful.*

"Can you sense anyone else? Any other spirits?" he asked mildly, careful not to let his disappointment show.

"No," Nicholas answered, this time without any hesitation. "There is no one here. Only me."

"Only me."

Something about the hollow way he said that made Ward look at him more closely.

This was one of the days, Ward realised, when Nicholas

grew melancholy in his trance. Sometimes he got this way, though it was difficult to tell only from watching him.

"I am all alone," Nicholas said now. His tone was matter-of-fact, but there was an edge to it that made Ward's chest ache.

Ward hesitated, unsure how to answer. "You are not alone," he said at last. "I am here with you."

Nicholas laughed at that, but there was no humour in the dry chuckle. "No. You are there. Only *I* am here."

Ward frowned. Where was *there* and where was *here*? Sometimes he didn't understand the things Nicholas said when he was in his trance state. He was given to opaque utterances that probably made perfect sense to him, but were impenetrable to Ward.

Ward wanted to comfort him though, so he said again, gently, "You are not alone, Nicholas."

His words didn't seem to have the desired effect. Nicholas just shook his head, rolling it from side to side on the back of the chair.

Ward's stomach was in knots from gazing upon Nicholas's naked unhappiness. He didn't know what to do. After a few moments, he picked up his pen and scratched inside the notebook, *NH asserts repeatedly that he is alone*, as if the mere recording of that truth would somehow deal with the matter. Which was ridiculous. Disgusted with himself, he scored the words out and closed the notebook with a snap.

"Rest for a few minutes, Nicholas," he said, pretending a confidence he did not feel. "Then, when you're ready, open your eyes, and wake up."

∼

Some time later, when Nicholas had roused from his customary post-trance nap, they sat down to dinner together.

Nicholas had unbent enough to stay for dinner every Sunday evening since his second visit.

Snow lay peacefully curled up under the table at Nicholas's feet while they ate. Nicholas seemed to be enjoying the meal, but Ward's appetite was off. He toyed disinterestedly with his dinner, musing bleakly on the unremarkable results from the last few Sundays' work.

He had put Nicholas into a trance a number of times now, and today, for the first time, Nicholas had given every appearance of fully cooperating with what Ward had asked of him. That was progress, at least. On the previous occasions, whilst he'd consented to being hypnotised in the first place, once in the trance state, he'd demonstrated a reluctance to comply with Ward's requests, in particular, refusing to attempt to contact spirits.

Today he had co-operated though. And yet despite that, he'd still made no contact with any spirit, not his mother nor anyone else. In fact, he hadn't seemed to be able to detect any kind of presence at all—not even Ward, who had been sitting right beside him.

Rationally, Ward knew he shouldn't allow himself to feel discouraged. It was early days still. But it had been weeks since he'd started working with Nicholas, and their progress was so slow, it felt as though they were going backwards. It was only after today's failure that he realised he'd presumed that once Nicholas really tried, *something* would happen.

"You're not eating," Nicholas observed, setting his cutlery down and fastening his bright gaze on Ward.

Ward shook his head. "Don't mind me. I'm not especially hungry, and I'm bad company this evening besides."

"Yes, you are," Nicholas agreed. "And I think I know why."

Ward gave him a look. "Oh, really? Why don't you tell me, then, since I don't know myself."

Nicholas seemed unfazed by that testy reply. "You're

coming to understand that I'm not what you'd been hoping for. You convinced yourself at the outset, despite my protests, that I had some mystical connection to the spiritual plane—probably because of what Jed Hammett said to you in the Admiral's Arms that day—but now you're beginning to realise that I really am just as ordinary as I told you I was."

Ward scowled. Nicholas was about as far from ordinary as it was possible to get in his opinion. Not that he was about to tell Nicholas that.

"It's far too soon to be reaching any conclusions about anything," he said instead. "As I told you when we began, I need to test many combinations of conditions. So far, we've been working only with the application of one potential factor, namely a trance state. I would have been surprised if we'd had any real results as yet."

Nicholas didn't respond to that, just raised one brow.

Ward pressed on, manfully. "My intuition about my experience on the *Archimedes* is that it was all the conditions working together—my exposure to a strong concentration of natural electromagnetism, the presence of ozone, my hypnotic state—that enabled George to reach me. In all honesty, I'm not hopeful we'll see any positive results until we're able to combine most or all those factors in appropriate concentrations. But that doesn't mean this exercise is unhelpful. I'm building up detailed records of my observations of your responses, and all of that data, even that showing nothing happening, will assist me."

Nicholas plainly wasn't convinced. "Why do you look so defeated then?"

Ward sighed. "It's the magnitude of it," he admitted. "Realising that it's taken six meetings with you to get to this point and that we've scarcely begun yet. And we only have a few more Sundays left."

Nicholas eyed him. "We should be able to go down the Zawn soon, shouldn't we? Will that help?"

"Perhaps. I hope so. I just wish…"

"What?"

"I wish there was a quick way of re-creating all the conditions I experienced on the *Archimedes*. To see if you sense anything at all."

Nicholas considered that. "One big storm," he said. "I see that. You could ascertain once and for all whether I'll be any use to you. Save yourself some time."

Ward glanced up quickly. "I didn't mean that."

Nicholas smiled. "I'm not offended."

But Ward wasn't sure that was true. He thought Nicholas looked sad.

"Anyway," Nicholas said, more briskly, "you might get one soon. They come in off the sea all year round."

"The chances of one conveniently arriving on a Sunday aren't very high," Ward pointed out drily.

Nicholas regarded him. He was wearing his smile-frown, Ward's favourite of all his expressions, especially this particular one with the emphasis firmly on the smile, and only the tiniest frown pleating his dark brows. This smile-frown was mostly pleasure, with only a very little bewilderment.

He said, "Are you trying to ask me something? If so, I'd rather you just came out and said it."

Ward sighed. He'd been hoping Nicholas would take the hint graciously but apparently Ward was going to be forced to give voice to his wishes.

"Would you be willing to come here if there was a storm?" he asked. "Even if it was not on one of our Sundays?"

Nicholas said, "Well, it's nice that you posed it as a question this time."

Ward flushed. He couldn't think how to respond to that. They hadn't spoken of how Nicholas had been persuaded to assist Ward since that very first day, but each time Nicholas came to Helston House, it felt to Ward that he'd thawed a little more, making it a little easier for Ward to forget how this had started. Until now, that was, when Ward was forced to recognise that their bad beginning still lingered between them, like a sore that wouldn't heal.

He was about to apologise and withdraw his question, when Nicholas sighed and said, "How about this? If I feel a storm coming, I will try to come over here. Other commitments allowing, you understand."

Ward stared at him, astonished by his generosity. At last he said, his hoarse voice disguising the emotion that overwhelmed him, "Thank you. I appreciate that more than you could possibly know."

Nicholas just nodded an acknowledgement and picked up his cutlery again, turning his attention back to his dinner.

After a while, he asked, "Have you managed to find any other subjects yet?"

"Not quite yet," Ward said. "But I've corresponded with a gentleman in Truro, a Stephen Bryant, who claims to be a medium. He's invited me to attend one of his séances in a fortnight's time."

Nicholas's dark brows drew together in a small frown. "Are you going to go?"

"I may as well," Ward said. "He appears to have a reasonable reputation from what I can make out. It's worth investigating further, I think."

Nicholas's frown deepened. "Has he asked you to pay him?"

Ward opened his mouth to admit that he had—and that Ward had sent the money already—only to be struck by a sudden, awful realisation. Nicholas had now come to Helston House on numerous occasions, and Ward hadn't paid him so much as a halfpenny for his trouble. And after all his talk of paying handsomely too! Heat flushed up Ward's neck and blazed from his cheeks.

Nicholas immediately noticed his agitation. "What's

wrong?" he said. Then, incredulously, "You haven't already sent him money, have you?"

"I— Oh, hell, Nicholas—" Ward's voice was breaking up even more than usual, as it was wont to do when he was feeling strong emotion, "I am—I am *mortified*. You must forgive me—" He stood up quickly and crossed the room to ring the bell for Pipp.

"For God's sake, what's wrong?" Nicholas looked alarmed now.

"The thing is, I get so taken up with things, so obsessed with my own interests, that I forget you see—" Ward was babbling now. He gave a groan of dismay.

"Forget what?"

"You must think me the worst sort of opportunist."

"Opportunist? I don't know what—"

Just then, Pipp opened the door. "You rang, sir?"

Ward turned to his servant, relieved. "Ah, Pipp, yes. I have just this moment realised, to my utter shame, that I have not yet paid Mr. Hearn for any of his time. Could you please bring me the household ledger and the wages box?"

"Very good, sir."

"*What?*" Nicholas exclaimed, standing up so violently that his chair rocked on its back legs. Snowflake let out a little yelp of surprise and scrambled out of the way.

"I'll just be a moment, sir," Pipp said smoothly and withdrew, closing the door behind him with a quiet *snick*.

Ward turned to face Nicholas. To his surprise, the man looked furious.

"I never asked you for money," Nicholas snapped. I can't believe you thought I was hinting about that when I asked if you'd sent money to that medium."

"Nicholas, I didn't intend to suggest—"

"If I'd wanted paying, I'd've come right out and said so," Nicholas interrupted. His colour was up, his words pouring out, quick and bitter. "I've never asked you for anything, Ward!"

"Nicholas, please." Ward's voice was useless. Harsh when it should be pleading, no tone to it, no inflection. Nevertheless, he forced himself to go on. "I did not mean to insult you, but I promised you payment, and I do not want you to think I do not value your time!"

Nicholas wouldn't meet his gaze. He stared at the door, chest heaving. Snowflake, sensing his master's unhappiness, pressed his sturdy body against Nicholas's calf and looked up at him, his single eye darting anxiously.

"Nicholas—" Ward said again, and winced. The name on his lips sounded like a scold, when he only meant it as a plea. He could have wept with frustration.

The door opened, and there was Pipp again. He held the household ledger in one hand and the cast-iron money box he paid the other servants' wages from each week in the other.

"Go away!" Ward howled, and Pipp's confused expression was almost funny, might even have made Ward laugh his awful toneless laugh on another day.

Pipp pressed his lips together in a firm line and snapped the door shut again. The click of his boot heels was audible as he marched back down the corridor.

There was a long silence, then Nicholas said flatly, "Well, you'll be out of favour with Mr. Pipp after that outburst."

His fury seemed to have abated. Still, Ward lifted the verbal olive branch with great care, offering a wary half smile as he replied, "You don't know the half of it. Pipp may seem like an obedient servant to you, but he scolds me terribly when we're alone."

Nicholas shrugged. "I see more than you think. You're like an old married couple, you and Mr. Pipp, smiling at each other through gritted teeth and thinking no one notices when you're in a bad mood with one another."

That observation was so unexpectedly astute, it startled a short bark of laughter out of Ward.

Nicholas raised a brow. "I surprise you?" he asked lightly. He gave a dry, humourless laugh, then added, "Perhaps I'm like a talking dog to you. Or a bearded lady?"

"I beg your pardon?"

"You don't expect me to notice things, do you? Or even to be interested—*really* interested—in what you're trying to achieve. In your eyes, I'm here because you ordered me to come—and for the money, of course. Just a Gypsy looking to fleece you."

"That's not fair," Ward protested, hurt. "I don't think that. I was only surprised you noticed how things are with Pipp and me because *I* would never notice such a thing."

Nicholas didn't say anything to that, just watched Ward silently.

"As for the money," Ward went on doggedly, "you can refuse to take it if you want. I can hardly force it upon you. But I promised at the outset to compensate you for your time, and to find myself in breach of that promise—well, I'm appalled at myself. Can't you understand that?"

In that moment, Nicholas's thin-lipped anger gave way to a pained expression that was ten times worse than his ire. "But I don't want your money, Ward," he said quietly. "That's what *I* told *you* at the outset."

"I already have a position that pays me well enough…"

Ward's gut twisted with belated comprehension. Nicholas had indeed said as much, and Ward had insulted him by treating him like a servant—on top of blackmailing him.

"Oh," Ward said. He swallowed hard. "I'm—I'm sorry, Nicholas. I should have thought before I spoke." When Nicholas remained silent, his gaze averted, Ward said, "I truly didn't mean to offend you. Quite the opposite. I'm just hopeless at understanding other people, at least that's what Pipp says." He stepped closer, laying a hand on Nicholas's forearm. "Please. Forgive me."

Finally, Nicholas looked up and met his gaze. He sighed. "You *are* hopeless at understanding people," he agreed. "Which is shocking given how bright you are."

The faint whiff of humour in that response made the tightness in Ward's chest ease minutely. "Mother said I spent too much time with books and not enough with other children when I was a boy."

"She's probably right," Nicholas said, and shook his head. "I dread to think of how you'll get on at that séance."

Impulsively, Ward said, "Why don't you come with me then?"

"What?"

"Come to Mr. Bryant's séance in Truro with me. It's a week on Saturday. You can keep an eye on me that way, can't you?"

Nicholas opened his mouth—Ward was sure to refuse— then he closed it again and thought.

"All right," he said at last, surprising Ward. "Why not? I've not been to Truro in an age."

Ward's grin widened. He felt quite suddenly and giddily happy. "I was planning to leave on Friday afternoon. The séance isn't till Saturday evening but I thought to stay the extra night and spend the day in town, then return on Sunday. Will that suit you?" As soon as the words were out, it occurred to him that Godfrey Tremain might not like his land steward disappearing for several days and added quickly, "I can amend my plans if it does not."

"No, that sounds fine," Nicholas said, "if you're sure you've the stomach for so much of my company."

"I think I could bear your company for a sight longer than three days," Ward replied. "You will be the one begging for respite from me."

"You think so?"

"I'm a terrible travelling companion. I tend to forget I have company."

Nicholas shrugged. "Well, if that's the worst of it, I think I'll be all right. I'm capable of amusing myself."

They gazed at one another for a long moment, Ward still smiling like a fool. Nicholas was the first to look away, a faint flush over his high cheekbones.

"All right, then," he said briskly. "Now that's settled, I'm going to finish my dinner, though it's probably cold by now."

He took his seat again. Ward did likewise and discovered that he was hungry after all.

CHAPTER TWELVE

19th June 1853

The next Sunday, when Nick arrived at Helston House, Ward once again suggested they go down to the Zawn.

"The upper platforms are all in place now. I thought we could climb down and have a go at putting you into a trance down there."

Nick raised a brow. "What about the sea spurts? How can I possibly concentrate while I'm being soaked with saltwater spray?"

Ward grinned. "Let's give it a try. I don't think it's impossible. After all, I managed to go into a trance on board ship in the midst of a violent storm."

"Hmmm."

Ward elbowed Nick. "Come on. We'll take oilskins with us so you won't get too wet."

Nick sighed. "Fine. I'll give it a try."

He tried to ignore the warm feeling Ward's triumphant look gave him. The satisfaction he got from pleasing Ward troubled him.

It was a blustery day and the whistling, buffeting winds made conversation nigh on impossible on their way to the Zawn, but Nick was happy to walk in silence. These last weeks, he'd discovered that Ward—sometimes eccentric, sometimes difficult—was actually a surprisingly easy person to be with. Not just easy to talk to, but easy to be quiet with too.

Ward seemed to understand Nick's occasional need for silence, a need that went hand in hand with a somewhat contradictory and bone-deep loneliness right at Nick's core. He found it difficult to reconcile these warring aspects of his character: his need for isolation, and how alone that isolation could make him feel.

From what Ward had said of his life, especially of that long period of childhood sickness, it was plain that he too had spent a great deal of time alone. Despite that—or maybe because of it—like Nick, he chose to go about his life in a way that guaranteed the continuance of his solitary ways.

Nick had thought that loneliness was the price he paid for protecting something more important to him. But since he'd met Ward, Nick did not feel so lonely, not even when they were apart. He wasn't sure why that should be, and in truth, it troubled him sometimes. What business did Ward have, easing Nick's loneliness? Nick hadn't asked to be his friend.

He glanced at the man who plagued his thoughts. Ward was trudging along beside him, one hand deep in the pocket of his coat, the other holding his hat in place, an overstuffed knapsack, packed with oilskins, bumping against his hip.

He must have sensed Nick's attention because he returned Nick's glance, a smile just touching his lips, a faint question in his eyes—till his attention was arrested by something over Nick's shoulder, something that made him give one of his odd croaky laughs and exclaim, "Bloody hell, where's he off to?"

Nick turned his head, looking for whatever it was. A second or two passed before he saw it: Snow, running hell for leather after a white-tailed rabbit he was nowhere near fast enough to catch. Actually no, it was two rabbits. The dog swung his head from side to side as the rabbits diverged, now running in different directions, before picking one and pelting after it.

Nick laughed too. "He can't resist a rabbit. Don't worry, he'll come back once he tires out."

They were nearing the Zawn now. Nick pointed at one of the lightning rods Ward had erected around the crevice.

"Why did you put those up?"

"The rods? So I can work out here in a storm without fear of being struck. They should draw off any lightning strikes before they get anywhere near a person."

The pointless fence round the Zawn had been removed now, so Nick was able to step right up to the edge and peer inside without having to clamber over anything. And yes, there were the upper platforms Ward had spoken of, three of them, the first perhaps eight feet from the top and the next two at similar intervals further down.

Ward explained how the platforms were constructed and pointed out the ladders attached to the craggy wall of the crevice from which each platform could be accessed in turn.

"Very impressive," Nick said. "Though I'm still doubtful you'll be able to hypnotise me down there." He glanced at Ward to share his amusement, but the man wasn't looking at him—he was looking past Nick, his expression first merely frowning, then suddenly horrified.

"Oh hell," he said, launching himself past Nick at a run. "Snowflake, stop!"

Nick whirled around on his heel as Ward sped past him to see that Snow's sturdy white body was barrelling towards them, far too fast. With his blind eye on the side of the crevice, and his whole attention on the rabbit that streaked ahead of him, the dog didn't seem to realise he was about to hurtle over the edge.

Ward pitched himself at Snow.

"Ward, no!" Nick yelled—he was already running, but he was one endless second behind Ward and could only watch as Ward's upper body slammed down on the ground in front of Snow, bringing the dog up short, and his legs slid into the mouth of the Zawn, his weight immediately dragging him down.

"*Ward!*" Nick yelled again, closing the distance between them as Ward scrabbled for purchase, desperate fingers clawing at the short, rough, cliff top grass, while his boots sent clods of mud and rocks tumbling down the yawning chasm.

Nick threw himself to the ground beside Ward, grabbing for the man just as he was about to slide right in. Somehow he managed to grasp one of Ward's wrists, then reached down with his other hand to seize his elbow.

"Grab me with your other arm!" he cried. There was no platform below Ward, only the sheer drop to the sea below.

Gasping, Ward obeyed, reaching up to grip Nick's sleeve with his free hand. Nick's body shifted forward an inch or two in response to the man's weight pulling at him, and he cursed. How could such a reed-slim man feel so suddenly, overwhelmingly heavy?

Ward stared up at him, green-gold eyes wide with panic. "I don't want to pull you down!"

"You won't," Nick hissed, wrapping his free arm round a rocky outcrop at the edge of the crevice. "I'm steady now— but you have to try to pull yourself up. I can't hold you like this for too long."

Ward nodded. He looked terrified, but he firmed his jaw and swung his legs a few times—making Nick feel as though his arm was about to be torn out of its socket—till he managed to brace one foot against the wall of the crevice to steady himself. Then, white-faced, he used the wall and Nick's aching arm and shoulder to slowly haul himself up, knotting his fingers into the sturdy tweed of Nick's coat, and finally winding one arm round Nick's neck, his grip painfully hard, the side of his face pressed up against Nick's.

"Almost there," Nick panted against Ward's cheek, relief flooding him at that needy embrace. He began to edge his own body backwards in tiny increments, until Ward was able to inch his hips over the edge of the Zawn, then get one leg up and over. Only then did Nick loosen his death grip on the rocky outcrop, bringing his other arm around Ward's upper back and yanking him all the rest of the way out, out of that greedy maw.

Nick rolled onto his back, away from the edge, dragging Ward with him till Ward lay on top of him, his chest to Nick's, their faces so close the ends of Ward's dark-gold hair brushed Nick's forehead. They were both breathing hard, and Nick's heart was pounding with exhaustion and fear—and something else too. An undeniable excitement at Ward's nearness, at the intimacy of his body lying flush against Nick's while he stared into Nick's eyes.

Neither of them pulled away. Neither sought to bring to an end this moment that had already stretched too long.

There was a question in Ward's eyes.

Nick didn't really make a decision as such. It was instinct that drove him to grasp Ward by the back of his neck and haul him into a hard, desperate kiss. He half expected Ward to wrench himself away, maybe even hit Nick. But it seemed Nick's instincts were all right, because Ward didn't do any of those things. Instead, he melted against Nick with a helpless groan, bringing their bodies even closer together and fisting his hands around the lapels of Nick's tweed coat as he returned the kiss with urgent fervour.

Ward's mouth was hard—painfully so—pressing Nick's

lips against his teeth. Nick drew back a little, then parted his lips to soften the kiss, and Ward's small jerk of surprise at that was oddly touching. Loosening his rigid grip on Ward's nape, Nick tunnelled his fingers into the man's silky hair and slid his free arm around Ward's waist, steadying him as Nick shifted their bodies into a more comfortable position.

Tentatively, Nick stroked his tongue over the seam of Ward's closed, almost chaste mouth, his own mouth curving slightly when Ward finally opened to him with a small, surprised gasp. Ward was plainly unused to kissing, and that thought made Nick strangely giddy. He coaxed Ward into a deeper kiss, with tender, suckling pulls at his lips that soon had Ward writhing against him and Nick's cock growing achingly hard in his drawers.

Somewhere at the back of his mind, Nick knew they were getting too carried away. That this was dangerously reckless behaviour, out here in the open. With a huge effort, he broke the kiss, rolling them over again till Ward was under him, flat on his back in the scrubby grass. Ward seemed dazed, his light-brown eyes darker than usual as his pupils pushed back the band of tawny iris.

"Kiss me again," he whispered, lips barely moving.

When Ward whispered, his voice sounded quite normal. There was an inflection of yearning in it now that could not be discerned when he spoke in his customary bark.

Nick obediently lowered his head and brushed their lips gently together, even as he murmured, "We have to stop. It's madness doing this out here in broad daylight."

"You started it," Ward said, arching up his hips for more contact. Nick could feel the subtle prod of his prick, muffled by layers of clothing. He moaned softly, shifting his own hips away.

"You're right, I did," he said, pressing his forehead against Ward's before adding, "I think I lost my mind for a moment. I thought— Christ, Ward, I thought you were going to fall. I thought you were going to *die*. What possessed you? I've never been so damned relieved in all my life as when you finally dragged yourself out of there!"

Ward gave a breathy chuckle. "You kissed me because you thought I was going to die?"

Nick smiled, but he was serious when he answered. "I wouldn't have had the nerve otherwise."

Ward was silent for several moments. Then he swallowed and whispered, "In that case, it was worth it—almost dying, I mean."

Nick's heart thudded so hard he was sure Ward must feel the beats as well as he did.

"It was very foolhardy of me," he said. "I had no reason to believe you were like me. You've never—" He broke off suddenly, eyes widening. "That is— Oh Christ, *are* you like me?"

Ward's eyes danced with amusement and he gave a croaky laugh. "Oh, yes. You don't need to worry about that, Nicholas."

God, but he was comely.

Nick stared at Ward, unable to drag his gaze away, even as he said faintly, "We need to get up. What if someone sees us like this?" Ward didn't argue with that, but when Nick made to shift away, Ward lifted a hand to his face, halting him. Keeping their gazes locked.

"All right," he whispered urgently. "But stay with me tonight. Instead of going home after dinner, come to my bedchamber." When Nick hesitated, he added, "Pipp is the soul of discretion, I promise you. All my servants are."

Nick closed his eyes briefly. It was a terrible idea. He had a score of objections. And yet he found himself yearning to agree.

He settled on a compromise.

"I won't stay the whole night," he said at last. "But I'll stay for a while after dinner. How's that?"

Ward's smile was dazzling.

"Wonderful," he said.

CHAPTER THIRTEEN

From *The Collected Writings of Sir Edward Carrick*, volume I

From time to time, my father would ask me to perform some of my experiments for one of his guests or a curious neighbour. It felt rather like conducting a magic show—I must admit I rather enjoyed provoking gasps of surprised delight with my demonstrations of static electricity and electromagnetic current and Leyden jars. The difference between a scientist and a magician, however, is that while the magician's purpose is to pretend he is producing things out of thin air, a scientist's purpose is to explain that there is no such thing as "thin air." To show instead that the air around us is a complex, luminiferous ether through which invisible forces and subtle bodies move, if we could but see them.

∽

Ward didn't taste a single bite of his dinner. He put food in his mouth, chewed and swallowed, and nodded his agreement when Nicholas asked Pipp to pass his compliments on to Mrs. Waddell. But once it was over, he couldn't even have said what he'd eaten. Instead, he spent the whole meal dwelling on what was to come after, his stomach knotted with nerves and excitement.

"We'll take a glass of port in the study," Ward told Pipp as he cleared their dishes away.

Pipp was expressionless. "Very good, sir."

Ward's nerves had grown more and more jittery throughout the meal. By the time he and Nicholas were climbing the stairs together, he felt positively tongue-tied. Nicholas was equally silent, a serious expression making him look somewhat grim.

Was he having second thoughts?

Ward opened the study door and gestured for Nicholas and Snowflake to precede him into the room. Nicholas didn't even glance at Ward as he entered, but despite that, despite the fact that his sleeve did not even so much as brush Ward's as he passed him, Ward could *feel* him, as though Nicholas's life force pulled at Ward like a magnet. Or perhaps his presence influenced Ward's world in some unmistakable way, like the weather. Like when the air grew thick and heavy with the promise of an impending storm.

"Pipp'll be up with the port in a minute," Ward told Nicholas. "Then we'll get some peace."

Yes, they'd be alone at last, after the torture of sitting through too long a dinner, too many plates being put down and taken away again, when all Ward had wanted to do was push everything off the table and crawl over the polished wood to get to the man sitting on the other side.

Nicholas gave a strained smile and went to examine Ward's bookshelves. He looked like Ward felt—nervous with expectation and impatience, unable to settle to anything but the long-delayed promise of what was to come. He stared fixedly at the spines of the books, but Ward would have wagered he did not see any of the words.

When at last Pipp came, Ward watched with sorely tried patience as his servant unhurriedly unloaded the contents of his tray.

"Will that be all, sir?" Pipp asked at last.

"Yes," Ward said, suddenly unable to look his servant in the eye. "You may take yourself off for the night now, Pipp. I can see Mr. Hearn out when he's ready to go."

Pipp replied, "If I may be so bold, sir, it's rather late. If it's more convenient, I could have one of the guest rooms made up for—"

"That won't be necessary, Mr. Pipp." That was Nicholas, turning away from the bookshelf to quickly interrupt. "I'll only be here another hour or so."

Another hour or so?

Ward felt a stab of disappointment. That wasn't much time at all.

"Of course, sir," Pipp murmured, inclining his head at Nicholas. He tucked his tray under his arm and left.

And finally, they were alone.

Nicholas moved slowly towards Ward, a tentative smile tugging at the corner of his mouth as Ward stepped forward to meet him, heart thudding with anticipation, only to halt when the click of nails on the wooden floor made them both glance downwards. No, they weren't alone quite yet—Master Snowflake was still with them. The dog gazed worshipfully up at Nicholas, big head canted to one side.

Nicholas sent Ward an apologetic look. "I need to settle him down somewhere first. Where can I put him?"

"How about in here? Will he be all right if he knows you're just next door?"

Nicholas thought about that. "I think he'll be fine if I make him a little bed up, like the one he has at home. Would that be all right?"

"Of course. What do you need?"

"Do you have an old blanket, or maybe some rags?"

141

"I'm sure I can find something along those lines. Follow me." He went to the door that connected the study to the bedchamber, beckoning Nicholas to follow him. "This is where I sleep," he said, glancing over his shoulder at Nicholas, whose eyes were wide as he took in the opulence of the large bed dominating the room.

"You could sleep ten in that bed," Nicholas joked weakly, seeming unable to take his eyes off it.

Ward chuckled and opened up the linen chest at the foot of the bed, pulling out a soft woollen blanket of palest blue, trimmed with ivory satin. He handed it to Nicholas. "Will this do?"

Nicholas stared at it, seeming appalled. "I can't let a dog sleep on this."

Ward waved that off. "It's fine. I never use it—I'm always too hot in bed. Besides, it can be laundered if he makes a mess on it."

"But it's—"

"Nicholas, *please*," Ward interrupted, his already harsh voice even rougher than usual. "Let's not waste any more time."

Nicholas stared at him, his expression taken aback. Then his lips twitched and he nodded. "All right. Just give me a minute."

Ward watched from the doorway as Nicholas made a little nest in the study with the blue blanket and coaxed Snowflake over. Snowflake approached, sniffed the blanket cautiously, then eventually stepped inside, circling three times before he settled himself down. For a few minutes, Nicholas sat with his dog, hunkered on the floor beside him, petting his ears and broad, round head. Slowly, Snowflake seemed to relax, resting his head on his paws and closing his single, rheumy eye.

When Nicholas finally stood again, the dog was far from asleep, his eye immediately popping open to gaze at his owner pleadingly, as though begging him to stay. But after Nicholas soothed him again with more of those low murmurs and petting, he finally put his head back down, though he kept his watchful gaze on Nicholas as he and Ward tiptoed out of the study and entered the bedchamber, closing the door behind them.

"Will he be all right shut in there?" Ward asked.

"He should be fine," Nicholas replied with a smile. "So long as he knows where I am. Thank you for being so patient." After a moment, he added, "And for saving him. I didn't say that before, did I? I was too busy telling you how foolish you'd been."

"That's all right," Ward said. "You were quite right, I daresay. I just... didn't think how dangerous it was."

"You must never do anything like that again," Nicholas said seriously. "It was ridiculously brave, but my heart wouldn't be able to take it. Christ, if you'd fallen—" He shivered visibly.

Their gazes locked. There was just the smallest distance between them now, yet somehow that space seemed endless to Ward, and he couldn't think how to broach it. He was grateful, therefore, when Nicholas spoke, his voice low and somewhat tentative.

"What do you want to do?"

It felt like a huge question. A huge, undulating, unanswerable question. How to articulate all the things he wanted from Nicholas? All the things he'd been thinking about for weeks now. But Nicholas wasn't talking about that—he was talking about something specific and measurable. Something that could be fitted into an *hour or so*. Perhaps only one *hour or so* ever.

And still Ward couldn't formulate a sensible answer.

"Whatever you'll allow," he croaked at last with a painful honesty.

Nicholas smile-frowned, brows furrowing even as his silvery gaze gleamed with unexpected humour.

"All right," he said slowly, stepping a little closer, though not quite touching yet. "Tell me this. Have you done anything like this before?"

When Ward nodded, Nicholas looked surprised. "I thought—" he began, then cut himself off. "That is, if you don't mind me saying so, you seemed... rather unused to kissing."

Ward's cheeks warmed at that deduction. Had he been gauche? Obviously unskilled? It was a mortifying thought.

"I *am* somewhat unused to kissing," he finally managed to get out. "But I've had ample experience of other acts between men. Fellatio. Sodomy."

Nicholas's eyebrows rose at that bald assurance. "Sodomy!" he exclaimed. Then he gave a soft laugh and said, "My, you do know how to woo a fellow, don't you?"

Embarrassed as he was, Ward couldn't help but laugh at that and, for once, didn't even cringe at the barking sound of his mirth. "Wooing is not my forte," he admitted.

Nicholas's smile was amused. At length, he raised his hand and softly brushed the pad of his thumb across Ward's cheekbone. Ward shivered with helpless pleasure. He wanted to press into the simple touch and beg for more.

"What do you like best of the things you've done?" Nicholas murmured.

Ward swallowed, still feeling a little gauche. "All of them. I had a good teacher."

"A lover?"

"No," Ward replied shortly. "A whore."

Nicholas's eyes widened at that, and his stroking thumb stilled. He appeared shocked, and Ward felt ashamed for calling Alfie a whore.

"That's not fair," he said quickly. "He was a... a courtesan,

I suppose. Can a man be a courtesan? Well, anyway, he was very sought after. Very beautiful and skilled."

After a long pause, Nicholas said, "But he didn't kiss you?"

"No," Ward agreed. "We did most things together, but not that."

There was a brief, awkward pause, then Nicholas said, "Well, I can't match your experience. Gabe and I—the man you saw with me that evening, by the stream—we used to suck one another mostly, and once I let him bugger me—" He broke off, laughing shortly before saying, "That was awful."

Ward frowned. "Awful? Why?"

Nicholas seemed surprised at the question. "Well, it was painful, of course," he said, cheeks reddening. "And humiliating too."

"It oughtn't to have been," Ward said, reaching out. He placed his hand on Nicholas's forearm. Beneath Ward's palm, through the layers of tweed and linen, Nicholas was warm and vital and so very alive. And suddenly Ward wanted to just strip him, tear his clothes off, have his way with him. Show him just how good fucking could be, the way Alfie had shown him. How good it was when you were shameless and abandoned and pursued your pleasure as determinedly as a hound pursued a hare.

Nicholas had a mulish look about him now. "It mightn't be painful for the man dipping his wick, but I can assure you that the man being fucked knows all about it. Though I don't expect your courtesan told you about that."

"Actually, I've tried both—dipping my wick, as you put it, and being fucked—and I can tell you that I liked both very well." Ward smiled sweetly, enjoying the astonishment on Nicholas's face. "Though probably I most liked being fucked."

Yes, he knew how good it felt both ways, and he knew a great deal more besides. Knew how it felt to suck and be sucked, to have his balls played with and his nipples pinched, his cock rubbed and stroked by another man's hands, another man's shaft… Had Nicholas tried *those* things?

"You *liked* being buggered?" Nicholas exclaimed.

Ward stepped closer so that their chests were brushing, and he had to tilt his head a little to meet Nicholas's eyes.

"I loved it," he whispered.

Nicholas's chest rose and fell, his gaze flickering between Ward's eyes and his mouth. Ward could feel the warmth of the man's breath against his lips.

"If you use oil, or something similar," Ward continued in a low voice, "and spend time preparing your lover, there's no need for any pain. Or humiliation, for that matter."

Nicholas throat bobbed as he swallowed. "No?"

Ward ground his hips against Nicholas's, relishing the man's swift indrawn breath. "No. Not if you take your time."

Nicholas went very still at that, and Ward frowned, puzzled.

"What's wrong?"

"Nothing," Nicholas said. "Only when you say you need to take your time—well, that's something only a gentleman would say."

"Meaning?"

"Meaning people like you have plenty of time—and privacy—for these things, Ward. The rest of us aren't so lucky."

Ward didn't know what to say to that, but Nicholas didn't seem to require answer.

"When Gabe first came to Trevathany, he was lodging with Mrs. Bridges. My mother was still alive then, and living with me at the cottage. It wasn't till sometime after we met—one night when we were both drunk as lords—that we discovered our… mutual interest. But even after that, we had nowhere private to go. So we would meet at night, down by the mill stream, or walk over to the sands together and find a secluded spot in the dunes." He shrugged, looking away. "Our times together were always rushed. Furtive. We always had to be watching, listening in case someone came. When you talk about 'taking your time'—it's never been like that for me. It never could be."

Ward thought about that, and about what Nicholas had said about being buggered. About how painful and humiliating it had been. He lifted a hand to Nicholas's chin, turning him back to meet Ward's gaze.

"Did you even *want* to be fucked that time you did it?" he asked at last. "Or did you just agree to please your lover?" Ward winced at the words as soon as they were out of his mouth. As usual, without the softening effect of a sympathetic inflection, he sounded too harsh, too blunt. But Nicholas didn't seem offended by the question.

"Mostly, I agreed to please him," he admitted, making no move to pull away from Ward's gentle touch. "But I was curious too."

"And did he use anything to ease his way?" Ward whispered. "To stretch you?"

Nicholas tried to look away again, plainly mortified, but Ward's fingers tightened, and he stilled. For a long moment, Nicholas gazed at him unhappily, then finally he whispered, "He smeared some lard on his prick to help it in. But we had to be quick." He swallowed, then added, "I hated it. I was bleeding after."

"God, Nicholas," Ward whispered, stroking the man's jawline with his thumb. Such a strong, angular face. He wanted to examine every bit of it. Wanted to see every expression Nicholas had and catalogue them, every one, as though the man were a scientific mystery to be unravelled.

It was a terrifying feeling—Ward barely recognised himself. He'd never felt like this before about anyone, not even Alfie. Oh, he'd felt lust and even an easy sort of fondness for his erstwhile lover, but when he looked at Nicholas

Hearn, he felt turned *inside-out*. And now, as the man nestled his face into Ward's hand, stroking his cheek against Ward's palm like a cat seeking affection, the ache in Ward's chest was physical: an unfamiliar, unwanted, wrenching tenderness.

Why couldn't he want Nicholas in the easy way he'd wanted Alfie? That desire had been strong, but it had only been a physical need. An appetite, compelling as hunger or thirst. He felt the same intensity of physical desire for Nicholas, but there was something more besides, something much more dangerous to his peace of mind.

Nicholas's eyes were closed, his coal-black lashes quivering lightly. His cheek was warm and roughened by dark stubble, and when he pressed his lips against Ward's palm in an unexpected kiss, his mouth was soft and plush.

A moan escaped Ward, and at that sound, Nicholas's eyes flew open. It was no wonder—a moan from Ward was more like a bark after all—but his look of surprise changed to one of desire so quickly that Ward didn't have time to feel embarrassed.

"Why are we still talking when I could be kissing you right now?" Nicholas asked in a low, driven tone.

Ward's eyes widened and he croaked, "I have no idea."

"Me either," Nicholas whispered and leaned towards him.

CHAPTER FOURTEEN

Ward looked suddenly so flustered that Nick couldn't help but smile. The man was all assured experience when he talked of fucking and being fucked, using oil to stretch and prepare a lover, taking time to make everything pleasurable and good. And Nick had no doubt Ward knew what he was talking about—he was clearly very experienced, far more experienced in such matters than Nick. Yet the thought of a simple kiss seemed to make him as nervous as a maid.

As for Nick, well, kissing at least he knew how to do. He mightn't want women as bedmates, but he'd kissed plenty in his time, playing the part of a lusty lad when he'd had to. And of course, he'd kissed Gabe. He'd *loved* kissing Gabe. More than Gabe had liked kissing him back, he knew—Gabe had always been keen to get on with things, hurrying towards completion as though he were in a steeplechase, galloping hell for leather for the finish line.

Nick traced the pad of his thumb over Ward's mouth, loving the faint drag of damp flesh as he parted those delicious lips. So comely and so complicated, this lad. All that fire in his belly.

"I'm good at kissing," Nick murmured, dipping his head.

"I'll show you how. Then you can show me how to do the things you're good at."

"All right," Ward whispered.

Nick brushed his lips across Ward's, then, smiling, returned to press their mouths together more thoroughly. He framed Ward's face with his hands, tilting the man's chin up as he muscled closer.

He liked the contrast of Ward's slender, strong body with his own broader one. Liked too the similarity in their heights. Ward was only two or three inches shorter, so they were chest to chest, groin to groin, making everything easy and good.

Nick slid his tongue against Ward's, loving the thick moan that elicited. He did it again, and again. And then, finally, Ward mimicked him, tentatively entering Nick's mouth with his own tongue, his hands going to Nick's hips, tugging him closer, impatient for more.

Christ, but that mix of boldness and inexperience was intoxicating.

Groaning encouragement, Nick skimmed his hands inside Ward's open coat, sweeping his hands up and over the man's shoulders to remove it. Ward released Nick's hips to shake his coat free of his arms before stroking his hands up Nick's chest to do the same to him. Plainly Ward was more confident with this part in the proceedings—undressing his lover ready for a thorough bedding.

As Nick tossed his coat aside, Ward reached for his necktie, tugging the knot free, then sending the wilted linen sailing across the room while Nick wrestled with the buttons of Ward's waistcoat. And then it was frantic and messy, clothes flying as they kissed, stripping each other's layers away until finally they stood there in the bedchamber, naked in each other's arms. Naked and together, safe in this room, with no danger of discovery or interruption.

Nick stepped back, for no other reason than to look Ward over. A lamp in the corner of the room suffused the bedchamber with gentle light that kissed the planes of Ward's slim body. And Ward just stood there, quiet, letting Nick gaze at him, as though he realised Nick needed to do it. Needed to have this, if only once in his life.

Nick stretched out his hand and laid it on Ward's chest. Ward's skin was pale and smooth, and unlike Nick's, his chest was hairless. Further down his body, though, a trail of hair led from his navel to a light-brown brush at his groin, from which his cock thrust, straight and eager and flushed at the tip.

Nick traced his fingertips downwards, grazing chest, belly, and hip, till finally, dry-mouthed, he reached that lovely, jutting prick and took it in hand, circling his fingers loosely round the shaft. He slid his hand up, then down the length, glancing at Ward to make sure this was all right.

Ward's eyes were closed, but when Nick's hand stilled, he opened them again, his expression slightly stunned, as though he were waking from a dream.

"Don't stop," he pleaded. "I like you touching me."

"I want to touch you everywhere," Nick murmured. "Want to take my time."

Ward whispered, "You can do whatever you want—we have all the time in the world."

They didn't, not really, but there was certainly no hurry. Not tonight. No need to stay alert for anyone passing along. For the first time in his life, Nick was free to immerse himself wholly in another person. And he did. He touched Ward all over, first with his hands, and then with his mouth, pressing kisses to Ward's warm skin, loving every shiver and gasp of pleasure Ward gave him.

After a little time, Nick took Ward's hand and led him to the enormous bed, pressing him down onto the mattress. As he covered Ward's body with his own, he was filled as much with wonder as with lust. Just having Ward naked against him, in this light-filled room. God, but it was like sunshine on

Nick's skin after the longest and darkest of winters, and he soaked the good feeling up, greedy for it, mute with wonder.

They kissed again and again, each kiss long and deep and heady. Nick began to thrust his hips against Ward, hardly aware of what he was doing. His cock was so hard he felt liable to burst out of his own skin, yet he'd never felt so happy to wait to come. He never wanted this evening to end —though the very instant he had the thought, his body decided to demand otherwise, his hips beginning to move faster, only stuttering briefly to a halt when his shaft thrust awkwardly and a little painfully against the sharp blade of Ward's hip.

"Let's try this," Ward whispered in his ear. He shifted so he was lying next to Nick on his side, encouraging Nick to mirror him, till they were facing one another. Then he reached for Nick's cock while thrusting his own hips forward.

Nick watched, stunned, as Ward took both of their shafts into his grip and began stroking them together. And Christ, but that was extraordinary, that touch—the velvety kiss and drag of their naked pricks in the circle of Ward's hand, warm and strong and sure. Nick had felt nothing like it before. He stared at Ward, amazed for a moment, then leaned in close, pressing his mouth to Ward's again, sweeping his tongue inside and capturing Ward's gasp with his kiss. And God, it was perfect, his kiss and Ward's skilful hands, together.

Ward stilled, just for an instant, and then he was moving again, hand stroking with practiced ease while Nick ravaged his mouth, their hips rocking as their pricks slid back and forth, in and out of Ward's warm grasp in the same desperate rhythm. Nick wanted it to last forever, but all too soon, they were breaking apart, breaths heaving as they strained for release, their cocks jerking unevenly in Ward's hand, covering his fingers in their mingled spend.

~

They lay there afterwards, still tangled together. Nicholas's leg was thrown over Ward's, Ward's hand on Nicholas's hip. Ward closed his eyes and let himself drowse a little. This was an unfamiliar experience for him. Alfie's habit had been to get up and dressed as soon as their business was finished.

At first it was good, lying there with his new lover, suffused with soporific pleasure. But after a little while, when the fog of bliss began to dissipate and cool reality set in, Ward's sense of connection to Nicholas began to fade. He became aware of Nicholas's body as something separate from himself. Sensed a growing tension and began to wonder what the man was thinking.

He opened his eyes to find Nicholas staring up at the pristine white ceiling.

As though he sensed Ward's regard, Nicholas turned his head. "I should go. It's getting late."

Disappointment flooded Ward. "You're sure you won't stay?" He wished the croaked words unsaid as soon as they were out of his mouth—Nicholas's alarm at the question was unmistakable. His gaze flashed with brief panic, and though he schooled his expression quickly, he wasted no time tugging himself free of Ward.

"No, I need to get back," he said, rising from the bed, his back carefully to Ward. "I'm up early tomorrow."

Since Nicholas wasn't looking Ward's way, Ward allowed himself the luxury of staring as the man gathered his discarded clothes. It was no hardship to look at him. Nicholas had a strong, masculine frame, broad in the shoulders and chest, with lean, well-muscled thighs. A horseman's thighs, Ward thought absently, propping himself up on his elbows. He stifled a groan at the sight of the man's taut arse as he bent down to retrieve his rumpled necktie.

Nicholas began to dress. Once he had his shirt and drawers on, he turned to face Ward. He looked calm now, and steady, but Ward couldn't help wondering if he regretted what they'd done. He certainly seemed keen to leave.

"Are you all right for Friday still?" Ward blurted. For once he was glad of the harsh monotone that disguised the craven desperation behind his words.

"To go to Truro with you?" Nicholas asked. "Yes, of course."

"Just checking," Ward murmured, swinging his legs out of bed. "Let me get dressed and I'll let you out. Pipp will have locked up by now."

"All right, I'll get Snow," Nicholas said. "He's probably fast asleep."

Nicholas disappeared through the door to the study while Ward pulled on his trousers, fastening the buttons at the placket with nimble fingers. Without his suspenders, his trousers settled loosely on his hips, and he sighed, irritated. He couldn't be bothered getting dressed properly, so he fetched a dressing gown out of his wardrobe, a sumptuous garment of crimson satin, and put it on. By the time Nicholas returned, Snowflake at his heels, Ward was fastening the black silk frogging that ran down the front.

"What are you wearing?" Nicholas said. He was frowning.

"A dressing gown." Ward cocked a hip, raised a brow, and said, "Do you like it?"

Nicholas didn't even answer. "What will your servants think if they see you like that?"

"Oh, they've gone to bed." Ward waved his hand in an airy gesture. "The only person who might still be around is Pipp, and he won't think anything of it. He understands how things are with me."

"Well, he doesn't understand how things are with *me*."

Ward shook his head. "Nicholas, you don't need to worry. Truly. I often dress like this in the evenings. None of the servants would think anything of me wearing a dressing gown if they saw me—it doesn't signify anything."

Nicholas gave an impatient shake of his head. "Men like you don't seem to think the people who serve you have the ability to form thoughts or opinions of their own. You just assume they will accept whatever you tell them, whatever you want them to think."

"That's not true," he protested. "What you don't understand is that I know Pipp, probably better than anyone else in this world, and he knows me, and—"

"And Mr. Pipp isn't the only servant in this household," Nicholas interrupted flatly. "You have a cook, several maids, a groom, a gardener. You think they don't have eyes and ears?" He looked away, shaking his head, as though astonished by Ward's obtuseness. "I've sat around plenty of servants' tables in my time, and I can tell you they *all* talk, they all gossip."

Ward tried again. "Pipp is very discreet—"

"I daresay he is," Nicholas said. "But you are not."

Ward bristled at that, but Nicholas wasn't finished.

"I realise you don't need to be as wary as I do," he said, holding up a staying hand. "You've plenty of money to protect yourself. You could buy off a gossiping servant if you wanted, or up sticks to go and live somewhere else." He paused, settling his silvery gaze on Ward. "But you have to understand that I am not in the same position. If gossip starts up about me in this village, it will never be forgotten. I will have no choice but to deal with the consequences of that or find myself a new position." He shook his head. "And that would be no easy business for a man of my birth."

He was right, Ward realised with a stab of shame. Ward was always assuming that Nicholas shared the same privileges that he himself enjoyed, but that was not the case.

Slowly, Ward began to undo the black silk clasps on his dressing gown, then he peeled off the garment and tossed it aside, reaching for his shirt instead.

"Thank you," Nicholas said.

Ten minutes later, fully dressed, Ward led Nicholas downstairs. As they reached the bottom of the staircase, Pipp appeared—in his dressing gown as it happened, though his was a sight less ornate than Ward's ostentatious, crimson one.

"Allow me, sir," he said, drawing out his enormous key ring and flipping through the many keys there.

"Thank you for dinner," Nicholas said to Ward, politely. "And the, ah, conversation."

"Not at all. Thank you," Ward returned awkwardly. "I'll see you next Friday for our trip to Truro. Shall we leave around two o'clock? If that's not too early?"

"Two o'clock will be fine," Nicholas said as Pipp wrestled the door open and stepped aside to let him pass.

It was very dark outside, a cloudy night with no stars or moon to be seen. But Nicholas went out into it without hesitation, Snow a pale shadow at his heels.

"Good night, Sir Edward," he said and set off down the path.

"Good night," Ward echoed.

Nicholas didn't look back.

The shadows of the night had already swallowed him up by the time Pipp closed the door.

CHAPTER FIFTEEN

From *The Collected Writings of Sir Edward Carrick*, volume I

My brother and I went up to Cambridge together, though my brother only stayed a year. At the end of that year, George persuaded my father to purchase him a commission with the 80th Foot, his lifelong ambition having been to join the Army. Later, when George died in Burma, I took great comfort that we'd had that year at Cambridge together. We shared rooms, ate together most days, even attended the same classes—though George was not as interested as I. As the months passed, we regained that closeness we'd shared as boys, finishing one another's sentences, seeming sometimes to share the same thoughts—though no one would now have mistaken one of us for the other, with George topping me by several inches.

∿

24th June 1853

. . .

By the time the following Friday came around, Ward was on tenterhooks at the thought of seeing Nicholas again. The strange formality of their parting, after all that had gone before, had unsettled him. All week he'd found himself reexamining the things Nicholas had said to him about privacy and privilege and consequences.

"Spoken like a true gentleman…"

"The rest of us aren't so lucky…"

He was finishing his luncheon when Pipp announced Nicholas's arrival.

"Mr. Hearn, sir," Pipp said, and when Ward looked up, there was Nicholas, framed in the doorway of the dining room, wearing his customary tweeds and carrying a modest valise.

He was alone. No pale shadow at his heels today.

Ward rose from his seat. "Nicholas—come in, sit down." He glanced at Pipp and added, "Mr. Pipp, will you arrange a plate for Mr. Hearn?"

"Of course, sir," Pipp said. He took the valise from Nicholas, who looked faintly surprised at having to give it up, and left the room.

"You're always feeding me," Nicholas said, taking a seat. "It's quite unnecessary."

"Indulge me," Ward croaked. "I expect you've just had some bread and butter or some such thing. It's half a day's journey, you know. I don't want you expiring on the way."

Nicholas chuckled softly. "All right. Since you and Mr. Pipp are determined to fatten me up between you, I may as well let you."

"I was expecting to see Master Snowflake," Ward said as he settled his napkin over his knee again. "Have you left him downstairs?"

"No, I'm not bringing him. I've left him with my friend, Gid," Nicholas said. "Snow hates carriage journeys—just frets and frets. And Gid's good with him."

"I don't mind if you want to bring him," Ward said. "The journey only takes around three hours. I can tolerate a fretful dog for an afternoon."

Nicholas shook his head. "The last time I took him on a coach, he barked near enough incessantly and ended up vomiting all over the floor. The other passengers were ready to string the two of us up."

"Ah," Ward said. Then after a pause, "Will he be all right without you, though? I honestly don't mind if you want to bring him, barking and vomiting notwithstanding."

Nicholas's smile-frown made an appearance at that. He seemed both touched and amused by Ward's assurance. "That's kind of you," he said, "but it's not just because of the journey that I'm leaving him. Truro was where I found Snow in the first place. The one time I've taken him back there, he started shaking as soon as we got near. He probably thought I was going to abandon him there."

Ward pondered that. "It's true that some animals display the most astonishing sensory abilities. Dogs, of course, are renowned for their acute sense of smell. Perhaps Snowflake detected something in the air unique to that place—something you would not have noticed with your duller olfactory senses—" He broke off at Nicholas's sudden grin. "Is something amusing?"

Nicholas chuckled. "No, it's just that you're such a curious fellow."

Ward swallowed and looked away. He'd been told many times before that he was curious. An eccentric. A quiz. Usually he didn't care, but for some reason, coming from Nicholas, it stung.

How pathetic.

"What's wrong?" Nicholas said. Then comprehension dawned. "Oh for God's sake, I didn't mean curious like that! I meant *curious*. Interested. Fascinated by the world around you."

Ward glanced warily at Nicholas.

"Ward—I like that about you," Nicholas added softly, and some knot in Ward's belly loosened.

"I know some people think I'm rather odd," Ward admitted. "I daresay the villagers think I'm positively unhinged with my plans to communicate with spirits. But when an idea takes hold of me, I—" He halted, unable to find the words to express what it was that drove him.

"I know," Nicholas said simply. "You're passionate about what you do. About finding out why things happen a certain way. How they work."

Ward felt the oddest rush of gratitude. Gratitude that Nicholas understood this about him, and that he could put it into such simple words when Ward had been so entirely unable to do so. That he didn't think Ward was an odd duck —or perhaps that he did, but he didn't care so very much.

They set off for Truro after luncheon. Ward's carriage was the first word in luxurious travelling with wide seats upholstered in butter-soft leather and woollen travelling rugs folded at the end of each bench. As Nick climbed in behind Ward, he noted a large, flat wooden box on the floor of the carriage and a basket full of foodstuffs and beverages tucked in beside it.

"Bloody hell," he chuckled. "This carriage is fit for a king. Old Godfrey likes his comforts but he's got nothing on you. This must be near twice the size of his coach."

"I do a fair bit of travelling," Ward replied, as he sat himself down. "I'm fortunate that I have the wherewithal to do it in a manner that minimises the discomforts of long journeys and enables me to pass the time as fruitfully as possible."

"I'll say," Nick said, settling onto the bench opposite Ward and watching with fascination as the man lifted the flat wooden box onto his knee, turning it into a compact writing desk with a few practiced moves, the ever-errant lock of hair tumbling over his forehead.

Outside, the coachman shouted an instruction to the groom as he readied to depart.

"That basket looks as though it could feed the five thousand," Nick said, eyeing the hefty muslin-wrapped packages and cork-stoppered pot bottles that filled it. "And we've only just had luncheon. We'll certainly reach Truro before I'm peckish again."

Ward bit his lip, seeming oddly embarrassed. "Pipp has a tendency to over-provision—he's convinced I don't eat enough. I've tried telling him not to bother with baskets for such short journeys, but he gets ever so offended, so now I just let him do it and give the basket to the coachman."

The carriage lurched then, and they were off, though slow to start with as the coachman navigated the narrow path that led from Ward's front door to the road proper.

"How long exactly has Mr. Pipp worked for you?" Nick asked. He couldn't imagine any of Godfrey's servants ever being so familiar with him as it seemed Mr. Pipp was with Ward, at least in private. *Nick* wouldn't be so familiar with Godfrey and he was related to the man by blood.

Ward tapped his finger on his chin. "It's been a long while. Since I was twelve at least. He was a footman in my parents' house and my mother selected him as my personal servant."

"Your personal servant? You mean, your valet?"

Ward smiled. "Not quite. It was when I was convalescing. Mother wanted someone to see to my needs. Lift me in and out of bed and push me around in this ridiculous bath chair she'd obtained for me. She was quite determined that I should get up each day and take the air, you see. Even if it took me all morning to wash and dress." He gave one of his raspy laughs. "It drove me wild, but she was probably right."

"So Mr. Pipp was your nurse?"

"In a manner of speaking. As I grew stronger—and older —he seemed to naturally fall into the role of valet. And when I left home to attend Cambridge, it was convenient for him to join me as my general manservant. We'd become used to one another by then—it was obvious that he would be the head of my household when I came to set one up."

"You must know each other very well," Nick observed.

"We do. I trust Pipp absolutely. He knows me inside out."

"Even that you..?" Nick trailed off, raising a querying brow.

"Even about my preference for men? Oh, yes. It was Pipp who found Alfie for me—without my asking him to do so, I might add." He gave a loud bark of laughter. "That was a mortifying conversation, I can tell you!"

Nick pondered that revelation for a moment before asking, "Is he like us, then?"

Ward shook his head. "No. I gather there was a lady who disappointed him when he was quite young, but he tells me his taste runs to 'the motherly sort' these days. I understand he and Mrs. Waddell have had some sort of mutually beneficial arrangement for the last few years." He shuddered as if at the thought, making Nick grin.

The coach slowed, and Nick glanced out the window. They were at the bottom of the path now. The coachman executed a tight swing onto the main road—making the basket of food and drink slide across the carriage floor, till Nick stopped it with his foot—and then they were straightening again and the coachman was snapping his whip and urging the team of four into a smart trot. They were off, and Nick was conscious of a pang of excitement at the thought. He ruthlessly suppressed it, though, forcing himself to concentrate instead on pushing the basket back into place on the other side of the carriage and wedging it more securely with one of the travelling blankets.

When he straightened, he returned determinedly to their

previous topic of conversation. "It's strange to me that you and Mr. Pipp are so tight with one another. Old Godfrey isn't like that with his servants. He doesn't even look at them. He treats them like they're part of the furniture. Says things in front of them as though they don't have ears."

Ward frowned at that. At last he said, "Does he talk to *you*?"

"Yes, but I'm not a—" Nick began, then stopped. He felt suddenly queasy to his stomach. The words had come unprompted, before he'd really thought about the question. Only now did he realise how betraying they were, revealing that in his secret heart, Nick believed himself to be something more than a servant to his grandfather.

Despite all the evidence to the contrary.

Nick risked a glance at Ward—the man's gaze on him was painfully, unbearably sympathetic, and Nick looked swiftly away, turning his head to stare unseeingly out the carriage window at the hedgerows.

After a long pause, face burning with humiliation, he said quietly, "What I mean is, he *has* to talk to me. I'm his steward —there are always matters of business to discuss."

"Yes, of course," Ward said politely. "I can see that."

They fell into an awkward silence.

At length, Ward drew a sheaf of journals out from the single drawer in the travelling desk and began sorting through them. Selecting one, he put the others away and began to read, his brow furrowed with concentration. After another minute, he produced a pencil from his inside pocket and began jotting down notes in the margins. The pencil was a plain steel propeller one, quite short, and when he wasn't he using it, he stuck it behind his ear. Nick thought it made him look like a shopkeeper, and that made him smile. The thought of Ward measuring out sugar and tea leaves and lengths of fabric for sharp-eyed housewives was an amusing one.

Ward was too absorbed to notice Nick's attention on him,

and a couple of hours passed thus, in companionable silence. Nick didn't mind the silence a bit. He was a man who enjoyed his own company very well. He didn't need constant chatter —indeed, sometimes he craved silence more than anything. On days like that, if he could, he would set off from Rosehip Cottage with Snow at his heels and some bread and cheese in his pocket and just walk the whole day, not so much as a word passing his lips. Whenever he felt out of sorts, that would fix him, having the living earth beneath his feet and the wind on his face.

His mother had been the same. Sometimes she needed to be outdoors. She even used to eat her breakfast outside, hunkering down on the front stoop of the cottage, even though there was a perfectly good kitchen table inside. When Nick was a boy, he'd thought it was because she missed the travelling life, but it wasn't the moving around she longed for. Ma didn't mind being in one place—it was living on the land she missed. Sitting round a campfire at night with the heat on her face and the cold at her back. Sleeping under the wide sky.

She'd been so very alive, his mother. Even when she was thin and ravaged by disease, life had shone fiercely in her. Right up to the morning Nick had walked into her chamber and found her body. He'd stood there, at the foot of the bed, staring at her shell, wondering where she'd gone. Where her spark had disappeared to. Strange that she looked exactly the same in every particular, and yet the thing that made her Darklis Hearn was gone. He'd felt—*known*—her absence as soon as he'd walked in the room. Had known, with complete certainty, that she'd passed in the night and was no longer with him. That her small body was as empty as a house that no one lived in anymore.

~

When they reached their destination, it was almost six o'clock. Ward looked up from his reading, seeming surprised.

"Are we here already?" he asked, and Nick couldn't help but laugh. The man had been so absorbed in his reading he had no idea how much time had passed.

They climbed out of the carriage, and Nick looked about himself curiously. The Fox and Swan was a large and bustling coaching inn, its courtyard thronged with carriages, horses, guests, and ostlers. Ward started across the courtyard, and Nick followed, watching as Ward gave his name to the slip of a girl who came to greet them. She scurried off, and within moments, the innkeeper's wife was sailing towards them, a small, wide woman with a ruddy face and greying hair, mostly hidden beneath a lacy cap.

"Sir Edward," she gushed, "it's an honour to welcome such a distinguished guest."

"Ah. Good evening, Mrs..?"

She blinked at the sound of his rasping voice, then seemed to collect herself, saying hurriedly, "Bassett. Mrs. Bassett."

"Quite. Mrs. Bassett. Charmed," he said, inclining his head politely. He gestured at Nick. "And this is my companion, Mr. Hearn."

Nick inclined his head, and Mrs. Bassett did likewise, her gaze darting between himself and Ward.

"I've reserved you my best room, Sir Edward," she said then. "If you'll kindly follow me, I'll show you up."

She led them through two doors and up a flight of stairs, her step light for such a heavy lady, leading them to a pair of rooms joined by a connecting door. One of the rooms was large and well-appointed with a sizeable bed and a small writing desk and chair. The other was positively pokey with little more than a truckle bed in it.

She sent Nick a brief, apologetic glance as she showed them the smaller room. "I'd thought when Sir Edward asked for the second room, that it was for a manservant..."

She trailed off, meaningfully, glancing at Ward and raising her brows at him in silent query. But Ward, being Ward, didn't take the hint and made no move to explain Nick's position to her, though he had spoken of him in a manner that indicated a degree of equality between them.

Ward said merely, "Will this do, Mr. Hearn?" His face was expressionless. Was he thinking what Nick was thinking? That there was no need for Nick to use that truckle bed when they had locks on the doors that gave onto the corridor and a connecting door between the two chambers. That large bed in Ward's chamber would do very well for two...

Unless Ward had no interest in repeating what they'd begun a week ago? Well, even if that was so, Nick had slept on far worse than that truckle bed.

"It'll be fine," Nick replied. "It's only for two nights after all."

He was acutely aware of Mrs. Bassett's curiosity, could practically see the wheels in her brain turning as she tried to work out what Nick was to Ward. Astonishingly, Ward didn't even seem to notice her interest. For a man who was incredibly observant about the tiniest of details in his field of study, he could be remarkably dense about ordinary, everyday things.

"If Mr. Hearn is content, that will be fine, Mrs. Bassett," Ward said then, his rasping tone dismissive. "We'll dine at seven, if that suits."

The *if that suits* was a mere formality. There wasn't so much as a hint of a question in Ward's tone. These were the civil words of a man used to getting whatever he wanted, whenever he wanted it.

She smiled politely. "Of course, Sir Edward. I will make arrangements." She inclined her head and glided away, retreating downstairs again.

Nick chuckled as he closed the door of the little chamber,

shutting them inside. "She can't work out what I am to you, and it's annoying her," he observed.

"Do you think so?" Ward said.

Nick rolled his eyes. "For an intelligent man, you're rather oblivious at times."

Ward frowned, and all Nick could think about was how appealing he was with faint puzzlement pleating his brows. How ridiculously youthful.

Strange that this man—clever as an owl and rich as Croesus—looked like a boy sometimes. For some reason, it made Nick feel tender towards him, and when he stepped closer, he couldn't stop himself raising a hand and brushing back the wayward lock of dark-blond hair that was always falling over Ward's brow.

"How old are you?" he asked, curious.

Ward blinked, seeming surprised by the question, which had admittedly, rather come out of nowhere. "Twenty-six."

"You're a year older than me?" Nick said, wonderingly. "You look younger."

"No, I don't!" Ward protested.

Nick moved in closer. He slid his palms over Ward's hips and tugged him forward so that their groins met, and he could feel the fronts of Ward's thighs against his own. "Oh, but you do," he said. "You look like a lad sometimes. A right handsome one."

Nick saw that Ward liked that. Saw the gleam of pleasure in those tawny eyes before Ward's lashes fell. The shy smile he immediately tried to bite off, teeth sinking into his bottom lip. Oh yes, he was handsome, and there was that twisting feeling in Nick's gut again, making him feel exposed as a shucked oyster. He barely knew what to do with himself. It was all he could manage to keep his gaze on Ward as he leaned forward to kiss him.

Ward met Nick's questing lips with his own, and despite the urgent twisting desire in Nick's belly, it was a sweet kiss.

Ward's lips were warm, and he yielded to Nick with unexpected hesitancy. Despite all his impressive carnal experience with the former lover he'd spoken of, it seemed that in this one activity, Ward was more than content to let Nick take the lead.

"*Ayes*, you're a handsome lad," Nick murmured against Ward's lips. "And all mine."

Ward moaned again, seeming to like that idea, and Nick liked it too, though he knew they were nonsense words. Ward would never be truly his. Only for tonight and tomorrow, and for whatever other scraps of time they might share together before Ward grew bored of him or left Trevathany.

Pushing that depressing thought aside, Nick deepened the kiss and shuffled forward, urging Ward to step back, then back again, till he was leaning against the wall between the two chambers.

"I want you so much," Nick breathed against Ward's lips. "It feels like years instead of just a week since last time."

"I want you too," Ward whispered back urgently. "Nicholas—I want you inside me tonight. Will you do that with me? I've brought oil. I'll teach you how."

Nick groaned, far too close to climaxing just from this— from these kisses, and Ward's foolish, whispered promises. Nick loved Ward's whispers. The tone of Ward's speaking voice might be raw, but his whispers were just like anyone else's: rich with emotion and yearning.

Just then, a rap at the door invaded the silence.

Nick leapt back from Ward as though he'd been burned, lifting his hands to smooth his ruffled hair. Ward righted himself more calmly, with the confidence of the wealthy man who never expects anyone to open a door on him without invitation.

"Come in," Ward called out. The words emerged in his usual bark, and the expression on the face of the little maid-servant who opened the door a moment later was wary.

"Pardon me, sirs," she said. "But Mrs. Bassett sent me up to tell you she's set aside the small dining parlour for you for dinner and it will be served at seven and do you think you'll be wanting a bath brought up in the meantime?"

Ward didn't even consult Nick, merely nodded. "Yes, please. A bath each for myself and Mr. Hearn."

Nick opened his mouth to say there was no need to have two baths—he could just as easily jump in Ward's water when he was finished—but then it occurred to him that was very far from appropriate. What gentleman would want to share another's bathwater? So instead he closed his mouth and resolved to enjoy the rare luxury of a tub of hot water all to himself.

CHAPTER SIXTEEN

From *The Collected Writings of Sir Edward Carrick*, volume I

One evening, during that first year at Cambridge, George and I went to see a mesmerist, a Monsieur Beaumier, who was touring the music halls of England. The things we witnessed that evening were undeniably miraculous, and quite shocking. Beaumier put several assistants into mesmeric trances and having done so, was able to persuade one to hold her hand directly over a candle flame even as it scorched her palm; another to sit, unflinching, as Beaumier discharged a pistol next to his ear; and a third to sit quietly as a long, sharp needle was repeatedly stabbed into the tender flesh beneath her fingernails. Later, I would learn of the work of James Braid and come to understand better the true nature of the trance Beaumier's subjects had been in—what Mr. Braid called neurypnology, or hypnosis. I would learn that the bringing about of such a state was far simpler than the mesmerists would have it, and the state itself far more subtle. Mr. Braid had the most important of all qualities in a scientist: open-mindedness. He had heard tales of the mesmerists and felt sure they must all be tricksters, but when he went to see a performance for himself, he was open-minded enough to own that there was something to their claims. The difference between Mr. Braid and certain well-known supporters of Mesmerism was that, whilst he accepted the truth of what he witnessed, he rejected the explanation given to him as to why it had occurred. Instead, he sought out his own explanation, one that was consistent with rational scientific principle.

The "small" parlour contained a table big enough to seat eight comfortably, but Ward and Nicholas were dining alone. Ward asked the maidservant who showed them to their table where the other guests were and was told they were all eating in the common dining room. Mrs. Bassett apparently reserved the small parlour for "special guests," a class to which, as a titled gentleman, Ward belonged.

The inn was bustling with custom. Even with the door closed, Ward and Nicholas could hear voices from the common dining room a few doors down and, more noisily, from the taproom further along the corridor. When the maid-servant brought their soup, her gait was swift, her expression harried, and she'd barely put the dishes down before Mrs. Bassett was shouting for her again, her sharp voice impatient. "*Mary*! Where are you, girl?"

"You're run off your feet tonight," Nicholas said to her when she returned to clear away the soup plates.

Ward glanced at Nicholas, surprised by this idle conversa-tional gambit. Ward rarely engaged in everyday conversation with servants outside of his own home. Not beyond asking for what he wanted. Nicholas's casual observation—and the sympathetic smile that accompanied it—struck Ward as overly familiar. Perhaps that was unfair. Nicholas probably felt quite differently about such interactions than Ward did.

Whilst Nicholas's present station in life was far above the maid's, it hadn't always been so. Indeed, a girl such as this might even have looked down upon Nicholas when he was a mere stable boy.

The girl returned Nicholas's smile with a small one of her own. "Yes, sir, it's been ever so busy," she confided in a warm Cornish burr. "Mrs. Bassett turned the other girl off three days ago for thieving. She's not managed to get a replacement yet, so I'm having to do everything."

"You must be worn out," Nicholas said with a sympathetic smile.

"I am that," she said, heaving a sigh.

"Well, you can take your time serving us," Nicholas said. "We're in no hurry."

He got a grateful look for that before she hurried off again.

"*You* might not be in hurry," Ward said, when the door closed. "But I'd like to get back to my bedchamber." He smiled. "I have plans for the rest of the evening."

Nicholas smiled, foxy-like. "We can go now if you like. I'm not even especially hungry."

"Let's go after the next course. That should be enough of a showing to stave off any remarks from Mrs. Bassett."

"Done," Nicholas replied, eyes gleaming.

A few minutes later, Mary was back with a platter of roast chicken, suet puddings, and vegetables. Ward let her serve him a too-large portion and thanked her politely. Then he picked at his plate half-heartedly, barely tasting the food he was putting in his mouth as he watched Nicholas eat.

Nicholas was as bad, his attention all on Ward, his bright gaze lingering on Ward's mouth so often, Ward felt it almost like a touch. It was Nicholas who finally pushed his plate aside first, his dinner barely half-eaten.

"Aren't you hungry?" Ward croaked.

"I couldn't eat another bite," Nicholas replied, a tiny smile teasing the corner of his mouth.

By way of answer, Ward set his own cutlery down and leaned back. "Me either. I think I'm ready for bed now."

Nicholas's twitch of a smile grew into a grin.

Just then, Mary returned, a jug in her hand.

"Begging your pardon, sirs, I forgot your gravy," she said. Then, spying their half-full, pushed-aside plates, added worriedly, "Oh, didn't you like it?"

"The food was fine," Ward said. "We're just not very hungry."

Mary flinched at his harsh tone, and he couldn't help but be irritated by her reaction, even though he knew it wasn't her fault.

She glanced at Nicholas, as though begging for help.

"Is it because I forgot the gravy?" she whispered, eyes wide.

Nicholas said calmly, "No, no, not at all, it's just been a long day for us, and we're needing our beds more than food." He pushed his chair back and stood, drawing a couple of pennies out of his pocket and handing them to her. "Thank you for your service, Mary. I hope the rest of your evening is easier."

"Thank you, sir," the girl replied, hurriedly tucking the coins into the pocket of her apron. "Good night, sir. Sleep well."

"That was kind of you," Ward remarked as they walked down the corridor. He was conscious that it would not have occurred to him to give the girl a gratuity.

"It was just tuppence," Nicholas said, shrugging. "Still, I suppose she only earns... what? A shilling a day?"

"A shilling? Is that all?"

Nicholas glanced at him, his expression amused. "Don't you look at your household accounts?"

"Good heavens, no. Pipp deals with all that. I'm far too busy with my work."

"Hmmm," Nicholas said. He didn't sound particularly

impressed with Ward's ignorance of his servants' wages, and Ward felt unexpectedly embarrassed.

"I should know about such things," he decided. "I'll speak to Pipp about it when I get back."

Nicholas made one of his smile-frowns at that, puzzled and pleased at once, and for some reason, that did Ward's heart good.

As they began to climb the stairs, Nicholas leading the way, Ward wondered what salary Nicholas earned. How much of his daily earnings did tuppence amount to? Or a shilling? Even as he pondered, he felt downright traitorous just thinking such thoughts, because he knew, without a doubt, that Nicholas would hate it. For the first time, Ward felt glad, fiercely glad, that he hadn't paid Nicholas even a penny for his time. If he had, everything would be different between them; he saw that now. Nicholas would feel entirely differently about him. About them.

"Thank you for your service."

Service.

Service wasn't just work, it was paid work. Work that was instructed by a master of a servant for payment. The money that changed hands for that work shaped the relations of those two people in a way that could never be changed.

Ward realised, with sudden clarity, that if he had paid Nicholas, they would not be doing what they were about to do now. Nicholas would not have allowed it.

Tonight, Ward was going to undress Nicholas and be naked with him and take the man inside his body. The impossible intimacy of it made his head rush, not just because he wanted it so much, but because he knew this was going to be the first time Nicholas had known such intimacy, and that might just be the most astonishing and exciting part of this. That Ward was giving Nicholas something he'd never known before; that he was going to make this thing that had always been, for Nicholas, rushed and tainted by the fear of discovery, into something slow and languid, something to savour. At least, he hoped so. He planned to ready himself thoroughly, but it had been a while since he'd last done this, and he was very aware that there would likely be some discomfort, especially given how inexperienced Nicholas was. So yes, he felt a little nervous, but it wasn't a fearful nervousness —more a giddy, happy sort of nervousness, like champagne in his belly, ready to pop and overflow.

When they reached the door of the bedchamber, Ward drew from his pocket the large brass key Mrs. Bassett had given him earlier. He felt the weight of Nicholas's gaze on him as he fumbled it into the lock, all fingers and thumbs, and quickly glanced at the man. Something twisted in his chest to see the easy fondness in Nicholas's eyes. It was not a look he'd seen on any lover's face before, that pure, good-humoured... affection.

Affection and desire together.

What a breathtaking combination.

"Is the door to the little chamber locked?" Ward whispered, gesturing at it.

Nicholas nodded. He appeared calm and assured, even though he was the virgin here, so to speak.

At last the bedchamber door swung open and they stepped inside. It was barely eight o'clock and, at this time of year, still light out, but with the heavy velvet drapes closed, the room was dark, shrouding them both in deep shadows as soon as Ward closed—and locked—the door behind them.

Ward quickly crossed the room to light the lamp, the match he struck flaring brightly in the darkness, then quickly subsiding. He let the flame recover its strength before lifting the glass chimney from the lamp and touching the match to the oily wick. As soon as he replaced the chimney, the flame seared, rising high and bright—too bright. He fiddled with the knob till he'd dimmed it to his liking.

When he turned back to Nicholas, it was to find that the

man had already removed his coat, waistcoat, and tie. His shirt gaped at the neck, revealing a tantalising slice of shadowy, tawny skin and his dark hair gleamed in the lamplight. He was smiling faintly at Ward, his gaze warm and appreciative, and exuding that characteristic calmness that settled every jangling nerve in Ward's body.

"You look... very nice," Ward said hoarsely.

In truth, Nicholas didn't look *nice*, he looked beautiful. Not that he seemed to mind Ward's blandly decorous words. If anything, he was amused, one side of his mobile mouth kicking up in the charming half smile Ward liked so well.

"You do too, but you're a bit buttoned-up for my liking," Nicholas replied, moving towards Ward and reaching for the buttons of his coat. "Let's get you out of these clothes."

Dry-mouthed, Ward nodded mutely.

Nicholas dealt with his buttons in a matter of moments, pushing the coat from Ward's shoulders. It dropped noiselessly to the floor, and of one accord, they moved closer together, close enough to kiss.

"Such a handsome face you've got," Nicholas murmured, tracing his thumb over one of Ward's eyebrow. "Eyes like acorns."

"*Acorns*?" Ward repeated, amused despite himself.

Nicholas's smile was sheepish. "That's what they look like to me," he said. "But I'm no poet." He leaned in, his breath warm against Ward's mouth, lips near enough to capture without effort.

"You look into my eyes, and you see *acorns*," Ward repeated, grinning.

"I do," Nicholas confirmed, smiling. "Right now, they're a light, woody brown, like when acorns are properly ripe and they've fallen off the tree in the natural way. The way they are when you find them on the forest floor, with their little caps falling off."

Ward blinked, surprised by how much thought Nicholas seemed to have given this.

"But sometimes," Nicholas went on, almost dreamily, "they're more like those greenish ones that aren't so ripe. The ones that are holding tight to their caps, you know?"

Ward did know. He knew exactly the shade Nicholas meant, and it surprised him because if he'd been asked what colour an acorn was, he'd have said *brown*. Just brown.

"My mother says I have hazel eyes," Ward husked.

Nicholas looked interested. "Is that the proper word?"

Ward shrugged. "It's the word my mother uses."

"I'm sure it's right then," Nicholas teased. "Whatever colour you call them, they're beautiful."

"So are yours," Ward said with helpless honesty.

Nicholas laughed, amused. "You don't need to pay me back, compliment for compliment."

"I mean it," Ward protested. "They're like... starlight." And with that, he lifted his chin, closing the tiny gap between them, settling his lips on Nicholas's.

He didn't know quite what to do after that, but Nicholas appeared to be happy to take charge and Ward was very happy to let him. Moaning with pleasure, Nicholas slid his sleek, sinuous tongue into Ward's mouth, drawing Ward's into play.

Oh God, the things Ward had been missing with not kissing...

He grasped Nicholas's hips and pulled him closer, thrusting their groins together as Nicholas explored his mouth with his lips and tongue, suckling and nipping and licking at him as though he was a delicious treat.

When they finally broke apart, both breathing heavily, Ward reached for the hem of Nicholas's shirt. "I want you to fuck me," he murmured against Nicholas's lips as he pushed the linen up, uncovering the man's belly, then his chest. "I want you inside me."

Nicholas groaned at that, lifting his arms so that Ward could strip the shirt off him in one swift move. Ward threw the shirt aside and ran his hands over Nicholas's broad shoulders and down his hard, muscular chest, loving the rasp of chest hair under his palms, the way Nicholas's small nipples peaked under his touch.

"And I really want to feel your skin against mine," Ward muttered.

"God, yes," Nicholas gasped and began fumbling the placket of his trousers open. Ward followed suit, both of them stripping as quickly as they could, before coming together again, naked this time, for more deep, devouring kisses.

Nicholas's cock was like iron against Ward's, hard and flushed. Their shafts bumped and duelled, the blunt heads rubbing and nudging as they kissed, on and on. It was Ward who finally, regretfully, broke the kiss. He took Nicholas's hand in his and led him to the bed, urging him to lie down on his back before turning away to extract a small jar from his valise.

"What's that?" Nicholas asked roughly as Ward approached the bed, removing the top of the jar and thrusting two fingers inside to extract a large gob of white grease that immediately began melting on his skin.

"Coconut oil," Ward said, putting the jar down on the bedside table. "Alfie introduced me to it." Nicholas frowned at the mention of Ward's old lover, and Ward couldn't help but smile a little at that. "It makes everything easier. You'll see."

He stayed standing, lifting one foot onto the mattress, exposing his hole to Nicholas's astonished gaze. And then, in one rough movement, he shoved his greasy fingers inside his body, gasping briefly at the first painful stab, even as his cock thrust eagerly upwards.

Nicholas's eyes widened as he lay there, staring, as Ward shamelessly pushed his first two fingers in and out of his hole several more times to make sure the grease was worked right inside his body. He withdrew them more slowly and began to use just his fingertips to massage his rim, pressing and rubbing at the taut ring, relaxing the stiff muscle while stimulating the tender, exquisitely sensitive flesh. The whole time, he watched Nicholas, lying on the bed. The man's cock strained upwards, swollen and flushed, and his silver eyes burned with lust.

"Ward," he whispered. Then, "My God. Look at you."

With a groan, Ward shoved his fingers back in. This time, he gave in to the temptation to fuck his desperate hole with a series of hard thrusts before he withdrew again and returned to the stretching and massaging. Already he ached to be filled. To be fucked. No one had ever looked at him the way Nicholas was looking at him now, his intent gaze darting between Ward's face and his fingers as they circled and rubbed and slid inside his body. The rosy head of Nicholas's cock wept, a thread of clear fluid stretching from the straining tip to his flat belly.

"You can touch your cock if you want," Ward said roughly, and Nicholas's hand immediately shot forward to take hold of his shaft, a moan escaping him as he stroked himself.

"You like doing that," Nicholas said, almost disbelievingly, as he watched Ward work.

Ward croaked a laugh. "I love it."

"I want to do it," Nicholas said. "To you, I mean." His face flushed scarlet but he watched Ward steadily as he asked, "Will you let me?"

Ward's answer was a groan and a wordless nod. Immediately, Nicholas sat up.

"Come here then," he said. "Lie down."

Ward obeyed. He lay on his back on the deep, soft mattress, spreading his thighs and bending his knees up, tilting his hips to expose his already loosened and slick hole to Nicholas's gaze while Nicholas got into position, kneeling between his legs.

At first, Nicholas just looked at him, eyes wide with wonder. Then, tentatively, he reached out his index finger and gently traced it over Ward's hole, eyes glittering when Ward jerked at the intense pleasure of that brief, whispering caress.

"My God," Nicholas murmured, and did it again, this time a little more firmly.

"I want your fingers in me," Ward breathed. His whisper-voice was soft and pleading, unfamiliar to him.

Nicholas glanced up at him, then he nodded and reached for the jar of coconut oil from the bedside table, extracting another glob of the white grease. Swallowing hard, he brought the already melting oil to the entrance to Ward's body. As soon as Nicholas touched him there, fingers gently circling and probing, Ward's hole flexed, then clenched, drawing the tip of Nicholas's index finger inside his body, just the tiniest bit. Nicholas gasped and stilled.

"Oh God, Nicholas," Ward groaned. "Don't hold back. Push inside."

"I don't want to hurt you," Nicholas whispered.

"You won't. I can take it—I'm ready for it." He met Nicholas's eyes and added desperately, "I'm *begging* you for it."

"All right," Nicholas said, and slowly pressed his finger inside, moaning softly as Ward's body sucked him in. "Oh God," he whispered. "That's... It's like silk. And the heat..."

"More," Ward pleaded. "Please."

Nicholas pulled carefully out before pushing in again, this time with two fingers. Then out. Then in again. After a little, encouraged by Ward's moans and desperately rocking hips, he quickened the pace, till soon his fingers were plunging swiftly in and out, whilst his restless gaze moved over Ward's writhing body.

"More," Ward begged again. "I can take more."

He could feel the slickness of the extra oil Nicholas had introduced, both inside his body and out. The rim of his anus was liberally coated now and three of Nicholas's sturdy fingers were able to shove in and out of him with ease. Ward closed his eyes as pleasure sparked inside him, only to be ravaged by a new sensation when Nicholas leaned down to take Ward's cock into his mouth.

Nicholas's mouth was hot and wet and clasping, and Christ, but all these sensations were enough to do Ward in: his arse being filled by Nicholas's thrusting fingers, and his cock being suckled by the man's sweet mouth. He gave a harsh cry, and Nicholas immediately broke off, lifting his head and stilling his hand to stare at Ward, appalled.

"Have I hurt you?"

"Christ, no," Ward gasped. "It's just... so good that I'm ready to spill. But I don't want to like this."

Nicholas's silver gaze glittered, a hint of smile itching the corner of his mouth. "How do you want to do it?"

"With your cock in me," Ward whispered. "Fucking me. Hard and deep."

Nicholas swallowed. "Tell me what to do. I've never—" He broke off, looking so suddenly unsure that Ward found himself reaching a hand out to him.

"Just come here," he said. "Come inside me and lie with me."

"Don't you have to turn over?"

"No, we can do it like this. I want to do it like this." Ward smiled. "I like looking you." He lifted his knees to his chest, exposing himself even more, and Nicholas whimpered.

"Come on," Ward urged. "I'm yours."

Nicholas nodded, still looking nervous even as he shifted on his knees to align his cock with Ward's entrance. And then, at last, he was pushing into Ward's slick hole, slowly filling Ward's arse with his thick, blunt cock, eyes closing and head falling back as the sensation of burying himself deep inside Ward took him over.

"Oh God!" Ward gasped. "That's good. So good."

It was better than good. It was everything. Being filled, possessed—in that moment, Ward felt like he'd never be able to have enough of it. Wanted it to last forever.

Nicholas's expression was all amazement. "You feel extraordinary." He pulled back and thrust again. And again, and again, until he was fucking Ward the way Ward most loved, with deep, rhythmic thoroughness. Owning Ward's body and using it for his pleasure.

He fell forward, bracing himself on his elbows on either side of Ward's head, and took Ward's mouth in a savage kiss. Oh, but this man loved to kiss! And now Ward did too. He opened to that seeking tongue, letting Nicholas plunder his mouth as he was plundering his arse, relishing the friction of Nicholas's flat stomach against his cock, which Ward realised with something like wonder he hadn't even touched yet.

Despite the lack of attention to his cock, Ward's crisis was building fast. He felt the churn and surge in his balls that told him he was about to come. He broke the kiss to tell Nicholas, but Nicholas spoke first, panting, "I'm going to spend. Can't stop it—"

"God, yes. Do it—" Ward hissed, giving himself up to the pleasure, holding nothing back. The final stuttering strokes of Nicholas's cock sawing in and out of him shoved Ward over the edge, and he came long and hard, a guttural cry in his throat that Nicholas silenced with his mouth. Wet heat splashed his stomach and filled his arse simultaneously, his own spend and Nicholas's too, mingling with the coconut oil and their sweat, leaving him sticky and satisfied and thoroughly marked.

"Thank you," Nicholas whispered in his ear. "That was… well worth waiting for."

Ward was smiling as he drifted off into a doze.

CHAPTER SEVENTEEN

From *The Collected Writings of Sir Edward Carrick*, volume I

I embarked upon my studies at Cambridge—philosophy, mathematics, and natural sciences—with the woolly notion of taking up a career as a clergyman. It was my father's idea and a common road for a second son. Long before I graduated though, I knew that the Church was not for me. On leaving Cambridge, and following a long argument with my then-disapproving father, I enrolled at King's College London to undertake further studies in the fields of chemistry and natural philosophy. It was there I wrote and published my first scientific paper and began—in my spare time and using the professors' equipment whenever they would allow it—to carry out practical work into the subject which gripped me at that time: identifying a more effective electrolyte for the production of electrical power.

～

The next morning, Nick woke early. A thin beam of sunlight had found its way into the bedchamber through a tiny aperture in the velvet curtains, falling across his face and dazzling him when he cracked his eyelids open. He groaned, lifting his arm to block out the blade of light. As he did so, his fingertips brushed against warm skin. Surprised, he turned his head.

Ward.

The man lay beside him, completely naked, contentedly sleeping.

In sleep, Ward's face was calm in a way it rarely was in wakefulness. Awake, the man was always thinking about something, fine brows drawn together in concentration. Nick rather liked his distracted look, but there was something uniquely appealing about his peacefully dozing countenance. Something oddly innocent too. Though innocent was the last word Nick would have used to describe what they did the night before, and the shameless, wonderful way Ward had seduced him.

He had been inside Ward, and somehow, amazingly, Ward had loved it as much as Nick had. The sensation of Ward helplessly spilling between their bodies while Nick fucked him, his cock buried deep in the man's tight arse, had been, without doubt, the single most wonderful thing Nick had ever experienced. So astonishing that it had even made Nick wonder if he might one day allow Ward to fuck him in return, despite having vowed never to allow that to be done to him again. But if he did it with Ward the way Ward had shown him last night, with coconut oil and all that preparation...

Christ, just the thought of it had him hard as stone again, and wanting more. He stroked his cock, curling his fingers loosely around his shaft while he watched Ward's sleeping face.

His moving arm made the covers shift, and soon enough, Ward was stirring. He gave a raspy sort of moan and blinked his eyes open, giving Nick a puzzled, bleary look for a moment before he seemed to realise where he was and smiled.

"Morning," he croaked. Strangely, Nick found his mouth curving just at the sound of the man's voice. No one could call Ward's voice beautiful, but Nick had grown used to it now. It was part of who he was. A reminder of how strong he was, and the obstacles he'd overcome.

"Morning," Nick murmured. "Did you sleep well?"

Ward's smile was slow and sleepy. "Like a top. What time is it?"

Nick considered the brightness and angle of the sunbeam penetrating the gap in the drapes. "I'd guess six or so."

Ward grunted and rolled away from him, reaching for his discarded pocket watch. Having retrieved it, he flicked it open.

"Not far off," he confirmed. "Ten past."

"Do I win a prize?" Nick teased.

"Like what?"

He grinned wide. "How about a kiss?"

A raspy chuckle. "I think I could manage that. Come here."

Nick leaned over him, bracing himself on one arm. For a few moments, he just looked at Ward, taking in the picture of him lying there, in bed with Nick. The morning sunlight kissed Ward's hair so that it gleamed dark gold against the white linen pillow, and his eyes, which had the greenish tinge of a ripe pear this morning, were warm with fond good humour.

Why was it that Nick never seemed to get bored looking at Ward? He had the same features as everyone else, two eyes, a nose, a mouth. Brow and chin. What was it about the particular configuration of Ward's face that fascinated Nick so much he could just lie here all morning and stare at the man?

"I thought you were going to kiss me," Ward said at last, seeming amused.

"Be patient," Nick scolded, mildly. "I'm looking at you."

"Why?" Ward's smile was satisfied. "Do you like what you see?"

Nick gave a growly chuckle. "You know I do."

Ward laughed, then his eyes went soft and he said, "So do I." He slid one hand up the length of Nick's braced arm and curled his fingers round the back of Nick's neck, fingers tangling in the thick hair at his nape. "Now kiss me."

And with a muffled groan, Nick obliged.

They breakfasted in the parlour they'd dined in the night before. After last night's coupling and this morning's more languid performance, they were able, finally, to concentrate on eating, and each polished off a large breakfast of coddled eggs, ham, sausages, and fried potatoes.

"What's your plan then?" Nicholas asked, dropping his napkin onto his empty plate and leaning back in his chair. "We've the whole day free, haven't we?"

"Yes, the séance isn't till evening," Ward confirmed. "Shall we take a turn about town? There are several bookshops I'd like to visit, but other than that, I'm happy to accompany you wherever you'd like to go."

It was only once the words were out that it occurred to Ward that Nicholas mightn't want to spend every moment with him. Quickly he added, "Unless— You'd probably prefer some time alone…"

Nicholas's eyebrows drew together. "Why would I?"

Ward tried—but probably failed—to hide his pleasure and relief at that swift response. His smile felt impossible to hide, even as he tried to rein it back in. "All right then. Is there somewhere particular you'd like to go, or shall we just have a walk around?"

"I wouldn't mind taking a look at the new railway," Nicholas said.

"Excellent idea!" Ward agreed. The line from Truro to Penzance had only just opened the previous year. "Anything else?"

Nicholas thought. "When I come down for the livestock auction, I usually go to the White Hare. They have the best stargazy pie I've ever tasted." He frowned a little then, looking at Ward. "Though it's a fairly rough sort of place, so… perhaps not."

Ward wondered if Nicholas was thinking of the day Ward had gone into the Admiral's Arms and seen Nicholas for the first time. He'd felt like a fish out of water, but look where his boldness had brought him. To this place, today with Nicholas. Which only went to show that sometimes one found unexpected treasures in the strangest places.

"I'd like to go there with you," Ward said. "I've been itching to try this famous Cornish delicacy everyone keeps telling me about. Although—" He patted his stomach and made a rueful face. "At this moment I can't imagine I'll ever eat again."

Nicholas chuckled. "Oh, I think your appetite will recover."

Ward grinned. "I'm sure it will," he said, and he wasn't talking about food.

They set off shortly after breakfast. The Fox and Swan was a mile or so west of Truro proper and as it happened, the railway was on the same side of town. They headed south to Higher Town where the small station was located, strolling down country lanes that were densely green with early summer growth.

It was a lovely day. The sky was a cloudless stretch of

blue, and the sun shone with early warmth and the promise of more heat to come. They'd scarcely been walking five minutes before Nicholas shrugged off his coat and slung it over his arm.

"Wish I hadn't brought the damned thing," he grumbled. He'd worn his usual tweed while Ward's light fawn coat was of cool linen.

"Your coat's too heavy," Ward pointed out. "You should have worn one like mine."

"Perhaps I would have, if I owned one like yours," Nicholas said mildly.

Ward immediately felt ashamed of his thoughtlessness. He had wardrobes of garments to choose from, some suitable for warm, summery days like this and others for cold, wintry ones. Nicholas's clothes were perfectly respectable, but they were clearly of a different order of elegance from Ward's and his choices were presumably much more limited.

Ward didn't usually notice the difference between their clothes, but here in Truro, he found himself doing so, and other things besides. The difference between his own cut-glass vowels and Nicholas's warmer, rounder ones, his stiff manners with the serving girl and Nicholas's easy good humour.

"Have you been to the railway before?" Nicholas asked, interrupting Ward's thoughts.

Ward glanced at him. "Yes, Pipp and I came down last year to meet with the architect of Helston House. Afterwards, I took the train to Penzance to visit a friend. What about you?"

"Not yet," Nicholas said. "I'd dearly love to go on a train, but I've no reason to visit Penzance." He smiled. "That's the trouble with this railway line. It doesn't go anywhere I need to be."

"Well, it won't be long before they finish the line between Truro and Plymouth, and then you'll be able to go anywhere.

All the way to London in a single day. And then from London all the way to Scotland."

"I've never been to London," Nicholas said, "or Scotland."

"I've not been to Scotland either," Ward admitted, "but I can tell you, you'll love London. I mean, it's dirty and noisy of course, and dangerous in places, but there are so many wonderful things to see. There's no place in the world more alive, I think."

"You miss it," Nicholas observed. "No wonder. It's so quiet in Trevathany."

"I didn't mean that I *miss* it," Ward said. "Only that I would like to show it to you."

As soon as the words were out, he felt colour flood his face at how thoroughly betraying they were. Nicholas turned his head to look at him in surprise, and Ward quickly averted his gaze, realising with something very like relief that they were almost at the station.

"Ah, here we are," he exclaimed, picking up his pace and striding towards the tiny office. "I'll ask the stationmaster if there's a train due anytime soon. I believe there are a few each day, so we might be lucky."

It turned out there was a train due in forty minutes, so they waited, standing side by side, leaning against a low wall that looked over the platform, while Ward explained how steam engines worked, and the problems that had been encountered with the rival atmospheric system, so recently abandoned by Mr. Brunel in neighbouring Devon.

"Perhaps they'd have finished the line from London to Penzance already if they'd stuck with steam engines," Nicholas said, sending a teasing glance Ward's way. "And then you could've taken me to London like you said you wanted to earlier."

Ward's face flamed, and Nicholas chuckled softly, though not unkindly. He turned his back, settling his hips against the wall so that he was facing away from the tracks, looking Ward directly in the eye.

"Where would you take me, if we could go there tomorrow?"

Nicholas's mouth was hitched in a familiar half smile and there was something wistful in his gaze that made Ward feel strangely tender to him, and that made his own embarrassment fade.

He said, "I'd take you to the British Museum to see the Rosetta Stone and the Elgin Marbles. And then to Hyde Park. You can walk for miles there. Perhaps we'd even go boating on the Serpentine. Or riding on Hampstead Heath—we could go up to Parliament Hill. You can see the whole city from there."

Nicholas's gaze was warm. "That all sounds wonderful."

Ward grinned. "Oh, that's just for starters! I'd take you to the zoo and to Astley's circus, and there are dozens of music halls and theatres we could go to. I'm not one for those sorts of entertainments usually, but I'd love to show you—" He was babbling so quickly, his voice cracked, the words petering out on a croaky rasp.

"I can't even imagine a place so lively," Nicholas said. "The most entertainment I've ever seen is the Christmas mummers, and the music hall here in Truro a time or two."

"Did you like the music hall?"

Nicholas gave a huff of laughter. "Some of it. There were one or two good singers, several awful ones, some decent acrobats, and a so-called mind reader my mother could have given a run for his money."

"Your mother read minds too?"

"No," Nicholas scoffed. "But she could read people. Why do you think all the village women came to her about their loved ones who'd passed? She was very astute. Very good at understanding what people wanted to hear."

It was in that moment Ward realised that Nicholas didn't

—*really* didn't—believe in his own mother's powers as a medium. It shouldn't have come as a surprise—he'd alluded to as much several times before, and yet Ward felt stunned.

Nicholas didn't seem to notice. He gave a sigh and turned back to look over the wall again. "My life has been small, Ward. I've lived all my life in Trevathany. Truro is about as far from home as I've ever been."

"There's nothing wrong with staying in a place you love," Ward said.

Nicholas gave a short laugh. "Well, it's true I've never felt a burning desire to leave Trevathany. And it would all too easy to live out my days there. But…"

"But what?"

"I have never truly belonged."

The pain in that confession was audible. Ward wished he could take Nicholas into an embrace and hold him tight, but of course it was impossible. The station master was pottering close by, and there were people gathering on the platform on the other side of the wall as the time for the next train's arrival approached.

"I was just the Gypsy woman's brat or the Tremains' bastard." Nicholas shook his head. "I didn't belong in the village, and I didn't belong at the big house. I didn't belong anywhere." He rubbed at the back of his neck, though his voice was deceptively calm when he added, "If I could've married, maybe things would be—" He stopped. "Well, there's no use thinking of that."

Ward's heart twisted.

"If I could've married…"

That very thought had crossed his own mind many times. How much easier life would be if he married. He could have children, creating a branch of his family that would be his to govern, and that would integrate in easy, predictable ways with his wider family, with his sisters and their husbands and children. For a man as wealthy as Ward, a suitable marriage could be arranged with ease. He could even keep a man on the side, to meet his own secret needs—that was what others did. He knew of several men like that, with a family ensconced in one house, and a male lover in another.

But Ward couldn't do that. He wasn't sure why it was quite so unthinkable to him, only that it was. To live intimately with a wife and family and yet keep the essence of himself from them—he knew it would eat away at his very soul. Yet the alternative, to never express the part of him that loved men, was equally impossible. Not because he was a slave to his appetites, but because those appetites were intrinsic to who he was and to suppress that would be like cutting off the air he breathed.

"If I could've married..."

When Nicholas had spoken those words, Ward had known he felt the same way.

And Ward had ached for him.

Ward stared at Nicholas's strong, square hands resting on the wall in front of them. He glanced around to see if anyone was looking at them, checking his surroundings with the ingrained habit of a man used to being careful. No one was watching. No one seemed the least bit interested, in fact, in the two men standing at the wall, at the back of the platform. No one saw Ward inch his left hand close enough to Nicholas's right that the sides of their hands touched, from the tips of their fingers, down the length of their pinkies, all the way to their wrists.

To the casual observer, it had the appearance of the lightest, most innocent of touches. Entirely unintentional. And yet Ward felt that touch with every particle of his being, warm and tingling, a spark that zinged between them as bright as the tiny blue flashes Ward had seen sparking above the brim of his hat on the *Archimedes* the night he'd last heard George's voice. Ward realised, with something like amazement, that even as he stood there quietly, staring straight ahead, his heart was thundering, and he was holding his breath.

When he finally worked up the courage to look up from their touching hands, it was to find Nicholas's gaze fixed on him, his silver eyes stormy and wild. In the distance, a long shrill whistle sounded through the air, signalling that the engine was nearing. The crowd on the platform shifted and murmured with excitement, straining their necks to catch their first glimpse of the approaching locomotive, but Nicholas's eyes stayed on Ward, and Ward's on Nicholas, even as the engine screeched to a noisy, gasping halt before them.

CHAPTER EIGHTEEN

After the steam engine had come and gone, Nick and Ward walked into the town proper, strolling at an unhurried pace towards Boscawen Street.

It was past noon now, and Truro was bustling. This was the biggest town in the county, and today, Saturday, its busiest day. The streets were crammed with market stalls selling all manner of things—bolts of fabric, spring cabbages, sprats preserved in vinegar, powdered remedies for every possible ache and pain—an unimaginable variety of goods compared to even the busiest of market days in Trevathany. Customers from all walks of life thronged the streets, gathering round the stalls to examine produce and bargain with the vendors, while hawkers circled amongst them, laden with baskets and trays that spilled over with bright ribbons, savoury pastries, shiny apples.

Nick had donned his coat again several streets back, before the crowds got busy. As warm it was, he felt better knowing his money was carefully tucked in his inside pocket, out of reach of any thieves in the crowd. Ward seemed far less concerned about such thoughts than Nick, even though he was a more obvious mark in his elegant, expensive clothes.

He strolled along with his arms swinging by his sides, seeming relaxed and at ease, practically inviting pickpockets, but Nick made up for his insouciance by glaring at anyone suspicious looking who got too close.

Ward paused to buy a Bath bun from a baker's boy with a tray of goods hanging from his neck. As they walked away, he broke it in half and passed one half to Nick.

"I thought you said you'd never be hungry again," Nick said with a grin, before tearing off a corner. It was sweet and tasty, with candied peel and raisins scattered through the warm, fragrant dough.

Ward grinned back. "I was thinking of you. I know you've got a sweet tooth and you're missing Mrs. Waddell's scones this week."

They finished the pastry between them, just as they reached Caddo's Bookshop. Ward brushed the final crumbs from his fingers before he pushed open the narrow door, Nick close behind him.

It was gloomy inside despite the brightness of the day, and the bell rang with a melancholy peal, but the man who sat at the high desk at the front of the shop wore a bright and merry expression when he looked up from his book.

"Sir Edward!" he exclaimed when he spied Ward, and hopped down from his stool. "How good to see you! I've several volumes set aside for you to look at that I think you may be interested in."

"I'm pleased to hear it, Mr. Caddo," Ward replied, stepping forward to greet the man. "I shall be delighted to take a look at them."

For the next half hour, Ward and Caddo did nothing but talk books. Nick browsed the shelves as he waited, soon realising that the shop sold mainly books of a scientific nature. A few handwritten signs scattered about the shop gave clues: *Geology, Mathematics, Natural Sciences.*

Ward ended up purchasing no less than four books and

two journals. Caddo wrapped everything up in brown paper and string, making a loop at the top that Edward could slot his fingers and thumb through to carry them easily, and then they were on their way again.

"Where's the next bookshop?" Nick asked.

"Oh, it's very close—only a few minutes' walk."

It was a glorious day, sunny and bright. Ward swung his package of books at his side as they walked and they talked easily of this and that.

After a while, Ward asked, "Do you read much, Nicholas?"

"Not as much as should," Nick admitted. "My mother couldn't read at all and saw little purpose in books—though she could tell a story better than anyone else I ever met. She had scores of them by memory. We never had any books in the house. I did all my lessons up at Tremain House, and she didn't like me bringing books back."

He saw Ward's expression shift into one of sympathy, and for some reason, that bothered him. Quickly, he looked away, adding lightly, "I'm not much of a one for reading anyway. I'm more the outdoor sort."

"What were your lessons at Tremain House like?" Ward asked.

Nick shrugged. "They were all right. I had them from four till seven each day. At first, my teacher was Harry's tutor. He was a nice gentleman. Mr. Price."

"Isn't that rather late in the day for a boy to be doing lessons?"

Nick was puzzled by the question. "I was a stable boy—I had to do my work first. I started at seven in the morning, but they let me finish early for the lessons, since Harry's were done by then and they couldn't have Mr. Price working all night."

At Ward's look of surprise, Nick chuckled. "You didn't

think Harry and I got our lessons together, did you? As though Godfrey would have allowed that!"

Ward just blinked. "And you were working? How old were you?"

"Twelve when the lessons began, eleven when I started in the stables. Godfrey wanted to get my measure before he wasted any time or money on me." He forced a smile, but had a feeling it was probably little more than a twist of his lips.

Ward looked troubled. "How long did the lessons go on?"

"Till I was nineteen. Mr. Price left when Harry went to school. After that, it was a mix of the village schoolmaster, the curate, and Mr. Lang—he was the steward before me."

"What did you learn?"

Nick shrugged. "When I was younger, the same as any other schoolboy: mathematics, grammar, history, geography, a little Latin. Then later, the business of being a steward: animal husbandry, bookkeeping, that sort of thing."

"Did you ever read a book just for fun?" Ward asked, his expression curious.

Nick frowned, thinking. He honestly couldn't think of one.

Ward must have read the answer on Nick's face because he didn't wait for a reply, merely said, "I'll wager I can find you a book that you'll enjoy reading. You wait and see."

They spent a long time in the next bookshop, wandering around together this time. Ward kept pulling out volumes and telling Nick about them. He seemed to like Mr. Thackeray and Mr. Dickens especially. After a while, he handed Nick a small fat volume bound in dark-red morocco leather. Nick opened it. The flyleaf read, *The Thousand and One Nights, commonly called in England, The Arabian Nights' Entertainments,*

a new translation from the Arabic with copious notes, by Edward William Lane.

He glanced up at Ward. "What's this about?"

"It's a series of tales, told by a woman, Scheherazade, to her husband, over a thousand and one nights."

"Hasn't she anything better to do with her time than sit around telling stories?"

Ward smiled. "Scheherazade is telling the stories to save her life. After he discovered his first wife was unfaithful to him, Shahryar decided to marry a fresh virgin every night, then behead her the very next day. He does this hundreds of times, till Scheherazade comes along. But Scheherazade is well-read, cultured, and clever so her stories are marvellous, and each night she leaves a loose end trailing so that Shahryar has to let her live to find out what will happen next."

"He sounds vile. Does she escape?"

Ward laughed. "No, she runs out of stories after a thousand and one nights, but he's fallen in love with her by then so decides to keep her."

Nick made a sound of disgust and shoved the book back at Ward.

Ward laughed again. "Honestly, Nicholas, it's good. Well worth it for Scheherazade's stories. I'm going to buy it for you."

Now Nick was laughing too. "But I don't want to read about a scoundrel like this Shahryar. I swear, if you dare to buy it for me—"

"*Nick?*"

That was a new voice.

Nick dragged his gaze from Ward to look at the man who was walking towards them.

His heart sank.

"Gabe," he said stupidly. "What are you doing here?"

Gabe had been smiling, looking pleased to see Nick, but at

Nick's tone his eyebrows drew together in a tiny frown. "Well, I *do* live here."

Immediately Nick felt foolish. "I didn't mean here in Truro. I meant here, in this bookshop."

Gabe's frown deepened. "I have been known to read, you know. I'm a schoolmaster, after all." His gaze flickered to Ward, curious.

Beside Nick, Ward rasped, "Introduce me to your friend, Nicholas."

Gabe's eyes widened a little at that, though whether it was his harsh voice or the sheer high-handedness of his words that surprised him, Nick wasn't sure. For his own part, he was bristling at being so blatantly told what to do, but he was used to hiding his feelings when he was provoked, so he only said mildly, "Of course. Gabriel, this is Sir Edward Carrick, Mr. Tremain's newest neighbour. Sir Edward, Mr. Gabriel Meadows. He used to be the village schoolmaster in Trevathany."

Gabe took a step closer to Ward, and the two men shook hands.

"Pleased to meet you, Mr. Meadows," Ward said, though his unsmiling expression gave lie to the words.

"Likewise," Gabe returned stiffly. "Nick and I are— Well, we used to be friends when I lived in Trevathany." He paused. "Good friends."

Nick glanced at him in surprise. *What on earth?* When Gabe returned Nick's look, there was something oddly defiant about his expression.

There was a brief awkward silence then. What was a man supposed to say in a situation like this, after all?

Ward—this is Gabe. We were lovers till he ran off and got married without telling me.

Gabe—this is Ward, my new lover. I fucked him for the first time yesterday and it was nothing like the time we did it. In fact, it was the most wonderful experience of my life…

"So, what brings you to Truro, Nick?" Gabe asked.

Nick wasn't sure what Ward would be comfortable with him saying, so he merely said, "Oh, you know how it is. Business to attend to. I tend to store up my errands and deal with them all at once."

"How long are you here for?"

"Just till tomorrow."

Gabe smiled. "Then perhaps we could dine together this evening? It's been too long. I've missed your company."

Nick was about to decline when Ward rasped, "I'm afraid that's impossible. We have a prior engagement."

Nick turned to look at him, astonished and irritated in equal measure by this possessive—and quite unnecessary—interjection.

Gabe said, "Both of you?"

"Yes," Ward said, again without waiting for Nick to speak. "Nicholas and I travelled down here together, and we've made arrangements for the whole evening." The words carried a distinctly dictatorial edge.

Nick's temper surged. How dare Ward presume to speak for him without first consulting him? And this possessiveness? It was flattering to an extent, but could Ward not see that such behaviour could expose them to conjecture? Even if Gabe could be trusted—and Ward had no basis for making such an assumption—the fact was that anyone in this bookshop might overhear their conversation. Oh, but it was this just sort of arrogance from the very wealthy that most riled Nick, this total lack of consideration for consequences. After all, why worry about consequences when you would face none? With his wealth and title, Ward simply didn't have to be as careful as Nick and Gabe did. That, Nick thought bitterly, was just a fact of life.

Shooting Ward a quick glare, Nick turned to Gabe. Somehow he managed to keep his tone even. "I'm afraid that we—that *I* am busy this evening, but if you've time for an ale just now, we could go to the White Hare? It's not far from here."

Nick felt Ward stiffening beside him, even though he was still looking at Gabe. Gabe, whose smile had returned now, wide and genuine.

"That would be wonderful," he said.

And somehow, it was Gabe's pleasure, more than anything else, that filled Nick with sudden, overwhelming regret. He turned to Ward.

"You're very welcome to come along," he said, offering a small smile. "The White Hare is the place with the stargazy pie I was telling you about."

But Ward wouldn't even meet his eyes. He pressed his lips together and shook his head. "I wouldn't dream of intruding. I'll let you catch up with Mr. Meadows in private."

Nick couldn't hear any tone in the rasped words, but he could tell Ward was unhappy from his averted gaze and unsmiling mouth.

"You wouldn't be intruding," he assured Ward desperately, even as the man nodded a polite farewell to Gabe and began to turn away.

"I'll see you this evening," was Ward's cool reply. "Enjoy the rest of your day."

Gabe waited till they were settled in a private little nook in the White Hare with two tankards of froth-topped ale in front of them before he mentioned Ward.

"So, what's going on between you and Carrick?"

"Nothing," Nick replied. "As I said, I'm helping him with his work." He'd already told Gabe that the man was a scientist and that Nick had agreed to be his subject. In fact, he'd babbled about electricity and ozone and lightning rods nonstop all the way from the bookshop to the White Hare in an effort to avoid precisely this question. Which was absurd, since there was plainly no avoiding it.

Gabe chuckled. "Come off it. He was practically pissing a circle round you in that bookshop."

"Oh, bugger off," Nick replied uncomfortably.

Gabe raised his eyebrows and reached for his ale, tipping his head back to take a long drink. His strong throat bobbed as he swallowed, and it occurred to Nick that once upon a time, just that sight would have be enough to get him hard. Even the last time he'd seen Gabe, down at the mill stream on May Day when they were already finished, he'd still felt a strong pull to him, one that had gone beyond simply finding the man attractive. But now, today, it finally felt as though those feelings were well and truly in the past.

"How's Jenny?" Nick asked when Gabe put his tankard back down on the table. "And little Peter?"

Gabe looked away. "Don't start."

"I'm not," Nick said. "I'm asking because I want to know. You can't think I wish them ill, Gabe. I wish you all happiness, I really do."

It was true. Even in his darkest moments, he'd never borne Gabe's wife any ill will. If anything, he felt sorry for her. Hoped that Gabe would treat her better than he'd treated Nick, though judging by Gabe's behaviour the last time he'd been in Trevathany, that seemed unlikely.

"All right," Gabe said shortly. "Let me tell you how we all are. Jenny and Peter are well. Peter's started babbling. He says *Dada* a lot. And *Mama*. Jenny wants more babies, but I'd rather wait and save for a bigger house first. I've taken on two private students three evenings a week—working men who want to improve themselves. That's a help with money. Jenny's mother's staying with us just now, which is driving me slowly mad, but she's going home on Thursday, thank heavens. And Jenny's cooking is getting better, which is a relief since I thought I'd expire from hunger when we first got married, and—and bloody hell, I *miss* you, Nick." He stared into Nick's eyes as he whispered those last words, his expression agonised, the hand clutching his tankard white-knuckled.

"Gabe—"

"I know you hate me," Gabe went on in a low voice. "And I know I deserve your hatred, but the truth is, even now, I still think about you. Every day, Nick. That's what I wanted to say that last time I saw you in Trevathany. That's what I *should* have said."

They stared at each other for long moments, till Nick looked away, shooting a quick glance about to check no one was paying them any attention. No one was—there were only a handful of others in the taproom and none of them were even glancing their way.

As used as he was to the endless need for watchfulness, Nick still hated it. Hated having to be always prudent, always aware, always lowering his voice even when he wanted to shout his frustration to the world. To just *be* and *do* without always second-guessing himself.

It was a feeling he'd been able to shed, for a few perfect hours, with Ward. First at Helston House and again last night. Wealth gave you the luxury of privacy. If Nick had arrived at the Fox and Swan with Gabe at his side, Mrs. Bassett would likely have wanted to know what they were about, instead of simply assuming their business was respectable and offering them her best parlour to dine in. That was a reality that Ward didn't even begin to understand. He was so used to his privileged position, he had no idea what it was like for others. And perhaps it was unfair to resent Ward for that privilege, when Nick himself had relished the brief, heady freedom it had brought him last night.

Nick dragged his gaze back to Gabe's. "I don't hate you, Gabe," he said wearily. "But we can't be to each other what we once were. You know that. You have a family now, and you need to look after them."

Gabe swallowed and nodded. "I do love them. Jenny's a good mother, and a kindhearted girl, but I—I just didn't realise how much I'd miss you. And I don't just mean the physical, Nick. You were my only real friend in Trevathany. I liked *talking* to you."

"I know. It was the same for me. It was hard when you left. I felt... very alone."

"Christ, Nick." Gabe's voice was pained. "I'm so sorry. I *left* you—"

"It's all right," Nick said. "I'm all right now."

"Are you really?" Gabe asked. He smiled sadly. "And is it terrible that I'm hoping the answer is no?"

Nick's mouth quirked in a rueful smile. "Yes, it's terrible," he agreed, then more gently, "And yes, I think I am."

"Because of him?" Gabe asked. "Carrick?"

Nick thought about that. These last weeks, getting to know Ward, their growing friendship and intimacy—it had been so consuming that there had been no room in him for loneliness or regret or bitterness. As for Ward's physical interest in him, his frank admiration, his *desire*... That had fed something in Nick that was utterly parched. What had passed between them last night had drenched the dried-out cracks in his soul, filling up every cavity and hollow so that, maybe for the first time in his adult life, Nick had felt... happy, however momentarily.

Frowning, he met Gabe's gaze. "Yes. Because of him, I think."

"You love him then," Gabe said. His Adam's apple bobbed in his throat.

Nick searched the other man's face. "Is that what this is? I don't know, Gabe. I've never felt anything quite like this before."

Gabe gave a huff of unamused laughter. "Not with me, I take it?"

Nick scowled at the table, irritated by that. "It's not quite the same, no."

"How?" Gabe asked. "How is he different from me?"

"Ward is—"

Extraordinary. Endlessly fascinating. Utterly infuriating at times. The most comely man Nick had ever seen, with the filthiest imagination. Demanding. Giving. And unapologetically just exactly who he was.

And Nick... loved him.

He dropped his head into his hands. "Bloody hell."

CHAPTER NINETEEN

From *The Collected Writings of Sir Edward Carrick,* volume I

In 1851, I finally set up my own laboratory in London. My father, softened then by ill health, had become reconciled to my refusal to join the Church and finally allowed me access to my portion to enable me to take this momentous step. I was excited beyond measure and embarked upon my work with the single-minded enthusiasm of a monomaniac. I would have thought that nothing could have diverted me from it. But a year later, as I returned home from a trip to Trinity College, Dublin, something happened to me during the sea-crossing from Ireland that would change the path of my life forever.

∼

Ward was dressing in his evening clothes when Nicholas returned.

He heard the scrape of the lock of the next-door chamber

first, then the tread of boots. Moments later, Nicholas appeared in the doorway that connected the two rooms.

"I'm back."

Ward's gut still burned with anger over the events of earlier—he kept his eyes on the mirror and continued to fasten his necktie. "We're dining at six this evening, so you should get ready."

"All right," Nicholas said, but he didn't move. After a pause, he added, "I'm sorry about earlier. I shouldn't have gone off with Gabe like that. It's just that when you said—"

"It's quite all right," Ward interrupted. He gave his necktie one last tweak then turned to meet Nicholas's troubled gaze. "But you really ought to get ready. The séance is at half past seven and we mustn't be late."

Nicholas didn't say anything for the longest time. He seemed to be considering how to respond, but at last he just nodded and turned away, saying, "I won't be long." Then he disappeared back into the small adjoining room and closed the door behind him.

He reappeared a few minutes later in fresh clothes, with his hair neatly combed, and followed Ward down to the dining parlour in silence, remaining subdued all through dinner. Ward was quiet too, both because of what had happened in the bookshop and at the thought of what the evening before him held. He wondered what sort of man Stephen Bryant would prove to be. A medium with genuine abilities, or just a fraudster, preying on grieving families?

At last, towards the end of the meal, Nicholas sighed and said, "Are you still angry?"

He looked and sounded irritated, and that made Ward's own annoyance spike. Even though Nicholas had apologised when he'd first returned to the inn, he didn't seem to feel truly sorry about going off with Gabe Meadows this afternoon. Indeed, from the scowl on his face, it seemed he had his own gripes about what had happened, though Ward couldn't imagine what those might be. On another evening, Ward would probably have asked Nicholas outright what the problem was, but not this evening. He was in no mood to entertain that argument now, not with his stomach clenched up with nerves at the prospect of the séance.

"I'm not in the least bit angry," he lied.

"Fine," Nicholas replied, looking away. "You're not annoyed with me at all."

His scepticism was obvious. Well, that was Nicholas, wasn't it? He was a sceptical character, and not just about Ward's stupid lie—most likely about the whole night ahead.

In fact, thinking about it, Ward found it difficult to remember why it was he'd asked Nicholas to come along tonight at all. One of the great ironies of their friendship was that Ward had initially wanted to get to know Nicholas because he'd believed that, with his unusual background, Nicholas would be more open to the idea of communicating with spirits than anyone else in Trevathany. In fact, it had transpired that the opposite was true. The only chink in Nicholas's considerable scepticism was his—possible—child-hood sighting of the Physic. And in truth, from what Nick had said during his trances, Ward wasn't convinced that the encounter hadn't simply been the fevered, if vivid, imagin-ings of a sick child.

Even when his own mother was mentioned, Nick would usually just make some throwaway comment that hinted at a lack of belief in her supposed abilities.

"She was very astute. Very good at understanding what people wanted to hear..."

Not that Nick's belief or lack of belief should make any difference, given that Ward was supposed to be approaching this evening's events with the objective disinterest of a scien-tist. He was here to assess Stephen Bryant, to find out whether he might be a credible subject for Ward's studies. Except the truth was, Ward didn't feel the least bit objective.

He felt... hopeful. Hopeful, and desperately afraid to be hopeful, that George might come to him again, as he had on board the *Archimedes*.

Because if Stephen Bryant was a true medium, that might well happen.

~

Stephen Bryant lived on the outskirts of Truro in an area of the town Nick was unfamiliar with. He and Ward walked there in silence, Ward still quietly remote after their mostly silent dinner. Nick wasn't sure how much of Ward's distance was lingering annoyance over Nick's going off with Gabe that afternoon and how much was preoccupation with the events of the evening still to come. Whatever it was, he wasn't minded to try coaxing Ward into a better mood.

The address Mr. Bryant had provided to Ward led them to a sizeable villa but when the front door was answered—by a sullen lad of around fourteen years in a grease-stained coat— it became apparent the house was divided into a number of separate apartments. The boy led them up two flights of stairs to Mr. Bryant's rooms, rapped at the door in an irritated way, called out "*More* visitors!" in a tone that suggested his patience was sorely tried, and stomped off without waiting to see if they'd get an answer.

A few moments later, the door inched open, revealing the lugubrious, jowly face of a middle-aged man. His hair was very black—too youthfully black for that sagging, lived-in face—and his eyes were heavy lidded and somewhat bloodshot.

"Good evening," he said in a deep, refined voice. "Are you here for the séance?"

"We are," Ward replied.

The man blinked at Ward's harsh voice, then said, "May I ask your name?"

"Sir Edward Carrick," Ward confirmed. "And this is my friend Mr. Nicholas Hearn."

At this introduction, the man opened the door wide and offered his hand, his sudden smile surprisingly wolfish. "Pleased to meet you, Sir Edward," he said. "Stephen Bryant at your service."

He shook first Ward's hand, ushering him inside, before taking Nick's. His palm was warm and rather damp against Nick's, though his grip was firm. Nick had to fight the urge to wipe his own hand on his trouser leg after. He walked past Bryant in response to his gesturing arm, waiting with Ward just inside the narrow hallway while Bryant closed the front door.

"Come through and meet the others," Bryant said. "First door on your left ahead."

The door he indicated gave on to a gloomy room that was evidently all set up for a séance. It was dominated by a round table surrounded by eight chairs of various shapes and sizes, all packed tightly together. The table itself was covered by a long black tablecloth, the edges of which brushed the floor. A few lone candles were scattered here and there about the room. Just enough to see by and no more.

"The others are in the parlour," Bryant said, leading the way past the table, to a door on the other side of the room through which a few low-pitched voices could be heard.

This room was more brightly lit and contained five people. On one couch sat an older woman and a girl of around seventeen or eighteen. Their features were so similar, it seemed reasonable to assume they were mother and daughter. They wore mourning clothes of unrelieved black and the older woman wore several large pieces of jet jewellery: a brooch, earrings, and a thick rope of beads that she twisted between black-lace-clad fingers.

"Mrs. Harris and Miss Harris," Bryant advised Nick and

Ward, gesturing at the ladies. Then to the ladies, "Ladies, this is Sir Edward Carrick and his friend Mr. Nicholas Hearn."

"Pleased to meet you, ma'am," Ward said, addressing his comments to the older woman.

She nodded gravely. "You are fortunate to be granted entrance to this circle, Sir Edward," she told him. "Mr. Bryant is a highly sought after medium. He has a waiting list for his séances, you know."

Bryant gave Ward a modest shrug. "My gatherings are small by necessity, Sir Edward. Too many listeners tend to discourage the spirits."

"Why would that be?" Nick asked. It was only once the words were out that he realised how combative they sounded. He hadn't intended to voice his sceptical thoughts aloud, certainly not so early on. Already, though, Stephen Bryant was demonstrating the signs of the professional show-man, planting the seeds of the excuses he might need later. It irked Nick. He hated the thought of Ward being taken in by such a man—and he feared Ward would be taken in. Because for all Ward's talk of objective scientific observation, it was plain that he desperately wanted to believe in this. Wanted to believe his brother's spirit lived on in some way. And that was precisely the sort of hope that men like Bryant preyed on.

Bryant regarded Nick and his expression was calculating. "The spirits can be volatile," he said at last. "And shy. Especially when there are coarse, insensitive souls in the room." The look he gave Nick left him—and the others in the room—in no doubt that Nick was in possession of just such a soul.

Nick pressed his lips together to stop himself retorting—or worse, laughing. Ward would not forgive him if they were thrown out before the séance even started.

Bryant moved on to the next guest. "This is Mr. Wallace," he said, gesturing towards a shrunken elderly man with wispy white hair and an old-fashioned, though elegant coat that fairly drowned his wizened form.

"Sir Edward," the old man said in a high, reedy voice. "Mr. Hearn." They nodded back politely.

"And finally, Mr. and Mrs. Peasland."

The last two members of the group were a younger couple, perhaps in their late twenties or early thirties. The woman, who was quite pretty, looked like a rich man's idea of a Gypsy woman. Her simple black gown was cut low over her bosom, imperfectly veiled by the lacy red shawl she wore draped about her shoulders. Her glossy brown hair was woven into two thick plaits that she wore down, past her shoulders, and a bracelet made of string after string of tiny gold coins adorned her left wrist. Her husband was dressed in a similarly Bohemian fashion, in a sort of loose tunic-coat worn over wide-legged trousers.

Mrs. Peasland rose from her chair to greet them, gravitating to Nick first, her expression all avid interest.

"Pleased to meet you, ma'am," Nick said.

"I'm very pleased to meet *you*, Mr. Hearn," she replied archly. "You have—oh, quite a *look* about you, I must say." He wasn't sure what that was supposed to mean, but instead of offering an explanation, she gave him a brilliant smile before turning her attention to Ward. "And Sir Edward." She waved a vague hand, still smiling, though less brilliantly now. "Delighted, of course."

Mr. Peasland offered his hand to each of them in turn, murmuring a quieter welcome.

"It's not often we get visitors from London, here in Truro," Mrs. Peasland said, directing her comment solely to Nick. "I do hope you're not here to steal our dear Mr. Bryant away from us."

"Oh, I'm not from London," Nick said. "Sir Edward here is the city man."

"Are you a Truro native then?" she asked.

"Trevathany," he confirmed briefly, not much liking her close attention.

"Of course, I should have *realised*," she gushed. "That Cornish black hair... and I'd hazard a guess you have some Romany blood. Am I right?"

"I'd wager you are, Mrs. Peasland," Bryant said, before Nick could respond. "Mr. Hearn has a distinctly *Gypsy* cast to his features."

Realising that every eye was upon him, Nick nodded stiffly. "My mother," he said.

"How wonderful," Mrs. Peasland breathed. "The Gypsy people are very highly attuned to spiritual matters. I have always felt a great affinity to them."

Well, that explained her costume, Nick supposed.

"As it happens, Mr. Hearn's mother was accounted something of a medium in her day," Ward said, beside him.

Nick scowled at Ward, giving a minute shake of his head. He didn't want his mother discussed here, in front of these people. Ward's faint smile withered, his brows furrowing with concern.

"Is that so?" Bryant enquired, drawing Nick's attention away from Ward. "How very fascinating. As Mrs. Peasland says, there are certainly *some* Romany people who have an innate talent for spiritualism, but I must say that I have found them quite inconsistent in their practices. They tend to rely on a sort of native intuition, rather than having a firm grasp of the science of spiritualism. I'm afraid they've done little but harm the reputation of the movement as a whole."

The room was very quiet when he finished talking, every eye darting between Bryant and Nick as they awaited Nick's reaction. He didn't respond though, despite the anger churning in his belly at Bryant's insults. Instead, he made his expression carefully neutral, just as he always did when he was provoked, whether it was Godfrey Tremain defaming his mother or Jed Hammett calling him a *Gypsy's bastard*—or this charlatan.

A ripple of unease went around the room at the awkward

silence, and still Nick said nothing, while Bryant's face grew flushed.

Finally, the man was forced to speak. "We may as well get started then," he said shortly, heading for the door. "If you'd all like to follow me."

CHAPTER TWENTY

Once everyone sat down, Bryant extinguished most of the candles in the séance room, leaving only one—little more than a stub—burning in the middle of the table. As the room was windowless, it was now very dark indeed.

Bryant took a seat between Mrs. Peasland on his right and Mrs. Harris on his left. Miss Harris sat next to her mother, then Ward, Nick, Mr. Wallace, and finally Mr. Peasland beside his wife.

Bryant asked them all to hold hands. Despite the discord between them, Nick welcomed the warm slide of Ward's palm against his own, the intimate curl of their fingers and thumbs in a loose grip. Just that simple touch steadied him, quieting his unease over the tense atmosphere.

Mr. Wallace's hand brushed Nick's other sleeve, and Nick fumbled for the old man's hand, taking it in his own. Mr. Wallace's skin was dry and papery, but for a frail-looking old man, he had quite a grip on him.

"We ask the spirits to offer their guidance," Bryant said. "To come to our circle and answer the questions in our hearts."

Was this an announcement, Nick wondered. A prayer? If so, to whom was he praying?

"Some of our number," Bryant continued, his voice raised as though he was indeed addressing a larger audience than their small group, "are here because they are weighed down by grief. Others are here because they seek answers to great questions. But all of us come into this circle with humility and open minds and hearts."

There was a chorus of muted *Amens* around the table. Nick and Ward were silent.

"Now, ladies and gentlemen," Bryant said in a lower voice —evidently he was finished addressing whoever had been intended to hear his previous assurances—"please place your hands *lightly* on the table before you, palm-down. Do not exercise downward pressure please. I do not want any of you inadvertently influencing the movement of the table."

No, Nick thought sourly. *That's your job.*

They obediently let go of each other's hands and set their hands down on the table. The heavy black fabric covering the surface of the table muffled Nick's sense of touch.

"Spirits," Bryant announced, again in that louder voice. "We invite you to our circle." He paused. "Is anyone there?"

Silence.

Silence.

Bryant repeated, "Is anyone there?"

The table rocked. Someone gasped.

It wasn't much, but it was a distinct tilt towards the Harris ladies. The table came to a rest again.

"Are you the spirit of one of our loved ones?" Bryant asked, and the table tilted again, again towards the ladies. Mrs. Harris gave a half sob.

"Tell us your name," Bryant demanded, and he began to recite the alphabet slowly. At last, at *J* the table tilted again, then at *O* and *H* and *N*.

By the end of that routine, Mrs. Harris was crying in

earnest. It was interesting, Nick thought, that after the first letter had been selected, Bryant hadn't returned to the start of the alphabet again, but had moved straight to *I* and the letters that followed, quickly reaching the *O*. He had corrected himself on the next two passes though, starting at *A* each time. Nick wondered if Ward had noticed that detail.

There were questions for John Harris, from his wife: mundane, domestic questions about whether she ought to send their youngest son to boarding school this year—*Y-E-S* —and whether the new kitchen maid was to be trusted—*N-O*. After a while, it seemed Mrs. Harris had run out of questions, and Bryant moved on, inviting any other spirits to the table.

The next visitor was, apparently, well-known to Bryant. She announced her presence not with table-tilting but with a series of thuds and raps that Nick couldn't quite locate. Some sounded as if they came from under the floor, others from the tabletop, and still others from the walls.

"Is that you, Miss Violet?" Bryant asked in that same raised tone as before. In his normal voice he added, apparently for Nick and Ward's benefit. "Miss Violet has been my spirit guide for many years."

She was certainly active. As well as the raps and the thuds, she violently knocked over a chair in the corner—Nick made a mental note to check later for any sign of string attached to the legs—and apparently extinguished the candle on the table, leaving them in full darkness. She also answered numerous questions for Bryant, confirming amongst other things that three people at the séance would have their questions answered this evening, one of them a man who would speak with his brother.

Nick was aware of Ward stiffening at that, the telltale brush of shoulder and thigh. For now, he could only wonder whether Ward was actually believing this nonsense, or if he felt as sceptical as Nick himself did. He feared not, and his gut burned with resentment at Bryant's easy manipulation of Ward's grief.

Miss Violet went on for some time after that without any further veiled references to Ward. She seemed to have a word or message for nearly everyone before she finally departed.

After that, Bryant began the same routine of calling on the spirits again, inviting them into the circle and assuring them of *open hearts and minds*. It was amazing, Nick thought, what effect language could have. How it predisposed people to believe. Other than people like Nick, of course, who'd come here tonight not looking for comfort or answers but to watch out for Ward. To try to make sure he wasn't taken advantage of.

"We are listening, spirits," Bryant said. "Is anyone there?"

A bell rang.

It was a low, quite loud bell, with a sad echoey sound.

Ward went rigid.

"Who's there?" Bryant asked.

Again the bell. It sounded like—like—

Like a ship's bell.

"Your name, spirit!" Bryant demanded. He began to recite the alphabet, and sure enough, when he reached *G*, the bell tolled again. And again at *E* and again at *O*. Bryant was going through the alphabet painfully slowly. Nick was sure he was deliberately increasing the tension, and Nick's anger was growing with every moment.

It wasn't until Ward made a small, choked sound of distress though, when the bell tolled again at *R*, that Nick finally snapped. Finally decided he couldn't bear it any longer and stood up so abruptly that his chair fell over, clattering loudly to the floor.

"What was that?" a female voice cried.

Bryant cried out, "Mr. Hearn, you have broken the circle!"

"What are you *doing*, Nicholas?" Ward croaked, his voice close to giving out with too much emotion. He got to his feet, his chair near toppling when he pushed it back with his knees so that he had to reach out a trembling hand to steady it.

All he could think of was George. That bell—the bell from the *Archimedes*—tolling in the darkness. Was George gone now? Already? Ward's heart still thudded with the panicky excitement that had flared in him at each of those chimes, an excitement that was already beginning to fade as disbelieving fury set in.

"Ward, come on! You must be able to see what's going here," Nicholas exclaimed. Ward caught the glitter of his eyes in the gloom, his vague outline. "You can't be that blinded to reality."

"What do you mean by that?" a female voice demanded from the other side of the table. That was Mrs. Peasland. "What on earth's going on?"

Nicholas's outline moved as he turned his head in the direction of her voice. "What's going on is that your precious Mr. Bryant here is a fake." His voice was scathing. "There are no spirits here, just cheap parlour tricks."

"Now, look here," a frail voice quivered. Mr. Wallace. "You can't come in here, throwing around accusations like that!"

"No, you can't!" Mrs. Peasland agreed. "It's outrageous! Why, Mr. Bryant invited you here in good faith, to share his gift—"

"Gift?" Nicholas laughed without humour. "Is there anyone here who didn't pay to be at this séance?" He turned back to Ward and said, "Surely you of all people can see past this nonsense?"

In the far corner of the room, light began to bloom, slowly illuminating the players in the proceedings. The source of the light became visible first: Mr. Peasland had apparently left the table while everyone else was sniping and was carefully placing a chimney over the oil lamp he'd just lit. Now Ward could see all the shocked and angry faces clustered about the table, all of them staring in disgust at Nicholas, who stood with his hands clenched in tight fists by his sides; his jaw a hard, uncompromising line; and his silver gaze on Ward, angry and pleading at once.

"Ward," he said. "You have to see—"

"No," Ward bit out. "I don't." He shook his head, unable to believe what had just occurred. "You were my guest this evening. For God's sake, don't you know how to behave? I only asked you here to observe—"

"You *asked* me to watch out for you," Nicholas interrupted. "And that is what I'm doing."

"Oh, please!" Ward replied. "You knew perfectly well I wouldn't have wanted you to disrupt these proceedings. You should be ashamed of yourself!"

"*I* should be ashamed?" Nicholas cried in disbelief. "Truly, Ward, are you *blind*? Do you not see what has just happened in this room? The table tilting—a child could do it! As for the raps and bells, I'll wager there's someone else here making those noises, hidden somewhere, or rapping from the floor below. In your heart of hearts you know this as well as I do. Christ, Ward, you—"

"Stop it!" Ward snapped. "Stop blaspheming—there are ladies present! And stop calling me by my given name in company. For goodness's sake, show a little decorum!"

Nicholas froze and fell silent, his expression stunned.

The echo of his own words reverberated in Ward's mind, and immediately he wished he could call them back, knowing with sudden, sick certainty, there was nothing—not one thing —he could have said that could have been worse.

"Nicholas," he said hurriedly, "I'm sorry—"

But already Nicholas was stepping back, putting distance between them.

"I'm sorry. I truly didn't mean that," Ward babbled. He

held his hands out, palms facing Nicholas, as though pleading for calm.

Bryant had risen to his feet now too. "I realise that your people have erratic ways, Hearn," he said snidely. "But I cannot tolerate this sort of hostile behaviour at my séances. I must think of my other guests and ask you to leave."

"Well said, Mr. Bryant," Mrs. Harris piped up, and Mr. Wallace nodded his agreement solemnly. Mrs. Peasland fingered her gold coin bracelet, her pretty mouth set in a fractious line.

Nicholas had adopted that oddly neutral expression he wore sometimes, all emotion masked. Ward hated that expression, and how it shut him out. When Nicholas opened his mouth to reply to Bryant, Ward spoke over him, desperate to show Nicholas that Ward was on his side.

"We will be leaving together, Mr. Bryant," he said. "We will trouble you no longer."

Bryant's face fell. "Oh, there's no need for *you* to leave," he said hurriedly.

"No," Nicholas agreed icily. "No need for you to leave, *Sir Edward*. And no need to answer for me either, thank you. I've a voice of my own and can speak for myself."

He turned on his heel and stalked out the room.

Ward stood there, paralysed, flinching as first the parlour door, then the front door slammed behind Nicholas. His mind raced. Should he run after Nicholas or leave him to cool down? He wasn't sure exactly what had just happened, but he knew with complete certainty that he had wounded Nicholas badly.

"And stop calling me by my given name…"

Christ. He'd pulled rank on Nicholas, hadn't he? Knowing that was the sorest of all sore spots for him. And God, but he was regretting it now.

More words returned to him.

"Don't you know how to behave?"

"You should be ashamed of yourself!"

He closed his eyes. He knew with horrible certainty that Nicholas would not easily forgive him for this.

Into the silence, Bryant said, "Well, now that Mr. Hearn's done the decent thing and removed himself, shall we resume the proceedings?"

Ward blinked and looked up to find the others all watching him with curious expressions, all except young Miss Harris who was staring straight ahead.

"I think I had better go after my friend," he said, and his voice sounded distant to his own ears.

He felt oddly dazed, his mind already racing ahead to what came next. He'd go straight to the Fox and Swan—surely that was where Nicholas would be—and he'd apologise, profusely. Everything could be put right—they could get back to the way things were last night. That perfect night. Surely they would get that back?

They had to.

"Oh, come now, Sir Edward! Stay till the end of the séance at least," Bryant wheedled. "I felt sure we were getting somewhere before Mr. Hearn's outburst. There was—" he made a swirling gesture with his right hand and looked upwards, as though searching for words to explain, or perhaps waiting for divine assistance "—if not quite a presence yet, certainly a sense of something approaching."

Ward actually shivered. The theatricality of the man in that moment seemed so suddenly very wrong. Before he could respond though, Mrs. Peasland, who had been staring at Bryant with an enraptured expression, turned to Ward, clasping her hands at her bosom, and said, "Oh, yes, please stay, Sir Edward! Please do let us make the circle again and try to contact your loved one. Do not let your friend's lack of faith in the spirits prevent you from gaining the comfort of communicating with your dear departed again."

Mr. Wallace made another of those mumbling noises that

signified agreement, and Mrs. Harris and Mr. Peasland added their voices too, all of them urging Ward to stay.

Only Miss Harris was silent. And then, quite suddenly, in the middle of that cacophony of voices, she rose from her chair and left the table. She walked over to the other side of the room and… stared at the wall.

"Mathilda?" her mother cried. "What on earth are you doing?"

Mathilda Harris didn't answer, just stretched out one hand and ran the tips of her fingers down the wall. It was the oddest thing—till quite suddenly, Ward realised what had her so transfixed.

There was an *edge* sticking out.

It was, Ward realised as he peered, the edge of an almost invisible panel, the sides of which were designed to cunningly follow the pattern of the striped wallpaper.

A panel that happened to have been left the tiniest bit ajar.

"Miss Harris—" Bryant said hurriedly. He tried to get out of his seat, but he was hemmed in by the ladies on either side of him, and though both Mrs. Peasland and Mrs. Harris obligingly shifted their chairs to let him out, he was too late to stop the girl from sliding her fingertips down that errant edge and tugging the panel open.

The space behind was big enough—just—for a person to stand upright in.

And someone did. A young woman holding a bell in her hand.

CHAPTER TWENTY-ONE

From *The Collected Writings of Sir Edward Carrick*, volume I

The year that followed my brother's death was a difficult one. Six weeks after the news arrived, my father suffered an apoplexy. It was his second in as many years, but this time he was paralysed after, and died a few days later. My poor mother, having lost both her eldest son and her husband in a matter of weeks, was distraught. It was some months after my father's death that she heard of an American woman who had arrived in London, a Mrs. Haydn, who claimed to be a spiritualist medium. Mrs. Haydn was holding séances throughout the city at that time, and gathering quite a reputation. My mother begged me to take her to one of these séances, and so I did, and spent an extraordinary evening watching as Mrs. Haydn summoned numerous departed spirits who identified themselves by giving the dates of their deaths and accurately answering questions posed by their grieving relations. The spirits' responses were given by rapping noises, the origin of which were a mystery to all present, some sharp, some dull, and seeming to come from all about the room, even under the floor. There was a message for me, from George: *All will be well.* I wept to hear those words again, the same he'd used to me that night, months before, on the *Archimedes.*

When Ward got back to the Fox and Swan, Nicholas was not there.

Ward settled down to wait for him. He opened one of the journals he'd brought with him to read in the coach, but couldn't concentrate on the contents. His eyes slid over the words, unable to take them in. His mind was drifting elsewhere, his ears primed to hear the slightest approaching noise. He kept getting up to look out the window.

But Nicholas did not come.

Hours passed and he did not come. Eventually, at one in the morning, Ward retired to bed, only to lie there, awake and fearful, wondering where Nicholas was. If he'd tracked down that Gabe fellow or, worse, if he was lying dead in a ditch somewhere.

It wasn't until dawn that Nicholas finally returned.

Ward had fallen into a fitful doze, but his eyes opened at the scrape of a key in a lock and he sat bolt upright, not quite awake, yet somehow aware that this was important. Then memories of the night before flooded his mind, and he scrambled out of bed, looking for the source of the noise. It came from the other, smaller room.

Ward crossed the floor and pushed the connecting door open. Nicholas was in the act of closing the door that gave onto the corridor, apparently as quietly as possible. He turned at Ward's entrance, and his expression of dismay made Ward's gut wrench.

"I thought you'd be asleep," Nicholas said. "I'm just here to get my bag. The stagecoach leaves in an hour."

"The stagecoach," Ward repeated. "What do you mean?"

"I'm going home," Nicholas said calmly. He reached for his valise.

"You don't need to take the stagecoach, Nicholas. I have the carriage. If you wish to leave earlier—now even—we can do that."

Nicholas ignored him. He wadded up a discarded shirt and shoved it into his bag.

"Nicholas," Ward said, "please. I want you to travel back with me. We have things to discuss."

Nicholas looked up. "And I want to leave on the stage-coach," he said flatly.

For a moment, their gazes held, then Nicholas looked away, resuming his packing. It didn't take long. Within moments he was buckling the strap.

"I'll get going, then," he said, once he was done.

"Nicholas, please—" Ward's rasping voice was desperate. "I'm sorry about what I said at the séance. You're angry with me, and I'm sorry, truly sorry."

Nicholas turned. His expression was furious, silver eyes glittering. "I'm angry with *myself*," he bit out. "I'm angry that I was actually beginning to believe you saw me as an equal and not as someone who's here just to serve you. I'm angry because I know better than that. I know what your sort are like, and sure enough, you showed your true colours today in front of Gabe and again tonight."

The furious hurt in those words took Ward aback. "I do see you as an equal," he whispered. "I really do."

"No, you don't," Nicholas snapped. "You told me you wanted me to call you Ward, but the moment you thought I was getting above myself, you changed your mind. You only want to listen to me when I'm saying something you agree with. Otherwise, I'm to stay quiet and biddable."

"No—" Ward protested.

Nicholas's silver gaze was cold. "Yes. In your eyes, you

are the master and I am the servant. That's how things started between us, and nothing's changed."

"No!" Ward repeated, shaking his head. "That's not how it is at all. Christ, Nicholas, I let you *inside* me—how can you think I want to master you?"

Nicholas's lip curled with disdain. "You think that makes a difference? Because I *fucked* you?" He gave a harsh laugh. "I put my cock in you because you told me to put it there. It doesn't matter which one of us has a cock in his arse. What matters is who decides what's to happen—and that's always been you."

Ward stared at him, stung.

"I was a fool to let my guard down with you," Nicholas went on bitterly. "I'd actually begun to believe you truly saw me as a friend—a *lover*. But tonight I realised that's just how you treat me when I'm doing what you want. The rest of the time you expect me to know my place and hold my tongue."

"That's not true!" Ward protested. "Friends don't always get along, Nicholas. Sometimes they argue, like we did tonight. Tonight you interrupted that séance at a point when I believed, truly believed, that I might be about to communicate George. So yes, I lashed out at you. And I'm sorry for it— it wasn't fair and I'm not proud of it, but I wasn't pulling rank on you!"

Nicholas's lip curled again. "No? What about when you told me I should be ashamed of myself? That didn't feel like a man speaking to his equal. You were scolding me, Ward. Telling me off like a naughty child."

Ward's cheeks heated at that memory. "I regret my words, I do! I wish beyond anything I could take them back. But can't you understand how I felt? I was so *sure* that George was there, and I've waited so long to speak to him. This last year, I've risked everything—thrown away my very reputation—in pursuit of this, and then tonight, just when it seemed he might be near—" His voice gave out.

Nicholas was silent for a long moment.

At last, he said, very quietly, "Your brother is dead, Ward. At some point, you need to accept that."

"I know he's dead!" Ward cried. "Jesus, Nicholas, what do you take me for? An imbecile?"

Nicholas said evenly, "You haven't accepted it, though. This obsession of yours is testament to that."

"I'm not obsessed. I'm gathering evidence for my studies—"

"Was that what you were doing tonight?"

Ward opened his mouth but couldn't make any words come out.

"You told me you were coming to Truro to see if Bryant would make a good subject for your work, but the truth is, you just wanted to go to that séance to see if he could contact your brother. You were so caught up in that, you weren't paying the slightest bit of attention to what the man was actually doing, never mind studying him. If you had been, you'd know he's a fraud. Not even a very good one. Christ, my mother was better!"

Ward stared at him. "She wasn't—"

"Clairvoyant?" Nicholas laughed harshly. "No. She did what she did for money, because we were poor, and she had no other way of earning. She knew how to read people, how to manipulate their emotions. Mostly, she made them feel better, I think, but it was all lies." He shook his head. "So you see, I really *wasn't* the subject you were hoping for."

Ward couldn't understand why he felt so gutted. He'd already guessed that Nicholas's mother wasn't a medium—hell, Nicholas had disclosed *he* thought she was a fake with that comment about her mind-reading—but somehow, having it so bluntly stated was different. It was like that moment in Bryant's parlour all over again, when Mathilda Harris had prised open the panel in the wall, revealing the woman standing inside.

"I was foolish tonight," Ward croaked. "Gullible. But I won't let that happen again. No more looking for mediums—what I need to do is concentrate on re-creating the conditions I experienced on the *Archimedes* and—"

"And what? You achieve that and you'll be able to speak to George again? So what if you do? What can he possibly tell you that will benefit you, or anyone else for that matter? What is all this *for*, Ward?" Nicholas threw up his hands, exasperated. "Can't you see how absurd this is?"

Ward felt like he'd been knifed.

"Absurd?" he echoed, disbelieving. "*Absurd*, am I? You've got a nerve, criticising me, Nicholas. What do you think I am? An idiot? For Christ's sake, I've got more education in my little finger than you have in your whole—"

He stopped himself just before he finished the rotten, mean-spirited thought, but it was already there, between them. The silence rang with the final word of that unfinished sentence, and when Ward dared to meet Nicholas's gaze, the other man's expression was disconcertingly level.

"Nicholas," he said. "I—"

"It's time I went," Nicholas interrupted, lifting his valise in his hand. "Past time, in fact. Safe journey home, Sir Edward."

Ward searched for something to say in response, something that would breach the yawning gulf that had opened up between them, but he couldn't think of anything.

And then Nicholas was gone, and he was left staring at the closed door.

CHAPTER TWENTY-TWO

From *The Collected Writings of Sir Edward Carrick,* volume I

Several days after I attended Mrs. Haydn's séance, I spoke of what I had witnessed at a gathering of a number of scientists of my acquaintance. With the benefit of hindsight I can see how very raw my grief was then, but at the time I thought myself perfectly rational. When several of the gentlemen questioned Mrs. Haydn's abilities, I defended her with a passionate fervour that was quite unlike me—I was then and am still now of a generally even temperament, but that evening I was beside myself. The whole debacle ended with me storming out of the house in which we had met.

The debate prompted two of the gentlemen to attend the next séance held by Mrs. Haydn for themselves. They subsequently penned an article supposedly exposing her as a charlatan, to which I responded with a letter of rebuttal. My letter was published by the same newspaper, as were a half dozen replies from men of science I knew and respected, including the man I had considered my mentor, Professor Kenneth Arnold. Each of them expressed their astonishment at my naïve credulity and disapproval of my public support for Mrs. Haydn.

For five years I had been working and writing ceaselessly in my chosen field and in so doing, had built an enviable reputation for a man of my years. Now that reputation had been publicly savaged, not by one of my peers but by six of them. The episode rocked me to the core. The only comfort I could find was in my vow to prove them wrong.

~

8th July 1853

"I don't understand this," Godfrey said, scowling. The lines on his forehead seemed deeper than before. He had aged quite suddenly this year, and for the first time in Nick's life, the old man looked frail.

"It's very simple," Nick said. "I'm going to find my mother's family. I may even travel with them for a while, if they'll let me. If not, well, I'll see about that when it happens."

Godfrey sat back in his leather wingback chair. "I've never heard anything so ridiculous in all my life!" he snapped. "You live here. You belong here!"

It was an effort, but somehow Nick managed to keep his expression neutral. Words, though, were beyond him. He could not agree with that final statement and anything he did say would be far too betraying.

"What about your duties?" Godfrey demanded.

"You'll find someone else. All you have to do is advertise the position."

"You're not giving me enough notice!" Godfrey replied angrily. Then, pettily, "I'll have to hold back the wages owing to you for that."

Nick had grown so used to Godfrey's threats over the

years, he didn't even blink. "Well, if that's what you want to do, I can't stop you."

Godfrey's fury seemed to boil over at that. "I cannot fathom your ingratitude," he spat out. "I gave you that position! I gave you Rosehip Cottage—"

"You own the cottage still," Nick pointed out evenly, "so it's yours to do with as you please once I leave. As for the position: you've had my labour in return. The salary you paid me was the same as anyone else would've got."

For a moment they stared at each other, Nick implacable and Godfrey fuming. Godfrey was first to look away. Nick wondered what he was thinking. If he had any regrets. Probably not. Godfrey Tremain was not a man given to regrets. He was a man who believed himself right in all things and would defend his decisions to the bitter end, no matter how poorly made they might be.

He waved a hand now. "Fine, have the wages."

"Grand. I'll take them," Nick said. "Since I've earned them."

Godfrey just scowled, keeping his face averted, staring instead outside the window.

There was a long silence then. Just as Nick was about to break it—to take his leave—Godfrey finally spoke again, his voice gruff.

"Are you ever going to come back?"

He didn't so much as glance at Nick, but kept his gaze directed out the window, at the moody Cornish sky that was sending down a steady drizzle of rain. He looked old and melancholy.

"I don't know," Nick said honestly.

Godfrey closed his eyes. For a moment Nick thought that, perhaps, he minded Nick going. Maybe even that he was going to ask Nick not to leave. But in the end all he said was, "You'd better get back to work then."

Nick nodded once and left the old man alone.

Out of habit, he headed out via the kitchens. Mrs. Hughes was extracting a tray of figgy hoggans from the oven, and the familiar scent of warm, spiced pastry filled the air. It was a scent Nick had always associated with Tremain House. For some reason, today, it made him feel hollow and sad.

He stood there in the doorway to the kitchens, watching Mrs. Hughes close the door of the huge cooking range while two kitchen maids chattered and peeled vegetables at the table. He'd been coming to this kitchen since he was eleven years old. Back then, the cook had been an old battle-axe, Mrs. Crowe. Mrs. Hughes had come when Nick was seventeen and had just started working with the old steward, Mr. Lang. She had always been kind to him.

Catching sight of Nick, Mrs. Hughes smiled wide and beckoned him in.

"Have a cuppa, Mr. 'Earn?"

He shook his head and tried to force a smile. "No, thank you, Mrs. Hughes. I need to be off."

"Well, take an 'oggan at least," she urged, and he let her press one into his hands.

Snow was waiting patiently outside the kitchen door. He lumbered to his feet at the sight of Nick, giving his characteristic little grunt-wheeze of pleasure, and trotted to his side, giving the hoggan a hopeful look with his single eye.

Nick sighed. "These aren't for dogs, you know," he said. But he still tore a piece off and let Snow have it, rubbing the dog's silky ears as they ate.

"Come on," he said at last, patting his thigh. He might have just handed in his notice, but he was still steward here for a little longer and now needed to see Godritch about an extra field Godfrey had agreed to let to Jessop. There were papers to be drawn up—Godfrey always wanted everything tied up right and tight. "Let's go to the stables, Snow. You can wait with Gid while I ride over to the village."

It was late afternoon now and the stables were quiet with

most of the heavy tasks already done for the day. The stable lads sat on the grass on the sunny side of the courtyard, polishing tack, while Gid and John the groom played fivestones.

"You wantin' an 'oss?" Gid called as Nick approached.

"*Ayes.*"

"Is Val all right for you? 'E's needin' some exercise."

Nick nodded. "He'll do fine."

"Jem!" Gid yelled. The boy looked up from across the courtyard and started to rise, but Nick waved him back down.

"I'll get him," he said.

Gid shrugged. "Suit yourself."

He wasn't sure why he'd taken the notion to do Jem's job for him, but he quite enjoyed the old familiar rhythms of saddling up a horse. As he did so, he found himself thinking again, as he had in the kitchens, of how long he'd been coming to Tremain House, and of the years—six of them—he'd spent working in these stables, summer and winter.

God, those winters. Mucking out stables and carrying heavy buckets of ice-cold water and getting chilblains. Those had been some hard days for a young lad. And lessons after besides.

"Oh good, I caught you before you left!"

Nick looked over his shoulder.

Isabella.

"Well now, Miss Bella," he said. "What a pleasant surprise."

"Don't give me that," she said crossly. "You've got Grandy in a terrible tizz. What's this nonsense about you leaving?"

Nick turned back to his work, tightening the straps on Valentine's tack. "Oh, he'll be fine. He just needs to get used to the idea. You know how he is."

Isabella sighed. "Sometimes you're wilfully obtuse. He's upset. Don't you care about that at all?"

"Not much," Nick replied.

"Well, you should."

"Why?"

"You know why!" Isabella snapped. "You and I are the only people Grandy cares for even a little."

Frowning, Nick stepped out of Val's stall and faced her. "He might care about you, but make no mistake, I'm just a servant in this house."

Isabella scoffed, "You don't really think that."

Anger surged at that. "I don't just think it," he snapped. "I *know* it."

Isabella actually flinched at his tone, her expression so surprised it was almost funny.

"Nick, you can't think that! You're the only person he ever listens to for one thing!"

Nick gave a bark of laughter at her rose-coloured view of the world. "I've worked for the old man a long time," he said. "And I've learned how to get his ear. That's just what we *servants* do."

She eyed him unhappily. "Can you at least tell me *why* you're going?"

Nick regarded her as he turned that question over in his mind. Isabella was six years his junior, a bright, pretty, spoiled young woman with the world at her feet. She was the apple of Godfrey's eye, and he'd always indulged her shamelessly, showering her with gifts. When she was very small, and had taken an unaccountable liking to Nick, Nick had been outwardly offhand with her, but secretly fascinated by this tiny, demanding queen. But there had always been—on his side at least—a tension between them too. And yes, a resentment.

She was his cousin, his blood. And yet he would always be her social inferior. Part of the Tremain clan, but never truly one of them. Just as he would never be one of the villagers, even though he'd lived there all his life and played with the village children when he was a boy.

"I don't belong here, Bella," he said roughly.

She blinked. "What?"

"I don't belong here," Nick repeated. "Not really. I'll always be Darklis Hearn's Gypsy bastard in this place." He shrugged, feigning unconcern.

"Nick," she whispered. "I don't—I don't know what to say."

Somehow he managed to huff out a laugh. "Well, that makes a nice change. I've never known a more talkative person than you."

She gave a choked laugh of her own. "Grandy says I should try to be more like you—learn to keep my own counsel. Oh Nick, he does care about you, you know! He just can't show it, or say it—it's not his way."

Nick sighed heavily. "It's nice that you want to believe that, but the truth, as far as the old man's concerned, is that I'm an embarrassment. Jacob's Gypsy by-blow. Godfrey gave me a job and a home, and though I never asked for it, I wasn't too proud to take it, not when he got my labour in return. But he doesn't owe me anything, Bella, and I don't owe him or anyone else. Truth is, I'm free as a bird. There's nothing holding me to this place." He smiled weakly. "Isn't that grand?"

She shook her head. "I've seen you walking the cliffs, Nick. I walked them with you when I was a girl sometimes, and if ever someone was in love with a place, it's you. You love the Tremain land, and these horses and—" she looked around, found Snow lying dozing in the corner of the stable, pointed at him "—that ugly dog, and—and Grandy and me, a little bit too, I think. That's what's holding you here, or what should be."

Was that what held you to a place. Loving things?

Loving people?

Was that what made you belong? If so, then why did he feel lonelier than ever when he thought about what and who he loved?

And Christ, was it only two weeks since Truro?

It felt like a lifetime.

Isabella gazed at him hopefully, and he felt a strange mixture of emotions at that look, because perhaps he did love her a little, but sometimes he hated her a little too. For never seeming to mind that he worked in the stables while she just played there, or that he'd been schooled in the evenings after a long day of labour while she was taught French by a fancy governess and had dancing and drawing lessons, and Harry was sent off to school with the sons of the great and the good.

Perhaps she saw something of his thoughts on his face, because her own fell, and for a moment she looked so like the little girl she'd once been that, despite himself, he found himself sighing and saying, "You're a pain in the neck, Bella, but I suppose I don't mind you too much."

The hurt expression faded at that, though she still looked heartbroken.

"Oh, cheer up," he said, injecting a bit of humour into his voice. "I bet you won't even miss me once I'm gone!" He even managed a grin then, though he wondered how convincing it could possibly be.

"I wouldn't be sad if I thought you wanted to leave," she said. "But I don't think you do. Everything and everyone you love is here, Nick."

She had listed all those everythings and everyones a moment ago, but she'd missed the most important one. The one who dominated his thoughts every day. The one who made his heart wrench whenever Nick thought of him.

The one who was the reason he couldn't bear to stay another day.

Isabella thought that love was what held you to a place, and maybe that was true, mostly. But sometimes it was the very thing that drove you away.

CHAPTER TWENTY-THREE

22ⁿᵈ July 1853

Nick wanted to walk along the cliff tops one last time before he left Trevathany, but when he rose from his bed on the day of his departure, it was to find that a thick mist had rolled in from the sea, shrouding the coastal path in a dense, white veil. His planned walk—the one he'd intended to be a farewell to the only home he'd ever known—became instead a ghostly thing. As sure-footed as he was, he couldn't see further than two feet in front of him and eventually he turned back, disappointed.

Over the course of the morning, the mist slowly cleared, but as it did so, the sky grew steadily darker, the air thickening with the close, heavy promise of bad weather. It seemed, Nick thought, that Ward was going to get his storm, at long last. And if Nick was any judge, it was going to be a bad one.

The coach wasn't due to leave till four o'clock, so at noon, Nick went down to the village for a walk around and a tankard of ale at the Admiral's Arms.

"I hear yer off," Martha Trevylyn said, as she set his ale down on the bar and held her hand out for his coin.

"*Ayes*," Nick said.

"Talkative feller, aren'tcha?" Martha said, laughing.

Nick grinned at her. "*Ayes*," he agreed, and tipped back his tankard.

"Where are you goin'?" she persisted.

"Penzance," he said, offering the minimum information.

She seemed to consider that a moment. "Jed 'Ammet, said you was goin' to join your Gypsy folk. Is that right then?"

"Reckon it is," he agreed.

"You travelled with them before?"

He shook his head.

"You better watch yourself then," she said, with a sage nod. "I know you're half Gypsy, but the fact is, you're more like one of us, what with you growing up in the village. Not like your mother, rest her soul. She was always a wild one."

Nick knew that Martha meant her warning kindly, but he was glad when she was called away to serve another customer before he could answer her. He raised his tankard and drank.

A little later, Gid Paget walked in.

"Well, look who it is!" he cried. "I thought you'd gone." He clapped Nick on the shoulder.

"I'm leaving today," Nick said. "Coach doesn't go till four though."

Gid grinned. "You sure you don't want to stay? Old Godfrey's been unbearable since Wednesday. In a right temper, 'e is."

Wednesday had been Nick's last day. Godfrey had sulked in his study, never showing his face and never summoning Nick. When he'd finished up, Nick had considered going to see him uninvited, but in the end, he'd decided against it. It had been drilled into him over the years that if Godfrey wanted him, he'd call for him. There was no reason to change things now. He'd made it halfway down the drive before Isabella came racing after him.

"Come and say good-bye, Nick, please," she'd begged. "He's being a stubborn old fool, but I know he wants to see you."

"You don't know what you're talking about, Bella," he'd replied, and strode off, leaving her staring after him.

Now, he raised a brow at Gid Paget, and said, "Not likely. Where I'm going, there's going to be no orders from anyone. It'll be bleddy heaven."

Gid laughed. "Ah, it sounds it. I envy you."

They shared an ale together before Nick took his leave. After he left the inn, he walked another circuit of the village, chatting to the few villagers he saw on his way, confirming that yes, he'd given up his position with the Tremains and was off on his travels. And yes, Snow was going with him, and it would be grand indeed to be free to do as he pleased for a while.

The clouds were still heavy and dark with the threat of rain, but Nick walked on, down to the mill stream where he used to meet Gabe sometimes. Strange, how difficult it was to remember those nights with Gabe now. All he could think of, when he tried, was Ward. Ward standing here, half-shadowed in the trees, his cheeks burning as he admitted spying on Nick. Waiting at the top of the staircase at Helston House, bathed in golden sunlight. Tangled in the bedsheets beneath Nick, his warm eyes shining with happiness and his hair all mussed from their lovemaking.

Nick's chest ached with longing. He felt so broken he wondered if he would ever be whole again. When Gabe had left Trevathany, Nick had been unhappy, but not like this. He'd still been able to go about his daily business without thinking of Gabe, only feeling miserable at night as he lay alone in bed. When Gabe had gone, he'd mostly missed being touched, and having someone to talk to who understood his secret desires. Missing Ward was an entirely different thing. Towards the end, he'd come to feel as though he belonged to Ward, and Ward to him. That together, they were more than just Ward and Nick. A mated pair, perhaps, like the black swans that graced the village pond.

That was what he missed. Not just the companionship of someone like himself, but *his mate*. No one else would do.

He had to get away. Had to try to find a new place in the world, or at least fill his days with so many new things that he wouldn't have so much as a moment to dwell on his unhappiness. However he might feel now, he knew, rationally, that time would pass and things would get better. That was life. You lost people, and you had to live on. It was just that now, in this moment, it felt impossible.

Nick stood there, on the bank of the stream, and watched the water slowly moving past, the surface glassy smooth. He tried out a thought.

One day, the knowledge that I'll never see him again won't hurt.

His heart was unconvinced. It ached in a hollow way, pulsing with misery. He wondered if anyone passing would guess at his distress, or if they would just see a man standing quietly, peacefully, watching the water glide past.

Ward stared out the window of his study. The clouds were heavy and dark, but it still hadn't rained. It would though. The water swelled inside the clouds, dragging them down low in the sky. The air was oppressive. There was going to be a storm. The sort of storm Ward had been hoping and praying for since he'd arrived in Trevathany.

"You haven't eaten a bite."

Ward turned away from the window to find Pipp standing in the doorway, frowning at the untouched luncheon tray that sat on the desk where he'd deposited it the last time he'd come in. The soup in the dainty china tureen had gone cold and the neat little sandwiches were curled at the corners.

Ward shrugged. "I wasn't hungry."

Pipp pressed his lips together and marched over to the tray. "You barely ate any breakfast either," he accused.

"I'll eat at dinner," Ward said vaguely.

Pipp sniffed. "You're getting too thin."

"I'm fine."

"You've got no appetite and you mope around all day. It's about time—"

"I said I'm fine!"

Pipp sniffed again, unimpressed, but he lifted the tray and stalked out the room without another word. When the door closed behind him, Ward returned to staring out the window.

It had been a bad couple of weeks. Since his return from Truro, he'd been... melancholy. Melancholy in a way he couldn't remember feeling before, unable to concentrate on his work at all, his mind filled with thoughts of what had happened in Truro, and of how Nicholas had looked at him just before he left the inn to catch the stagecoach.

Ward's chest ached at the memory, every time.

He turned from the window. Whatever his inclination, he would have to work today. The great storm he'd been waiting for all these months was finally gathering.

He would go down the Zawn. Get himself as close to the conditions he'd experienced on board the *Archimedes* as he possibly could. He was going to open himself up to George—reach out to his brother's spirit with everything he had. He didn't need anyone else to help him do that. Didn't need Nicholas Hearn.

But, oh, how he *wanted* him.

Ward sank into the chair behind his desk and closed his eyes. Every time he thought of his behaviour at the séance and later, at the inn, he was filled with self-loathing. Self-loathing and the despairing knowledge that he had alienated Nicholas forever. That Nicholas was finished with him.

"In your eyes, you are the master and I am the servant. That's how things started between us, and nothing's changed."

That wasn't true—it *wasn't*—but over these last weeks he'd thought about that night, and everything that had gone before, and now he could see how high-handed and autocratic he'd been from the first. Hell, he'd even let Nicholas believe he was prepared to resort to blackmail to get what he wanted, so why should Nicholas think the best of him now, because it suited Ward for him to do so?

Outside, the sky was growing darker by the minute, and the air had an oddly still, yet threatening quality to it. The storm was coming—it was time he got going.

He rose from his chair and slowly began to pack his knapsack—he was all but ready when the first rumble of thunder came, with the low, threatening growl of a great beast. A few moments of quiet followed, then the rain came. Hard and fast. The sort of downpour that would drench someone in half a minute or less.

Hoisting his knapsack over his shoulder, he headed downstairs. He found Pipp and Mrs. Waddell in the kitchen, drinking tea at the scrubbed oak table.

"Pipp," he said from the doorway. "I need my mackintosh and boots. I'm going down the Zawn."

Pipp startled at the sound of his voice, then looked over his shoulder at Ward and glared. "You're not supposed to come in here, Master Edward," he complained, getting to his feet. "You're supposed to ring."

"I'd get them myself, but I don't know where you keep them," Ward grumbled back.

Pipp disappeared into the boot room, emerging moments later with a long mackintosh coat, hat, boots, and an umbrella.

"You're not really going down that bloody great cave in

this weather, are you?" Pipp asked worriedly. "What if one of those platforms falls down?"

Ward shook his head and reached for the coat. "They won't. They're perfectly safe."

"How can you be sure?" Pipp insisted while Ward began fastening the buttons. "Have you seen how bad the rain is? What if it washes all the mud and rocks away and loosens the fixings?"

"The platforms are all bolted securely into the bedrock," Ward said calmly, pulling on the boots now. "None of them are going anywhere."

Pipp continued to mutter unhappily about how ridiculous this all was, and how could Ward expect to take notes in these conditions anyway, but Ward just ignored him, and soon he was about as waterproofed as he could be, the mackintosh covering his body down to below his knees, the boots covering the rest of his legs, and an oilskin hat pulled low over his brow. He waved away the umbrella Pipp tried to press on him.

Another long rumble of thunder sounded. Pipp looked troubled.

"What if you're struck by a lightning bolt?" he asked, frowning.

"There's not even been any lightning yet," Ward pointed out. "And besides, that's what the lightning rods are for. They should draw any strikes well away from where I'll be, inside the Zawn."

Despite the persistent melancholy that had dogged him these last weeks, now that he was ready to go, a glimmer of Ward's old enthusiasm began to return, a stirring of the familiar excitement at the prospect of imminent discovery.

He offered Pipp a smile. "Don't worry, I'll be careful."

Pipp sniffed, but some of his tension eased.

~

He was halfway to the Zawn when he saw her: a young woman on a grey horse, soaked to the skin, her red hair half-up, half-down, long strands of it plastered to her pale face. Her elegant riding habit was sodden, and a tiny, crushed hat with a broken feather listed from her ruined coiffure.

As she drew closer, he saw she was frightened—frantic even.

"Are you all right, miss?" he called.

She came closer, halting her mount beside him. "Thank God I saw you!" she gasped. "I need help—I thought I'd have to go back to the village. My grandfather's been thrown by his horse—he's hurt! Please, will you come? He's very near."

"Of course," Ward said. "Where is he?"

"Scarce more than two hundred yards." She pointed in the direction she'd come from. "We can both ride Cally if you like."

Ward shook his head. "Since he's so close I'll stay afoot. Lead the way."

She nodded and turned her mount, setting off, Ward following at a brisk pace.

He saw the riderless horse first, its reins trailing on the ground, then the man lying there, unmoving. Christ, was he dead?

The rain was coming down in sheets, the thunder rumbling incessantly Ahead of him, the young woman dismounted and rushed to her grandfather's side.

As Ward drew nearer, he realised he knew the man. It was Godfrey Tremain. He'd called on Ward a few weeks after his arrival in the village to welcome him. They'd shared a polite half hour's conversation during which Ward had been struck by the old man's light-grey eyes, so much like Nicholas's.

Now those eyes were closed, the big, raw-boned frame ominously still.

Isabella Tremain—he assumed it was she—looked up at him, terrified eyes huge in her white face. "When he fell, he struck his head on a rock. I couldn't rouse him, but he was breathing when I left him."

Ward dropped to his knees beside her and bent to examine the old man. He was still breathing, thank God, though he looked to be in a bad way, a large, purplish bruise marring one side of his face. He mumbled inaudibly when Ward asked if he could hear him, but his eyes stayed closed and his complexion was waxy, his breathing thready.

"You'll be all right, Grandy," Miss Tremain assured him shakily as Ward checked him for broken bones. "We'll have you all sorted out in no time."

Godfrey just gave a faint moan.

"His limbs seem sound, but he could have injured his back or neck," Ward told Miss Tremain. "We'll have to be careful how we move him. I'll ride to Helston House and bring a carriage back for him while someone runs down to the village to fetch the doctor. Can you wait here with him while I'm gone? I'll be back as soon as I can."

She nodded. "Thank you, Sir Edward—you are Sir Edward, aren't you?"

He nodded. "Yes, and you are Miss Tremain. I am sorry to make your acquaintance in such circumstances."

She swallowed and nodded. "Take my horse," she said. "I don't want you getting thrown too."

While Ward, Pipp, and William the groom fetched Godfrey Tremain back to Helston House in the carriage, Mrs. Waddell readied a room for him on the ground floor. There were no bedchambers there so the bed was a narrow truckle one, but it meant they didn't have to jostle him more, carrying him upstairs.

Dr. Ferguson arrived soon after. Ward waited outside in the corridor with Miss Tremain, now dressed in a clean, dry gown provided by Mrs. Waddell, while the doctor examined the old man.

Every now and again the thunder would roll, and he would have to bite the inside of his cheek to keep himself from groaning his frustration that he was sitting here, instead of out in the storm, doing his work. Hopefully he would be able to escape soon—once the doctor had emerged to give his verdict, and Ward had dealt with whatever immediate arrangements were needed for the benefit of his unexpected guests. But even then, by that time, the storm might be over. Christ, but he could scream.

"I should have tried harder to stop him going out," Miss Tremain muttered, wringing her hands. "But he insisted he wanted to go riding despite the storm clouds, so I said I'd go with him. I didn't imagine for a moment that this would happen! There's no way a startled horse would've been able to throw Grandy in the old days, but he was all riled up about Nick and not paying attention—"

"Nick?" Ward repeated, his heart in his mouth. "You mean Nicholas Hearn?"

She looked at him. "Yes, do you know him? He was Grandy's—" a brief pause "—steward."

"Yes, I know him. Why was your grandfather upset about him?"

"Nick handed in his notice a fortnight ago. Told Grandy he was leaving Trevathany for good."

"He's leaving?" Ward croaked.

"He's already gone. He left today."

Ward's stomach turned over, and a lump rose in his throat. Thankfully, the door to the chamber opened and Dr. Ferguson stepped out before Miss Tremain could notice his reaction.

She jumped to her feet and went to the doctor. "How is he?" she demanded, her voice cracking with emotion.

The doctor looked grave. "Your grandfather has had a bad

fall, Miss Tremain. He was not entirely conscious during my examination. To be frank, I'm very concerned about him."

"Did he say anything?" she whispered.

"Yes. He asked for Mr. Hearn." After a pause, he added, "He was quite insistent about needing to see him, when he managed to speak at all. Do you think someone could fetch Mr. Hearn? I fear there may not be much time left for your grandfather."

Miss Tremain let out a little sob of distress and covered her mouth, her eyes filling with tears as she shook her head. She swallowed hard, getting herself under control, then said thickly, "Nick left Trevathany on the coach late this afternoon. I'm not even sure where he'll be by now."

Ward's mind raced. Despite Nicholas's insistence that he was no more than a servant to Godfrey Tremain, Ward had realised from his conversations with Nicholas that the relationship between the two men was more complicated than that. Nicholas felt something for the old man—of that, Ward was sure. So, if old Godfrey Tremain wanted to speak his heart to Nicholas before he died, shouldn't Ward do whatever he could to make sure Nicholas at least got the chance to grant that request before it was too late?

Even if that meant Ward missing out on the chance to go down the Zawn in the only storm he'd seen since he'd come to Trevathany months before?

"I'll go after the stagecoach and fetch him back," he blurted.

Isabella turned him. "Would you, Sir Edward?" she whispered, her damp eyes full of hope. "I'd be so grateful."

He nodded. "It's the least I can do."

CHAPTER TWENTY-FOUR

The stagecoach to Truro was very slow and very crowded. In this weather, it was also very wet. There were numerous leaks in the roof of the old carriage that let in the rain. It trickled down the corners of the carriage walls, pooling on the floor, and dripped from several places in the ceiling too. The passengers sat in hunched misery, angling their hats to stop the water running down their necks. There was much grumbling in the dark.

The stagecoach windows were obscured by scraps of curtain, but even if they hadn't been, Nick wouldn't have been able to see where they were. As if it were not enough that the stars and moon were obscured by the thick storm clouds, the driving sheets of rain made it impossible to see more than a few feet ahead.

Poor Snow shivered at Nick's feet, cold and miserable—though at least not barking or vomiting, thankfully. The floor of the carriage was wet and cold but when Nick had tried to have Snow on his knee, the other passengers had complained. He was lucky the coachman had allowed Snow on at all, he supposed. That was mainly thanks to the additional coins he'd slipped to the driver before they left.

The rain hammered on the roof of the carriage ceaselessly, a loud drumming that prevented either conversation or sleep. It was so loud that it took time for the sound of approaching horses' hooves to penetrate. Nick lifted his head, listening. Heard a distant male voice calling out, "Hold up! Whoa there!"

The passengers sat up, shifting in their seats, alarmed. What was this? Highwaymen?

The large woman next to Nick began to fret as the stage-coach slowed. "What's 'e stopping for?" she demanded of no one in particular. "They're not supposed to stop, are they?"

At length the stagecoach came to a halt. There was a rumble of voices outside—the coachman and whoever had been hailing him, Nick surmised, though with the rain hammering on the roof, he couldn't make out what they were saying.

A few moments later the door of the stagecoach opened and—to Nick's utter astonishment—there stood Ward.

It was dark as could be, both inside and outside the coach, but Nick knew him instantly despite the gloom. There were a hundred tiny clues in the outline of his form and the shad-owed planes of his face and in the way he held himself. In the slow sweep of his head as he looked over the huddled group of wet, miserable passengers.

In the way he froze when his gaze landed on Nick.

"Ward?" Nick said. "What are you doing here?"

"Nicholas— I—" He broke off, then a moment later said hoarsely, "Your grandfather's had an accident."

For a moment, Nick was genuinely bewildered. "My grandfather?" he said stupidly. Then, "You mean, Godfrey?"

Ward nodded. "He was thrown from his horse near Helston House. Your cousin came to me for help."

Nick felt as though his brain wasn't working. "Why are you here?"

"I've come to fetch you. Godfrey's asking for you."

"For *me*?" He was genuinely astonished by that. "Did he strike his head? Ward, I doubt it's me he wants. He'll be confused."

A pause.

"The doctor said it was you he wanted." Those rasped words were harsh and toneless, but for some reason, Nick felt soothed by them, by their quiet certainty.

"I suppose I'd better come then." His heart was pounding so hard, it was a surprise to hear how calm his voice came out. He began to extricate himself from his wedged-in position. "Come on, Snow."

"I think Snowflake had better stay with William," Ward said.

"William?"

"He rode down with me," Ward explained as Nick shuffled past the other passengers to the open door where Ward stood. "You'll ride his horse back with me while he takes your seat to the next stop. Then he'll get the next stagecoach back to Trevathany with your luggage and Snowflake."

"I'm not sure about that, Ward," Nick said. "Snow doesn't know William." He jumped down, landing in the mud next to Ward and no doubt covering them both in filthy splashes— the road was already a quagmire.

"The doctor said we need to be quick," was Ward's reply.

"Is Godfrey going to *die*?" Nick asked, surprised to find how hollow, how bereft that thought made him feel, when Godfrey had only ever treated him like a favoured servant, and sometimes not even that.

"I don't know," Ward said simply. He didn't offer anything else. No platitudes. No promises. Just the plain, unvarnished truth.

Snow's familiar grunt-wheeze made Nick turn back to the coach. The dog stood at the open door of the coach, shifting anxiously, his noisy breaths edged with a soft whine.

"Don't worry, Nicholas," Ward said. "William will take very good care of him. Won't you, William?"

Ward's groom nodded, striding past. "I will, sir."

William climbed into the stagecoach then, pausing to ruffle Snow's ears and take hold of his collar before settling into Nick's empty seat, with Snow at his feet. Snow gave one of his rarely heard whines and the heartbroken sound wrenched at Nick. He swallowed hard against the sudden lump in his throat. He hated leaving Snow, but he couldn't ride at any sort of pace and keep the dog safely beside him, especially in this weather. Snow shot him one last betrayed look as Ward shut the door behind them.

"Come on," Ward said, tugging at Nick's forearm. "The horses are over here."

~

It turned out that the stagecoach hadn't gone nearly as far as Nick had thought. The ride back to Helston House took little more than an hour. It certainly helped that they didn't have to contend with wheels that might get stuck in mud, and that their mounts were big, hardy beasts built for strength and stamina. Nick watched Ward's horsemanship with interest. He wasn't the natural horseman that Nick was, but he was competent and confident. Fully in charge of his animal.

As they rode, the rain continued to fall incessantly and the thunder rolled, over and over. Twice they saw flashes of lightning over the sea.

Ward had been waiting for a storm like this for months, but instead of working, he was here, fetching Nick back. Nick wasn't sure what to make of that, and he couldn't ask. The weather put paid to any chance at conversation.

It was just after nine o'clock when they finally reached Helston House. A boy was waiting for them as soon as they arrived to take charge of the horses, and Mr. Pipp stood at the front door.

Nick followed Ward up the steps and into the hall.

"How is he?" Ward asked Mr. Pipp once the butler had closed the door behind them.

"Hanging on, sir," the servant said gravely. He turned to Nick, his expression kind. "Let me take your coat," he said, letting his usual formal air drop away. "The sooner you get in there, the better."

Nick's gloveless hands were icy and numb from gripping the reins, but somehow, falteringly, he managed to work the buttons of his coat free, and shrug the sodden thing off into Mr. Pipp's waiting hands. He was just about as wet beneath his coat after riding through that deluge, and he shivered with cold.

"He needs fresh clothes," Ward said.

"No time," Mr. Pipp replied without ceremony. "Wrap this round yourself, lad." He handed Nick a woollen blanket, and Nick shook it out before wrapping it round himself like a cape.

"This way," Mr. Pipp said, and Nick followed him across the chequered marble floor and down the corridor of the west wing, his gut twisting with nerves. He was still finding it difficult to believe that Godfrey had asked for him. That of all people, it was Nick he wanted to see. Worse, a part of him—a small, mean part—felt like thumbing his nose at the request and walking away. But you didn't do that to a man who was, it seemed, on his deathbed. Nick knew he'd regret it forever if he refused such a simple, final request.

Mr. Pipp stopped in front of a closed door and softly knocked.

A moment later, the door opened to reveal Isabella. Her red hair was loose about her shoulders and she wore a simple maid's gown. It gave him the oddest feeling, seeing her dressed like that. This was how she'd have looked if she'd been born into the same circumstances as himself. He almost expected her to bob a curtsey, but instead she reached for him, taking hold of his shirtsleeve and pulling him inside.

"Thank God," she said. "Come in. He's been barely holding on, waiting for you."

Godfrey had been accommodated in a small sitting room. A chaise longue and a writing desk had been pushed back to make room for the truckle bed on which he lay. Eyes closed, breathing laboured, his thick mane of hair was like tarnished silver against the pillow beneath his head, and his skin had a waxy, clammy look to it.

Dr. Ferguson was sitting by the bed, but at Nick's entrance, he rose and stepped to the side, ceding his place.

"Mr. Tremain has been asking for you," he said, and Nick felt the same stab of disbelief in response to that assurance that he'd felt when Ward had said it.

Nick looked at the empty chair, then glanced uncertainly at Isabella. She gave him a nod of encouragement, and after a brief pause, he sat himself down, perching on the edge and looking down at the old man.

He cleared his throat. "It's Nick here," he said. "I hear you've been asking for me."

Godfrey's eyelids fluttered, and his hand on the blanket twitched. A long, silent moment passed then, impossibly quietly, Godfrey breathed his name. "Nick."

"*Ayes,*" Nick said gently. And then, because it seemed the right thing to do, he set his own hand on Godfrey's, something he'd never done before.

The old man's hand was cold, the pouchy, liver-spotted skin unexpectedly soft. Nick stroked it with his thumb, thinking, oddly, how this reminded him of stroking Snow's velvety ears.

"Wish I'd—" Godfrey began. Paused for breath. "—owned you to the world."

Pain stabbed Nick in the heart, stabbed him there and twisted so hard he felt like a fish being gutted.

"It doesn't matter," he said.

"Does," Godfrey whispered, his laboured breathing making it clear how difficult every word was to utter. "You're like me."

Like Godfrey? Christ, no!

Nick patted the old man's hand and said softly, "Not I. I'm a feckless Gypsy, just like you always said." He said it lightly, almost fondly, but long-held resentment soured the words in his mouth, and he wondered if Godfrey heard that bitter echo.

Godfrey shook his head minutely and turned his hand, clutching Nick's fingers. "I mean... you love this place." Long pause. "Like I do."

Nick was silent. He did love this place. He loved Tremain House, and the harsh, rocky coastline, and the tumbledown village he'd grown up in. He felt connected to these places in ways he couldn't express in mere words. That feeling of connection went beyond the land and the sea and all the little piles of bricks and mortar that made up Trevathany. He felt connected to this grim old man too, and to the tearful girl standing by the door, and to the villagers he'd grown up with. But now, most deeply, he felt connected to Ward. When the stagecoach had rumbled out of Trevathany earlier today, it was Ward who had been the first of all those everyones and everythings he had mourned, as well as the reason he'd needed to leave.

"I changed my will last week," Godfrey went on. "Been thinking about it since I sold this land to Car—Carrick." He had to stop for a bit then, breathing hard for a good half a minute before he was able to go on. "Left you the rest of the plot that you've been on at me to start working."

Astonished, Nick could only stare at him for several long moments. "What?" he said at last. "*Why*?"

Godfrey got his stubborn look. "You said you—" another pause "—wanted to farm it."

"But I'm not a Tremain. You always said you wanted to keep everything in the Tremain name. You didn't even want to sell this bit to Wa—Sir Edward at first." Nick felt himself flush at his betraying almost-use of Ward's name, but Godfrey didn't seem to notice.

"You're the only one who ever gave a damn for the place," he wheezed.

"Oh Grandy, that's not true!" Isabella interrupted, stepping closer. Nick glanced at her. Her face was white, her lips pressed together in a thin line. She looked genuinely hurt by Godfrey's comment, but Godfrey just waved her off with a weak gesture.

"He's the only *man* who gives damn," he muttered, and Isabella stared at Godfrey unhappily, her throat working.

Godfrey clutched at Nick's hand, the grip of his cold fingers weak but determined. "Stay here," he whispered fiercely. "Your name might be Hearn, but—but underneath that Gypsy skin, you've a good bit of me in you." He gave a harsh laugh. "Twice what Harry's got."

"Grandy—" Isabella began.

"Hush," Godfrey told her. "I'll have no complaints from you. You've a dowry fit for a duchess, and Harry's getting the rest. I just want—"

"I'm not complaining," she protested.

He went on as though she hadn't spoken, his eyes boring into Nick's. "I want *you* to have a bit of it. Something you can pass on to your children. And them to theirs."

Nick stared at Godfrey. At this old man who had dominated his life for so long. He'd been giving Nick scraps from the Tremain table for years and years. And yes, arguably this was just another scrap—the land he was supposedly leaving Nick was far from ideal farmland—but still, it was quite a recognition. About as public a declaration of Nick's paternity as Godfrey would ever make.

But why now? Right at the end of his life, and only after Nick had handed in his notice and left Trevathany once and for all. Had he intended to try to lure Nick back? But if so, why not just tell him before he'd gone?

"You're like me... You're the only one who ever gave a damn for the place."

Perhaps Godfrey had decided that Nick was his legacy—more of a legacy in some ways than Harry. Oh, Harry would carry on the Tremain name, but Nick would carry on something else. Perhaps something that, in Godfrey's eyes, was more essential, more personal than that precious family name.

Perhaps Nick was to be the keeper of Godfrey's dreams.

That was what happened when people saw death coming. They wanted their dreams to live on. It was the same with his mother. In those last weeks of her life, she'd become preoccupied with her estranged family and had begged Nick to go and find them when she was gone. It was why he'd headed for Penzance as soon as he'd decided to leave Trevathany. For more than a year now, that old dream of Ma's had been sitting in his pocket, demanding to be fulfilled.

But you couldn't live other people's dreams for them, he realised. It was hard enough to find your own dream. Hard enough to give it voice and pursue it. That was one of the things he admired about Ward. That Ward saw what he wanted and acted on it, even if what he wanted didn't meet with other people's approval. Even if it made no damned sense. At least he *had* a dream—what did Nick have?

What did Nick want for himself?

The answer was already in his heart, waiting. He didn't even need to think about it.

He wanted his mate. He wanted Ward.

He wanted love and a home. Wanted that ever-elusive

sense of belonging he'd only truly felt for the first time in Ward's arms.

And maybe, perhaps, Ward wanted that too? Nick would never have dared hope for that before tonight, but tonight Ward had come for him. On the night of the storm Ward had been waiting for since he'd arrived in Trevathany, he'd abandoned the work that had driven his every moment for the last year and instead ridden out into the night to find Nick, to bring him here, to his dying grandfather.

"Nick—"

His name was a whisper, carried on the lightest of breaths. A sigh, almost.

Nick looked down at the old man again. Godfrey was fading. His eyes were clouding over, growing vague.

"Bella," Nick said without turning. "Come here."

She came to his side, putting her hand to Godfrey's cheek. "Grandy."

Together they looked down at the old man.

"Ni—" he tried again, watery eyes pleading.

In this moment, Nick wanted only to be generous. He said carefully, "I won't leave, Godfrey. I'll stay for good and work that land."

The old man's tight, pained expression eased.

And then he was gone.

CHAPTER TWENTY-FIVE

From *The Collected Writings of Sir Edward Carrick,* volume I

In the following months, I became so preoccupied with finding a scientific explanation for what I had experienced on board on the *Archimedes* and at the séance conducted by Mrs. Haydn, that I entirely abandoned the work I had been pursuing for so many years before that. Disenchanted with London and with the circles I moved in at that time, and having inherited my father's sizeable fortune and title, I purchased a plot of land in Cornwall with the intention of pursuing my new studies there. In the spring of 1853, I began my new life.

~

Isabella Tremain was crying. Not in a pretty, ladylike way, but with great wrenching sobs that made her whole body shake. Ward stood aside, bowing his head in respect, as Mrs. Waddell led her upstairs, to the bedchamber that had been prepared for her.

It was over then.

A few moments later, Nicholas emerged into the hall where Ward had been pacing, waiting for news. Unlike his cousin, Nicholas was calm and silent, the only sound from him the quiet click of his boot heels on the marble floor. When he caught sight of Ward, he straightened slightly, his body growing somehow more attentive, more aware.

"He's dead," he said bluntly.

Ward nodded. "I thought as much. Miss Tremain seemed very upset."

Nicholas rubbed the back of his neck. He looked tired, and Ward wished he could step forward and put his arms around him. Wished he had the right to touch him with kindness and concern. To offer comfort. But there was an invisible barrier between them now that couldn't be breached. All Ward could do was stand on the other side, watching as Nicholas managed his own grief and exhaustion.

He cleared his throat. "Pipp's made a bedchamber up for you. Why don't you go and sleep? You look exhausted."

But Nicholas shook his head and said, "Let's go to the Zawn."

Ward blinked. That was the last thing he'd expected to hear.

"You've waited months for a storm like this," Nicholas went on. The corner of his mouth twitched with a small, rueful smile. "The least I can do is see you through what's left of it."

For a moment Ward was silent, then he said, "The worst of it's already passed, I think. It's just the rain left."

Nicholas shook his head. "I think there may be more to come. Possibly not, but it's worth a trip up there, isn't it? It won't take long."

"Are you sure?" Ward asked, doubtful.

Nicholas shrugged. "I really don't think I could sleep just now anyway."

Ward managed a nod. "All right then. If you insist, I'll be glad of the company."

~

Nick's clothes had mostly dried on him while he sat with his grandfather, but his coat and hat were still sodden, so Mr. Pipp looked out some oilskins and a cap for him. Mr. Pipp had a lantern for each of them too, which he handed them in turn as they went out.

"Careful," he said sternly to Ward, and Ward nodded, though he looked distracted.

Nick caught Mr. Pipp's eye and said, "I'll make sure of it."

The rain was brutal still. It had been driving down for hours now, and the ground was boggy with it, sucking at their booted feet as they walked the short distance to the Zawn. The wind howled too, whipping the rain into their faces as they trudged along and ripping at the flames inside their lanterns, which flickered weakly, tiny beacons against the great dark force of the storm and the endless night.

"Watch your feet," Nick called. "There's scores of rabbit holes round here."

When they reached the edge of the Zawn a few minutes later, Nick began to seriously doubt the wisdom of what he had suggested. The Zawn was bad enough in the daylight. In the dead of night, in the midst of a storm, it was terrifying: a dark chasm full of jagged rocks and wild sea spray, its edges blurry and indistinct. Holding his lantern up, Nick warily eyed the nearest platform and the ladder that led down to it. The platforms had looked reassuringly solid the last time he'd been here, but shrouded in shadow, they seemed fragile and rickety.

Ward didn't seem concerned though—he was already on his way, stepping onto the upper rungs and climbing nimbly down.

Nick wanted to protest. To shout *No!* and demand they return to the safety of the house, but this had been his own foolish idea, so instead he waited patiently till Ward had safely reached the platform and stepped aside before following him, gripping tightly to the rungs as he descended, half expecting to be blown off by a sudden squall.

He wasn't much reassured when his feet finally touched the solid platform—somehow the storm conditions felt even more intense here in the Zawn. Maybe the wind was spiralling up from the sea. It was certainly whistling all around him, plastering his oilskins against him, near ripping off his cap, and drenching him with seawater spray from the churning ocean beneath them.

Christ, it was dark...

"The smell of ozone is stronger down here," Ward shouted over the wind, his eyes a faint gleam in the darkness. Nick inhaled, but if there was any identifiable scent in the atmosphere, it wasn't one he could put a name to. He could only detect the indistinct, nameless smell of rain.

Ward knelt and unfastened his knapsack, drawing out something and laying it next to the lantern he'd set down on the wet surface of the platform. The silver match-safe box. Nick stared at it, suddenly dismayed. What had he been thinking, suggesting this?

Just then, a low, threatening rumble of thunder sounded. The first in a while. Ward looked up quickly from his kneeling position. With the lantern next to him, Nick could just about make out his expression—he looked happy and excited.

"You were right," he shouted. "The storm's coming back!"

Nick's stomach churned. He didn't want to be right anymore. He should have done what Ward suggested and gone to bed, only taking Ward with him—that was what he'd really wanted. He should have crossed the two impossible feet of space that had separated them in Ward's hallway and just told Ward he loved him, instead of embarking on this absurd quest. That was all this was anyway—Nick trying in his clumsy way to show Ward how he felt.

Another roll of thunder came, this one impossibly long and deep, like the rumbling growl of a slumbering dragon beginning to stir. The very earth seemed to shudder, and Nick couldn't help but picture the flimsy platform on which they stood shaking loose from the rocks, breaking apart, tumbling down, down, down to the sea.

"It's close," he told Ward, sounding calmer than he felt.

The thunder rolled again, closer still—Christ, it was coming in fast!—Nick dropped to his knees beside Ward. "Perhaps we should go back up. This doesn't feel safe."

Ward shifted towards him and raised his hand, cupping Nick's cheek. His fingers were cold and wet, but the touch was still comforting, easing Nick's sudden panic.

"We're safe," he said. "These platforms were carefully built to hold fast and the lightning rods will draw any strikes away from us."

Nick said nothing, transfixed by Ward's earnest gaze and the light brush of his fingertips against his cheek.

Then the thunder came again.

This time it was directly overhead, and no longer a rumbling threat, but the threat made terrifyingly good—a sharp crack followed by an immense bellow of godly rage, and on its heels, the first strike of lightning, like a fissure in the heavens. A bright white-blue vein. A celestial strike of pure 'lectricity that lit up Ward's awed face for an instant.

"Jesus," Nick gasped. "This is—" He broke off, unable to find words for the immensity of it.

Ward's eyes shone in the darkness. "Just like on the *Archimedes*."

They stared at each other.

All right then.

Nick swallowed and made himself ask, "Where do you want me?"

Ward had him sit with his back against the rocky surface of the Zawn, his legs stretched out in front of him while Ward knelt beside him. He held up the match-safe box, and Nick tried to focus his attention upon it.

It was impossible. He could barely make the box out in the darkness, and every time there was another roll of thunder or crack of lightning, he jolted, his concentration wrecked.

"You have to focus upon the box," Ward yelled after several minutes.

"I know," Nick cried. "But I can't even see it properly."

Ward looked about him, frustrated. "Let's try this," he said, lifting the lantern. "Look at the flame."

They tried the flame alone, then the flame behind the match-safe box, casting light on its silver surface. Nothing worked.

"I'm sorry, I can't," Nick said at last, sick at heart. "Between the noise and the wind and the rain, it's impossible to concentrate."

Ward sighed, his disappointment plain. "Why don't I give it a try? I've hypnotised myself before."

"All right. I'll hold the box for you," Nick said.

They switched positions. Nick held the box up, trying to keep as still as possible despite the ache in his knees from the wooden platform. But though Ward stared and stared, the trance state eluded him too. They tried the lantern then, both with the silver box and without it. Nothing worked.

As Ward's expression grew more desperate, Nick began to wish again he had not suggested this. What had possessed him to do so? He had never believed this would work anyway. It was just that... he had wanted to give Ward *something*.

"Let me hold the lantern," Ward said at last. "Perhaps that will be easier, since I can judge more accurately where it is if I am holding it and focus my gaze accordingly."

"I think it may already be too late," Nick warned as he

handed the lantern over. "The storm's moving on again." Over the last few minutes, the rumbles of thunder had grown quieter and further apart. "Perhaps it's time to stop."

Ward didn't respond to that suggestion. He knelt on the wet wood and lifted the lantern above his head, staring at the flame, his face frozen in an expression of grim determination. He stared so long and so fixedly that Nick began to think he might actually have succeeded, but just as he inched closer to check, Ward let out a bark of frustration and cast the lantern aside. It fell on its side and rolled to the edge of the platform.

"God damn it!" he yelled into the storm. Then he looked up at the sky and screamed, *"Where are you?"*

Nick could see that cry was ripped straight from Ward's heart, a gory, bloody thing. His chest was heaving, and his face was wet with rain or tears, or both. The lantern rolled in the wind, back and forth, back and forth, at the platform edge, and Ward kicked out at it viciously, sending it hurling down the Zawn to the sea below.

"How could you *leave* me?" he screamed at the sky.

Nick laid a careful hand on his arm. "Ward. Please." He didn't even have to raise his voice to be heard anymore.

He half expected Ward to shake him off, but Ward turned to look at him instead, his face a picture of agonised, naked grief. "I will never see him again, Nicholas."

Nick's heart ached. "I know," he said, and he did. He knew this feeling all too well. The immensity of that realisation. All the warning in the world couldn't prepare you for that, when it came. That knowledge of the finality of death.

The thunder pealed again, but this time it was little more than a distant echo of what had gone before. The storm had indeed moved on, was likely many miles away now.

The rain had been relentless all night, but as the storm departed, still heavier rain followed in its wake, like a courtier behind a monarch. It drove down on them as they sat there on the platform, defeated, steady rivulets trickling down the back of their necks.

"I'm so sorry, Ward," Nick said at last, though he wasn't sure what he was sorry for exactly. Suggesting they come here? Failing? Maybe he was sorry because he'd never believed in Ward's theories. Despite that, he *had* tried tonight, for Ward, though he wasn't sure if that was a good thing or a bad thing now.

Ward put his hand over Nick's. "It's not you who should be apologising," he said hoarsely. "I've been lying to myself. You were right when you told me I was searching for a way to believe that George isn't really gone." He swallowed, hard. "And you were right when you said he *is* gone."

"Ward—"

"And even now, I'm being a selfish idiot, behaving like this over my brother who died a whole year ago when you've just lost your grandfather tonight." He shook his head miserably.

"It's all right," Nick said gently. "Godfrey wasn't my family. This is different."

"Nicholas—"

"No, *really*," Nick insisted. "I know what it is to lose someone you love. It was different with Godfrey. I can't say I loved him, and I'm quite sure he didn't love me. I think the reason he asked for me tonight was because he felt, well, connected to me. The same way he felt connected to the Tremain land maybe."

"It couldn't just have been that," Ward said. "He already has a legitimate grandson to carry on his name. I'm sure he must have loved you, Nicholas."

Nick gave a small smile, oddly touched by that attempt at reassurance. "No, it's just that Harry's nothing like Godfrey, whereas I— Well, he probably thought I was cut from his cloth, at least as far as the land's concerned. That's a sort of connection, but it isn't love."

"Isn't it?" Ward whispered. "Then what is?"

Nick turned over the hand that lay beneath Ward's so that they were palm to palm. He spread his fingers, sliding them into the spaces between Ward's, and Ward gripped him back. He couldn't breathe, never mind speak, but at last he managed a breathless, "Don't you know? Don't you feel it?"

Ward stared at him, his throat working. He whispered, "Nicholas—"

"I love you, Ward."

Ward's eyes glittered in the darkness. He said hoarsely, "Don't say that if you're only going to leave again."

"I'm not," Nick whispered and leaned in, using his free hand to grasp Ward round the back of his neck and yank him close, pressing their mouths together.

They crouched there, on the wooden platform in that great chasm in the ground, with the rain pouring down on top of them, freezing, shivering, sodden, and kissing, and Nick was so intensely happy in that instant that his heart hurt with it, as though it couldn't quite hold all the love inside him. He clutched Ward closer, deepening the kiss, and Ward groaned into his mouth.

Eventually Ward broke the kiss, pulling back to stare into Nick's eyes. "You must know already that I love you."

"I know no such thing," Nick said, smiling foolishly, unable to hide his pleasure at that declaration.

"Well, I do," Ward assured him, and though his voice was little more than a croak, his words were the sweetest Nick thought he had ever heard. At some stage, Ward's ruined voice had become so dearly familiar to him, he didn't notice its ugliness anymore.

"Come home with me," Ward said. "I want you in my bed."

"God, yes." Nick longed to be naked with Ward again, skin to skin. To lose himself in the private cocoon they made with their bodies.

"And this time," Ward said, "you're staying."

"Yes," Nick agreed eagerly, kissing up the line of Ward's jaw. "This time I'll stay all night."

"That's not what I meant." Ward pressed Nick back, and Nick blinked at the loss of contact.

"What?"

"I don't just want you to stay one night," Ward continued. "I want you with me always, Nicholas."

Nick stared at him. There were a hundred reasons he could give Ward right now as to why that couldn't be. But if he started enumerating them, this would end before it had even begun, and he couldn't let that happen.

What was he to do? Jump over the edge and hope for the best? Trust he wouldn't perish on the rocks? There were so many rocks. But there was also Ward.

"All right," he said, rain dripping down his face. "For always."

∼

Helston House was solid and square, modern and defiant against the wild Cornish sky. Pipp must have been watching for them—he opened the front door before they even reached it, searching Ward's face with his careful gaze as Ward and Nicholas removed their sodden coats and hats.

Ward offered Pipp a small smile, and Pipp's tense expression eased.

"Do you require any refreshments, sir? I can have a tray made up."

Ward glanced at Nicholas, who shook his head. "No, thank you, Pipp. Just some brandy perhaps. We're both soaked through."

"Very good, sir. Shall I bring it to you in the—"

"Just bring me the bottle," Ward interrupted. "We'll take it up with us."

Pipp gave an uncharacteristic grin and hurried off. Minutes later, they were climbing the stairs, Ward carrying two empty snifters in one hand and a bottle of French brandy in the other.

Since Ward's hands were full, Nicholas opened the bedchamber door, holding it so Ward preceded him.

A gas lamp on the table in the corner gave off low, gentle light, and a well-banked fire glowed in the grate. Everything was warm and welcoming and cosy. Ward set down the glasses and bottle on the table and turned.

Nicholas was leaning against the closed door, his black hair wet and slicked back from his brow, his silver eyes startling as ever. The very space between them seemed to pulse, as though all the longing of the past weeks had built up like so much electrical charge.

In the end, it was Nicholas who moved first, crossing the floor in a few quick strides and pulling Ward into his arms, pressing a line of small desperate kisses along Ward's jaw till Ward turned his head with an inarticulate sound and their lips finally met.

Nicholas's tongue speared into his mouth, Nicholas's hands firm on his hips as he yanked him even closer. The noise that tore from Ward was part groan, part sob. Their tongues tangled, bristled chins scraping together, and it was so sweet and good.

Nicholas began to efficiently strip Ward of all his wet clothes, his hands working quickly to remove and discard each garment till they were surrounded by damp heaps of cloth. He gazed on each new area of exposed skin with possessive, burning eyes, sliding his hands reverently over Ward's sensitive skin.

"My handsome lad," he whispered. "My comely boy."

Ward whimpered.

Once Ward was fully naked, Nicholas quickly stripped his own things off before stepping forward again to run his hands up Ward's sides and over his chest. He brushed his palms over Ward's nipples, then returned to pinch them lightly, sweetly, between thumbs and forefingers, making Ward gasp at the sharp, biting sensation, each tiny painful twist making Ward's cock stiffen and leak. He arched his chest towards Nicholas in encouragement, baring his throat submissively, and Nicholas chuckled, bending his head to press a row of suckling kisses along Ward's collarbone, then up his throat, and all the way to his ear.

"You like that?" he said softly when he got there, his breath warm and damp, making Ward shiver helplessly.

"God, yes," Ward groaned. "More, please."

Nicholas chuckled again. "So demanding," he murmured, lips brushing the delicate curl of Ward's outer ear, before his teeth nipped lightly at the fleshy lobe and his tongue snaked briefly inside.

Ward shivered at that too, hunching a shoulder and giving a gasping laugh, his cock straining towards his belly. He liked this very much indeed, this—being mastered. He liked that Nicholas was making all the decisions and all Ward had to do was react.

Nicholas took his hand and tugged, pulling him towards the bed. "Lie down. I want to give you pleasure."

"But I want to give you pleasure too," Ward protested, even as he obeyed, the sheets cool and clean beneath his naked body.

Nicholas smiled. "We'll pleasure each other," he promised, and as he positioned himself beside Ward, Ward began to see what he had in mind.

Ward turned on to his side mere moments after Nicholas did, reaching for the man's cock a scant second later. As his own cock was drawn into the wet, perfect heat of Nicholas's mouth, he drove his lips down Nicholas's shaft, filling himself with Nicholas's flesh and inhaling his heady scent. And then it was a messy blur of mixed-up sensations. The insistent, unbearably good penetration of demanding flesh, pressing right into his throat till he felt dizzy with it and drool leaked from his mouth. The hot sucking grasp of Nicholas's mouth on his own cock, drawing him in. The snaking swirl of that agile tongue against Ward's sensitive shaft.

Ward's mind battled to reconcile these competing sensations, the push and the pull, one part of him opening to receive even as another demanded entry. It was all his mind could do to just keep up with those twin experiences—what he was doing and what was being done to him. It felt as though his attention were jumping around like a grasshopper.

As his impending climax intensified, it became more and more difficult to concentrate on Nicholas. He gasped, losing his rhythm, and Nicholas's shaft drew free of his mouth. Nicholas didn't allow him even a moment to recover. He pressed in closer, moaning around Ward's cock as he took him impossibly deeper, letting Ward push forward one last impossible fraction till the head of his cock bumped against the back of Nicholas's throat.

And God, but that did it. Ward grasped the back of Nicholas's thigh and erupted into his mouth with a harsh groan. His climax came in hot, helpless pulses, and Nicholas's throat closed as he tried to swallow it all.

Ward drew back, strangely, possessively, needing to see. When he saw Nicholas's face—his lips swollen and decorated with traces of Ward's spend—a very primal satisfaction filled him. He reached out, brushing his thumb over Nicholas's lips to collect the pearly remains before sucking his thumb clean.

Nicholas groaned. "Ward—"

"Your turn," Ward whispered. "Lie on your back and spread your legs."

Nicholas obeyed, his silver eyes hot as molten metal as he watched Ward shuffle into the space between Nicholas's legs, on his knees.

"Take hold of your cock," Ward said, sliding down to lie

flat on the mattress. He grinned. "Show me how you please yourself when you're alone."

Nicholas let out a shaky laugh at that, but again he obeyed, his teeth sinking into his lower lip as he circled his fingers round his hard shaft and began to stroke. He watched avidly as Ward stretched forward just a little further and, slowly, tenderly... kissed his balls.

"Oh Christ," Nicholas breathed. "*Ward—*"

Ward kissed and lapped and suckled, gently at first, then more firmly, loving the contrast of fragility and roughness. Loving even more Nicholas's astonished, helpless gasps. He captured the tender orbs between his lips and cradled them there, rolling his tongue over them, before gently suckling them into his mouth. Then he did it all over again, and again, till Nick was chanting his name like a prayer. He moved lower, dipping his head to explore the tender, sensitive patch of skin below Nicholas's balls, then lower still, so that his tongue skirted the very edge of Nicholas's tight hole. That glancing caress made Nicholas cry out with something like desperation, so he did it again, stretching his tongue to graze the tender ring, over and over.

"My God, Ward," Nicholas gasped. "I've never—"

He broke off, and the sentence went unfinished, forgotten even, because Nicholas was groaning now, his jerking hand moving ever swifter as he wrenched out his climax. At last his spend erupted from him, splashing his belly, his chest, even his throat as he came hard, his bright gaze fixed on Ward.

They lay tangled together in bed after. The lantern had gone out, but the fire in the grate, though low, gave off a faint glow.

Outside, the rain still fell, though now with diminishing force. The storm was well and truly over.

"So, what now?" Nick asked. "Do you intend to continue with your work?"

"My attempts to contact the spirits, you mean?" Ward asked. He'd been staring at the ceiling, but now he turned his head to meet Nick's gaze, his expression a little bleak. "No, I don't."

He didn't offer any explanation, and Nick didn't ask for one. Right now, everything was still rather too raw for that, he thought. Instead he propped himself up on one elbow and gazed down at Ward's comely face. "What will you do then?"

Ward thought about that. "I may go back to the work I was doing before," he said. Then he smiled faintly, just a small quirk of his lips. "Or perhaps I will find something new to occupy me."

"Do you have something in mind?"

Ward paused. Then he said carefully, almost diffidently, "I've become quite interested in weather prediction lately." A self-deprecating huff. "It's all that watching for storms, I expect."

Nick was hit by an unfamiliar surge of affection—the hint of uncertainty in Ward's expression was so unexpected. It was rare to see Ward look anything but entirely sure of himself.

"Well, I can certainly see the practical use of that," Nick said. "The fishermen round here would welcome it, I'm sure. Too many men are lost to storms at sea."

"It would be good to do something useful," Ward agreed quietly.

"Ward, I didn't mean—" Nick began, falling silent when Ward reached up to place cool fingertips over his lips.

"I know you didn't," Ward said. "But you were right when you questioned what good my reaching George would do anyone in this life. So yes, that's one of the reasons I won't be continuing with my previous studies. And yes, in the future, I would like to do something that benefits someone in a meaningful way." He smiled then. "Anyway, what about you? What does your future hold, Nicholas—apart from me, of course?"

"Apart from me." Those words prompted a helpless smile from Nick. His cheeks had begun to ache with all the smiling he was doing.

"Well," he said, dropping down to the mattress again, so that they lay facing one another, their heads on the same pillow, "if you can believe it, Godfrey's apparently bequeathed me some land."

"Has he? Where?"

"It's the other part of the plot he sold you. It badly wants improving—it's nothing but grass and rocks just now. I've been nagging at Godfrey for a while to put it to some use. He must've decided to just give me it and let me do my worst. Probably realised Harry would never rouse himself to do anything more with it than stake it in a game of cards."

Ward raised his eyebrows at that, but only said, "And how do you propose to cultivate it?"

"I'm not sure. I'd be starting from scratch. Most farmers round here have dairy herds so there's really no more call for that kind of thing. The land's not particularly apt for arable crops, but it's good for other crops, and when the new train line's built from here to Truro, I'd be able to transport any produce a good distance, so that might be a way forward—" He realised he was beginning to babble and came to an abrupt halt, embarrassed by the betraying eagerness in his tone.

Ward didn't look bored though, or even amused. His eyes were warm, a faint smile playing over his lips. "It sounds as though you have some thinking to do," he said softly.

"It sounds as though we both do," Nick said. He reached out to brush back that always-straying lock of Ward's hair from his forehead.

"There are some things I need to think about," Ward agreed. "But there's others I'm already decided on."

"Such as?" Nick asked.

"Such as, I love you," Ward said. "And I want to share my life with you. Fully." He stared into Nick's eyes, his gaze growing a little wary, a little careful. "What about you, Nicholas? Do you want that too? Really want it, I mean?"

The edge loomed, terrifyingly high, but Nick didn't hesitate. He didn't know what was on the other side, but he ran towards it full tilt.

"I really do," he told Ward, and leaned forward to seal that assurance with another kiss.

And they soared over the edge of the zawn together.

EPILOGUE

5th October 1853

Mr. Godritch leaned over his desk and poured Nick a large glass of sherry.

"It's a decent bargain you've struck, Mr. Hearn," he said as he filled his own glass, "but it's important that you're absolutely clear on what you're signing up to."

He proceeded to explain the deed that lay on the desk in front of Nick, line by line. Nick tried to listen, or at least give the appearance of listening. The content of the deed did not actually matter, but its existence did, and Nick had to demonstrate a credible degree of interest.

"The lease of your land is for a lengthy period, true," the lawyer was saying now, "but in return, you'll get the benefit of Sir Edward's capital to do all the land improvements that are needed and to get the farm buildings constructed. Now" —he wagged a finger at Nick—"you have to understand that the majority of the costs that relate to your part of the land will be set off against the rent Sir Edward owes you, so you won't see much benefit for the first few years, but those costs will be increasing the capital value of your land, and Sir Edward will bear the costs of improving his own land himself. And I did manage to persuade Sir Edward to let you take a small proportion of the rent each quarter along with the salary he's paying you as his steward."

Mr. Godritch pointed at the relevant clause that recorded this, and Nick bent his head, pretending to read, even as he worked to suppress his smile. In truth, none of the financial arrangements mattered to him or Ward, but to Ward's consternation, Nick had insisted the bargain must not appear too suspiciously advantageous to him. When Mr. Godritch had made his suggestion regarding Nick receiving some of the rent from the outset, Ward had been only too happy to agree.

"I appreciate your efforts, Mr. Godritch," Nick said, the pen twitching in his hand. "I'm more than happy with the terms you've achieved for me."

"Well, it's the best you'll get considering Mr. Tremain saw fit to leave you a great swathe of empty, unused land and not so much as a brass penny to enable you to actually do anything with it." He shrugged. "In short, it's this or sell it for a fraction of what it will be worth in ten years."

Nick chuckled. "That's old Godfrey for you. Not that I'm shedding any tears—it's not as though I expected anything from him at all, and this arrangement suits me well enough. At least Sir Edward wants to leave the management of the land entirely to me. He's too busy with his own work to second-guess every decision I make the way the old man used to."

Mr. Godritch laughed at that. "Oh, I can assure you, Mr. Tremain was equally critical of my work, Mr. Hearn. There was no deed I ever drafted for him he could not improve upon himself."

They shared a grin, then Nick pulled the deed towards him and signed it with a flourish before turning the paper round so the lawyer could add his own signature as witness.

Finally, it was done.

"I'd better be getting back," Nick said, rising from his chair. "I've a deal to do today. But thank you for all your efforts and advice, Mr. Godritch." Leaning down, he ran a hand over Snow's back. "Come on, boy. Time to go."

The dog lumbered to his feet with a grumbly wheeze.

Mr. Godritch accompanied them to the door of his office, but paused there, his hand on the doorknob. "Incidentally, I heard you had to give your cottage up."

Cousin Harry had proven to be unexpectedly churlish about the legacy Nicholas had received. Within two days of Harry's arrival in Trevathany after Godfrey's death, an eviction notice had been pinned on the front door of Nick's childhood home.

"Apparently it's the Tremains' steward's cottage," Nick said, shrugging. "Goes with the position, or so I've been told."

Mr. Godritch tutted. "What nonsense! Your mother lived there for years, and no steward ever occupied it before that. In fact, the steward before you, Mr. Lang, lived at Tremain House itself." He gave Nick a long look. "If you wish, I'll take it up with Mr. Tremain. I'm quite sure this is not what Godfrey would have intended."

Nick was touched by that offer. Harry Tremain was the most powerful man round these parts now—apart from Ward, of course—and was not to be crossed lightly. And Mr. Godritch wasn't to know that the eviction notice had actually been rather serendipitous, creating an urgent need for Nicholas to find new accommodation.

"That's kind of you, but I've already decided to let it pass," Nick said. "For one thing, I'd already given up my position and the cottage just before Godfrey's death, as I'd been planning to leave Trevathany. More importantly though,

Sir Edward's given me accommodation at Helston House." He grinned. "Now I know why Mr. Lang liked living at Tremain House so well. My laundry's done without me even having to ask, and Mrs. Waddell's cooking is delicious. The next time you see me, I'll be twice the size I am now."

Mr. Godritch chuckled. "Ah, well then, perhaps it is for the best. We working men need our home comforts, do we not?"

~

Ward spent the morning reviewing the first set of daily logs he'd received from his weather observers and plotting the information on his weather map. He was becoming increasingly convinced that, given enough time, miles, and data, not to mention a reliable means of swift long-distance communication, it would be possible to predict the weather far enough ahead that it might actually make a difference—might actually save lives.

His main difficulty at the moment was getting the evidence to analyse, but he'd made arrangements to have daily weather logs prepared by a handful of people located throughout Cornwall. Within a few months, he hoped to have enough information to begin carrying out some early analysis to test some of his theories on weather systems.

As for long-distance communication, it was coming. There was already talk of laying a telegraph cable all the way across the ocean to the Americas. Just the thought of that was dizzying. If weather information could be telegraphed from places as far away as that within the next few years, who knew what might be possible?

A soft knock at the study door had him looking up. A moment later, Nicholas slipped inside. He was windblown and grinning.

"Well," he said, closing the door behind him and leaning back against it, "it's official."

Ward slid out from behind the desk and walked towards him. "You signed the lease?"

"I did," Nicholas confirmed, "I am now your landlord."

"Good heavens," Ward said, "I shall have to keep you happy if I am not to be evicted." He took hold of the lapels of Nicholas's coat and leaned in close, laying a kiss on his warm, curving mouth.

When they broke apart, Nicholas grinned and said, "You don't really need to worry about that since I am also officially your servant now. Which of course makes you my master." He quirked a brow at the last word.

"Well," Ward husked. "I must say, I did not feel like your master this morning."

Far from it. On his hands and knees and begging for Nicholas's cock while Nicholas teased him slowly, mercilessly.

Nicholas laughed softly.

"Honestly though, do you mind?" Ward asked, watching Nicholas anxiously. "Being my servant in the eyes of the world?"

They'd been over this before, but it still worried Ward. He remembered Nicholas's bitter words, that night in Truro.

"In your eyes, you are the master and I am the servant..."

Nicholas shook his head, his gaze soft and warm with affection. "It doesn't matter to me what the world thinks we are—landlord or tenant, master or servant—all I care about is what we truly are to each other. And we know that now, don't we?"

Ward swallowed against the lump of emotion that swelled in his throat. "Yes," he whispered. "You own my heart, Nicholas. And there's nothing to be done about it."

"Nothing except thank God for it," Nicholas murmured,

leaning in close to whisper in Ward's ear. "And for you. My lover, my friend, my soul mate, my helpmeet…"

Ward's mouth curved. "The keeper of your heart?"

"That too." Nicholas agreed, trailing kisses towards his mouth, the nibbling caress of Nicholas's lips making Ward shiver and shift as he wound his arms round Nicholas's neck.

"Forever?" Ward pressed, shamelessly.

Their lips were just touching now, and Nicholas's breath was warm against Ward's lips. "Such a demanding fellow," he murmured. "Forever and always—will that suffice?"

"I suppose it will have to do," Ward whispered, and captured Nicholas's lips again.

The End

THANK YOU, DEAR READER

Thank you for reading Nick and Ward's story!

Of all my books, this is probably the one I've done the most wide-ranging research for. From the discovery of electricity to the invention of batteries, and from the phenomenon of St. Elmo's Fire to the outrageous actions of Victorian mesmerists and spiritualists—I even read into the history of the conflict in which Ward's brother died, though those details didn't make it into the book... As much as I love these historical details, though, it's the connection between the characters that really matters, so I hope the connection between Nick and Ward resonated with you.

Let me know what you thought! You can find all the different ways to connect with me below—I love hearing from readers.

Finally, if you have time, I'd be very grateful if you'd consider leaving a review on an online review site. Reviews are incredibly helpful for book visibility and I appreciate every one.

Joanna x

~

CONNECT WITH ME!

Email: authorjoannachambers@gmail.com

Website: www.joannachambers.com

Newsletter: go to https://tinyurl.com/joannachambersnews
to subscribe for up to date
information about my books, freebies
and special deals.

All new subscribers get a free novella and two exclusive
bonus stories from the Enlightenment series.

Other ways to connect with me:
Website: www.joannachambers.com
Amazon: amazon.com/author/joannachambers
Goodreads: goodreads.com/joanna_chambers
Bookbub: bookbub.com/profile/joanna-chambers
Instagram: @joannachambers_auth
Facebook: https://www.facebook.com/joanna.chambers.58/

ALSO BY JOANNA CHAMBERS

ENLIGHTENMENT SERIES

Provoked

Beguiled

Enlightened

Seasons Pass *

The Bequest *

Unnatural

Restored

* exclusive bonus stories for newsletter subscribers

CREATIVE TYPES SERIES

(WITH SALLY MALCOLM)

Total Creative Control

Home Grown Talent

Best Supporting Actor

WINTERBOURNE SERIES

Introducing Mr Winterbourne

Mr Winterbourne's Christmas

The First Snow of Winter

The Labours of Lord Perry Cavendish

CAPITAL WOLVES DUET

Gentleman Wolf

Master Wolf

Total Creative Control (*Creative Types 1*)

Sunshine PA, meet Grumpy Boss…

When fanfic writer Aaron Page landed a temp job with the creator of hit TV show, *Leeches*, it was only meant to last a week. Three years later, Aaron's still there…

It could be because he loves the creative challenge. It could be because he's a huge *Leeches* fanboy. It's definitely *not* because of Lewis Hunter, his extremely demanding, staggeringly rude…and breathtakingly gorgeous boss.

Is it?

Lewis Hunter grew up the hard way and fought for everything he's got. His priority is the show, and personal relationships come a distant second. Besides, who needs romance when you have a steady stream of hot men hopping in and out of your bed?

His only meaningful relationship is with Aaron, his chief confidante and indispensable assistant. And no matter how appealing he finds Aaron's cute boy-next-door charms, Lewis would never risk their professional partnership just to scratch an itch.

But when Lewis finds himself trapped at a hilariously awful corporate retreat, Aaron is his only friend and ally. As the professional lines between them begin to blur, their simmering attraction starts to sizzle

… And they're both about to get *burned*.

～

Home Grown Talent (*Creative Types 2*)

Are you for real?

From the outside, it looks like model and influencer Mason Nash has it all—beauty, fame, and fortune. With his star rapidly rising, and a big contract up for grabs, Mason's on the verge of hitting the big time.

When an opportunity arises to co-host a gardening slot on daytime TV with his ex's brother, Owen Hunter, Mason is definitely on-board. And he intends to use every trick in the book to make the show a hit—including agreeing to his ruthless producer's demand to fake a 'will-they/won't-they' romance with his co-host…

Owen Hunter is a gardener with a huge heart and both feet planted firmly on the well-tilled ground. He's proud of the life he's built and has absolutely no desire to be on TV—yet somehow he finds himself agreeing to do the show.

It's definitely *not* because he's interested in Mason Nash. The guy might be beautiful—and yeah, his spoiled brat routine presses all Owen's buttons in the bedroom—but Owen has no interest in a short-term fling with a fame-hungry model.

As the two men get closer, though, Owen starts to believe there's more to Mason than his beautiful appearance and carefully-curated online persona—that beneath the glitz and glamour is a sweet, sensitive man longing to be loved.

A man Owen might be falling for. A man who might even feel the same.

But in a world of media spin and half-truths, Owen is dangerously out of his depth. And when a ridiculous scandal explodes online, with Owen at its heart, it starts to look as though everything he thought was real is built on lies—including his budding romance with Mason...

~

Best Supporting Actor (*Creative Types 3*)

Lights, camera...attraction!

When Tag O'Rourke, struggling actor-slash-barista, meets Jay Warren, son of acting royalty, it's loathing at first sight. Loathing...and lust.

Tag's dream is to act, but it's a dream that's crumbling beneath the weight of student debt and his family's financial problems. If his career doesn't take off soon, he's going to have to get a real job. After all, feeding his family is more important than feeding his soul.

Luckily, Tag's about to get his big break...

Jay never had to dream about acting; he was always destined to follow in his famous mother's footsteps. But fame has its price and a traumatic experience early in Jay's career has left him with paralysing stage fright, which is why he sticks to the safety of TV work—and avoids relationships with co-stars at all costs.

Unfortunately, Jay's safe world is about to be rocked...

After an ill-judged yet mind-blowing night together, Jay and Tag part acrimoniously. So it's a nasty shock when they discover that they've been cast in a two-man play that could launch Tag's career and finally get Jay back onto the stage where he belongs.

Sure, it's not ideal, but how bad can working with your arch-nemesis be?

All they have to do is survive six weeks rehearsing together and navigate a cast of smarmy festival directors, terrible land-ladies, and vengeful journalists. Oh, and try not to fall in love before the curtain rises...

Break a leg!

~